Terri Parsell Hilmey

IF IT COULD HAPPEN TO HER

IF IT COULD HAPPEN TO HER. Copyright© 2010 by Terri Parsell Hilmey. All rights reserved.

No part of this volume may be reproduced or transmitted in any form or by any means, graphic, electronic, or mechanical, including photocopying, recording, taping, scanning, or by any information storage retrieval system, electronic or otherwise, without the written permission of the author, who owns all rights.

Printed in the United States of America

ISBN 978-1-456-35816-7

For Peter, Elsie, Charlotte and Henrietta

If it Could Happen to Her

Chapter One

Ingrid Musgrave sat quietly watching "American Idol." Priding herself on her culture – she was, after all, the largest donor by far to the Metropolitan Museum of Art – sometimes she lowered her standards a bit and watched something that was pure fun. Besides, Bart liked it.

She looked over at Bartolomeo Molina and smiled. He was dozing peacefully in his overstuffed floral chintz chair, feet up on a matching ottoman, his head tilted a bit to the side. Devastatingly handsome, with thick, nearly black hair, and a firm body kept fit by rounds of polo, Bart was Argentinean in origin, and 22 years younger than her – and he made her very happy. She knew he probably wouldn't be sitting there if she weren't as wealthy as she was, but they did have fun together. She could never marry him – the checks from Geoffrey would stop coming if she did – but she thought what they had was quite good enough for now.

She turned back to the television briefly, and then sat up straight. Was that a knock on the door? Was she hearing things? She picked up the remote control and turned the volume down. She sat listening for another few seconds and then, again, distinctly heard a rapping on the front door. "That bloody woman," she thought, as she rose from her chair.

Ingrid Musgrave's security system had motion detectors that should have warned her when someone so much as stepped foot on her property. There was an elaborate web of cameras all around the periphery that should have shown her who her visitor was. And there were lights that should have lit up all along the driveway, and up to the house, as they approached.

Of course, none of it worked if her stupid housekeeper, Greta, didn't turn the damn thing back on before she left for the day. "I'm spending hundreds of thousands of dollars on a security system that can be rendered completely useless by Greta," she grumbled to herself as she went to the front door.

Ingrid Musgrave wasn't really concerned. After all, many of her equally privileged neighbors in their little haven of Cambridge, Connecticut had a habit of stopping by before bedtime to share a cocktail and a bit of gossip. She was only mildly annoyed. That is, until she opened the door.

The first man she saw – she was pretty sure she saw three, dressed all in dark green work clothes that reminded her of her grounds crew – pointed a gun at her and shot her through the forehead.

She fell, crumpled to the floor – dead before she even hit it – but he leaned over her and shot her two more times in the head.

The three men moved quickly into the house, fanning out. The second man into the house was the one to find Bart sitting in the chair in front of the television. Bart woke from his dose, and started to get up, a question in his eyes. That question was answered quickly by a bullet through his head. He fell back into the chair, quite dead, but was also shot once more to ensure he wouldn't rise again.

The three men searched the rest of the house, silently at first, and finally shouting to each other, "Clear!" They methodically searched the enormous house, from the top floor, where they removed all of the valuables lying about in any of the bedrooms. They also took tools and removed the entire safe from Mrs. Musgrave's dressing room, using a heavy-duty dolly to haul it to the window and toss it out, where it embedded itself four inches deep in her lovely lawn. Then they proceeded throughout the house, not bothering to take stereos or televisions, but rather skillfully choosing pieces of art from the walls, pieces of sculpture from the tables and shelves, and first-edition books from Mrs. Musgrave's library.

They were in and out of the house in about thirty minutes, politely closing the door behind them when they left. With everything secured and stored in the back of their SUVs, they drove one by one down Mrs. Musgrave's driveway, took a left at the end, and headed toward the highway.

Georgina Emerson Adams woke slowly that morning. She felt the cool comfort of her Frette pillowcase against her cheek before she turned over onto her back and opened her eyes, and, once she did, felt her long eyelashes fluttering against the black silk of her sleeping mask. She pushed the mask up onto her forehead, and lay looking at her ceiling, 12 feet above her head, with its intricate scrollwork and antique chandelier. She blinked her lovely, unusually vivid blue-green eyes and thought for a moment to herself, wondering why she had a headache, and why her stomach wasn't feeling very well.

Then she quickly turned to her right, and saw a familiar shape under the covers next to her. Georgina's perfectly-arched eyebrows drew together as she frowned, and she said, "Will I never learn from my mistakes?"

"Wally," she said, kicking him under the covers. Walter Grentham Grant, Georgina's ex-husband, groaned slightly, and rolled over to look at her. He smiled easily, and said, "Good morning, Georgie."

"Get out of my bed," Georgina said, throwing off her covers. "And don't call me Georgie."

He watched appreciatively as she stood and stretched her arms up over her head, wearing only a tank top and pajama bottoms. Her light brown, expensively-highlighted shoulder-length hair fell down her neck as she pulled the sleeping mask off her face. "How are you feeling this morning?" he asked, pushing the covers aside and putting his feet on the floor. "We actually did tequila shots, you know," he said, rubbing his temples. Walter's neat, usually tidy brown hair stood up in random spikes all over his head, and he ran his fingers through it, giving his scalp a good rub at the same time. He stood and stretched all of his 6'2" frame.

"I don't want to remember," she said, her stomach rumbling and reminding her. "And, on top of it, because you're here, Armeda won't bring me my breakfast tray." She threw her sleeping mask onto the bed, and grabbed the pale gray cashmere robe that lay at the foot of the bed. "The Frickin' Frick," she said, smiling for a moment and showing lovely white teeth.

Wally grinned, too, enjoying the smile he saw far too rarely. "You know you just go to the Young Fellows Ball to make fun of everyone."

"It's an excuse to wear a pretty dress and get drunk," Georgina said, pulling on the robe.

"And see me," Wally said, reminding her.

Georgina rolled her eyes. "My parents were devoted to the Frick," she said, "I couldn't *not* go."

She walked toward the double mahogany doors of her bedroom suite, as Wally got out of bed. "I'm in for a shower," he said, heading toward her marble and granite spa-quality bathroom.

"And then be on your way," Georgina said.

"Nonsense. Armeda can make me some breakfast," he said, going into the bathroom.

"She doesn't even like you," Georgina said as she walked out.

"She loves me – it's you she can't stand," Wally said, closing the door behind him.

Georgina pushed open the double doors, feeling their substantial weight, even though they operated as smooth as silk. Everything in Georgina's bedroom was substantial, from the king-sized thickly-carved mahogany bed, to the large French doors which led out onto her limestone terrace. She exited her room and strode to the kitchen, her robe swinging to and fro behind her as she made her way barefoot down the long marble hallway, past highlighted works of fine art, in her 10-room pre-war Park Avenue apartment. It had belonged to her parents before they died, and though she owned a house on Long Island, and another in Wellington, Florida, it was where she spent most of her time. She walked past the entry foyer on her right, decorated with matching consoles, mirrors and elaborate floral arrangements, and the enormous formal living room on her left, as she made her way toward the kitchen.

When she pushed through the kitchen door, she found her short, plump housekeeper Armeda sitting at the counter reading the New York Post.

Georgina had changed few things about the apartment, but the kitchen was one of them. The building had risen back in the early 1900s when people really knew how to build things, and Georgina did little more than occasionally restore what was already there, and occasionally reupholster furniture that was showing wear. But the kitchen had been built for a time when the owners rarely saw, and frequently neglected, the room, while Georgina liked to eat in there quite often. She had the cupboards redesigned, creamy white, with lavish scrolls and moldings, but with a slightly weathered look, making them look as old as the apartment, and brushed silver handles and drawer pulls that were also of the period, but all of which opened and closed with the barest touch of a finger. Greenish-black granite topped all of the counters, and the center island was a very dark brown wood, similar in design and style to the other cabinets, but adding a bit of contrast. It was one of her favorite rooms.

"Shouldn't you be working or something?" Georgina asked, as she pulled open the refrigerator door, paneled with the same creamy white cabinetry, and reached in for a Diet Pepsi.

"I'm not walking into your den of iniquity to bring you food," Armeda said, folding up the paper, dramatically making the sign of the cross, and turning toward the stove. "And I didn't know what time you'd be getting up. What do you want?"

"I want a Bloody Mary," Georgina said, climbing onto one of the tall chairs at the large center island.

"Well, I'm not making you one," Armeda said. "I'll make you an omelet with cheese and tomatoes and mushrooms," firing up the royal blue La Cornue range, turning and pointing at Georgina with her spatula, "and two pieces of wheat toast to soak up some of that alcohol."

Georgina sneered at her and turned the New York Post around, so she could see it herself. She thumbed through it while Armeda filled the kitchen with wonderful scents, and then put a plate in front of her. Wally strolled in a

If it Could Happen to Her

few minutes later, and Armeda put an identical plate in front of him, too, complete with a look of disgust. He smiled generously back at her, and said, "Armeda will you marry me?"

"You need to marry this one again," Armeda said, pointing at Georgina, "not just this sinning whenever you feel like it."

"Pray for me, Armeda," Wally said, digging into his breakfast, and pulling the New York Times closer.

"Oh, I do," she said. "Every day."

Wally finished his breakfast first, and went out through the back doors of the kitchen into Georgina's study. She turned to see him go, then put down the paper and followed him in there, crossing her arms, leaning against the doorframe and watching him. He was looking at some of the papers on her massive desk, and then up at her bookshelves, made of the same dark solid wood as the desk. "I'm glad you got out for some fresh air," he said, finally. "What were you working on this time?"

"The limitations of qualitative research," Georgina said

"Where's it being published?" he asked.

"The American Journal of Evaluation," she said, watching as he went around and browsed her bookshelves. He pulled out a study from the Australian Institute of Criminology entitled "Contract Killings in Australia."

"Why do you do this to yourself, Georgina?" He asked, putting the study back in the same spot where he found it, among many other similar studies, and reference books on psychology and crime.

"People are scum, Wally," she said. "It's interesting."

"Most people aren't," he said, turning to her. "You'd know that if you let a few more in."

"I have people in my life," she said.

"That you don't pay?" he asked.

"Paying them makes them very easy to get along with, and very dependable," Georgina said.

Wally sighed and turned to give her a kiss on the cheek as he left. They'd had this discussion many times before. "Will you marry me again, Georgina?" he said, holding her by her two shoulders.

"Maybe someday," she said, as she always did.

He smiled, patted her bottom to make her angry, and went out to give Armeda a big hug before he left. "Get away from me, you heathen!" Georgina heard her scream. Georgina smiled, and went over to her desk. She looked at

If it Could Happen to Her

the papers, books and files neatly organized on its surface. She was finished with her latest research project, and it was time to file all of the materials away. She had boxes ready to be assembled, so that she could begin the process of storage, but she had been avoiding it. It was something she found sad and exciting at the same time.

She walked out into the hallway, and into her formal living room. It was easily 1,000 square feet on its own, and it, too, had large floor-to-ceiling bookshelves on nearly every wall, these with sliding glass covers to protect the contents, filled with expensive collections of books, current fiction and non-fiction, first editions and reference books, all neatly and exactly organized into the Library of Congress system. Georgina had a librarian come and overhaul it for her about once every six months, because she read so much, and added so many books to the collection. The room was currently decorated in shades of blue, from pale to navy, with many floral prints and stark white cut-out fabrics, which she found soothing and stimulating at the same time. She walked past the very good furniture, stuffed with fancifully-trimmed down cushions, and the even better art, and pulled open the French doors that led out onto the large terrace that ran the length of this side of her apartment. She braced herself against the chilly mid-March weather, as a quick frigid breeze lifted her hair off her shoulders and made her eyes water, and she pulled her robe tighter around her.

She took a deep breath, and looked around her view of the Upper East Side. It *was* nice to be out again, she thought to herself.

A few hours later, Georgina lay on the buttery black leather couch of her therapist, Dr. Max Gregson, her ankles crossed neatly on one of the arms, and her arms behind her head. She was dressed in faded jeans and ballet flats, and an oversized black turtleneck sweater. Gregson's office was soothing, in a typical therapeutic sort-of way, but clearly reflected taste, with very expensive, rather stark architectural furniture.

Dr. Gregson almost didn't seem to fit into his surroundings, with a rumpled look which didn't quite match the tidy order of his office. He was short and balding, with wire-rimmed glasses perched on the end of his nose. He wore a pleasant, unruffled expression, and a worn-looking grey herringbone jacket with patches on the sleeves, a blue patterned bow tie and black, faded trousers. "You seem a little more relaxed today," he said to Georgina.

"I am," Georgina said. "I just finished a project. That always feels good."

"Yes, it's good research," Dr. Gregson agreed. "I'm glad you gave me the opportunity to review it for you." He changed the subject quickly. "But you also mentioned you got out of the apartment again."

Georgina stiffened a bit, moved her arms from behind her head, and laced her hands together over her belly. "Well, yes. I went to a party last night. It was a social obligation."

"And other than coming to see me, it's the first time you've been outside of your apartment in nearly four months," he stated the simple fact.

"Yes, and if you'd come to my apartment for our appointments, it would make my life much easier," Georgina said sharply. "I'm not merely 'isolating,' as you like to call it – I'm actually working, and it's easier to do from home. I have everything I need there."

"Well, I think that's debatable, Georgina," he said. "Your life might seem easier, but a lack of honest human interaction can tend to limit your growth as a person. When you insist you have everything you need there, it's because you're not properly including everything you need."

"I'm 30 years old now," Georgina said. "I think I know what I need."

"I see," he said, writing on his notepad. "And you told me you saw Walter last night," he said. "How was that?"

A little smile flickered at the corner of Georgina's lips for a moment, and quickly disappeared. Not so quickly that Dr. Gregson missed it, however. "It was fine. He was the typical Walter."

"Tell me about the typical Walter," he said.

Georgina inhaled deeply, knowing she was being drawn out, but being tolerant of the process. "Walter. Walter is Walter. I've known him since forever. We grew up together, and got married when I was 23. We got divorced when I was 25."

"And what is Walter like?" Dr. Gregson said. "You married him, and you still maintain a relationship. People tend to bore you easily. What is it about Walter that keeps you interested?"

"He's just Walter," she said. "He doesn't pay attention to me when I'm being nasty. Nothing bothers him. He's smart, and he's hard-working. With all of his money, he doesn't have to be, but he is. He's unusual in that way. He's intelligent, a decent person... It's hard to find fault with Walter." She nodded to herself, thinking that was a very good way of putting it.

"Did he ask you to marry him again?" he asked.

If it Could Happen to Her

Georgina sighed, but looked slightly pleased, "He always does."

"And how does that make you feel?" he asked.

"I guess I like it," she said. "It feels nice to know he's there."

"Do you ever think of saying yes?" he asked.

"Oh, no," she said, firmly. "I like things the way I like them. In my apartment, everything is where I put it, or where I directed it should be. If you're married to someone, you're living with them, and they're leaving their things all over – they're moving your things, so you can't find them. It's awful."

"Well, that's true. In order to have a relationship with another person, you have to let them into your life. You have to allow your lives to intertwine."

"Right. I don't like that," Georgina said. "That's why we divorced."

"It's been five years," he said, "do you ever worry Walter will meet someone, and stop being available to you?"

She shifted uncomfortably on the couch. "I guess I do. I like having him available." She took a deep breath, and sat up rather abruptly. She crossed her legs and sat back, crossing her arms in front of her as well. "I don't want to talk about Walter anymore."

"That's fine," Dr. Gregson said, making some notes on his pad, "we can talk about other things. How about what you're going to do next? You've just finished a project, you've been out socially – have you been riding?"

Georgina finally gave a full smile, "I haven't yet, but I'm going to. I'm going out this afternoon for a good, long ride on Three Winds." Three Winds was her favorite horse.

"That's wonderful," he said. "It might be nice for you to take some time off, and perhaps take a vacation – spend some time on the shore, or down South?"

"No, actually, I'm thinking about working again," she said, raising her chin a little, as though preparing herself to hear his objections.

"You mean for Konig?" he asked.

"Yes, for Konig. I'm going to call Daniel Levine either this afternoon, or first thing tomorrow morning," she said. "He's been leaving messages, and I'm going to call him back."

"Do you think that's a good decision?" Dr. Gregson asked. "You always want to work after you've isolated, but then it tends to set you back."

"I don't think that's true," Georgina said.

"The work you do for Konig reinforces your belief that people can't be trusted, don't you think?"

"Maybe," she agreed. "But it's not as though these things don't happen. They do. There's a certain value in the fact that I usually find out who did it."

"Yes, absolutely. And you're extremely talented. But, I think what concerns me most is the fact that you usually isolate again after you've worked. It does have a negative effect on you."

"No, I don't think so," she said. She paused for a moment, and considered, "Maybe you're right. But I usually have a really good sense afterward that there's a rightness to it. That I've put things back together the best way they can possibly go back together."

"Would you say you feel compelled to do it, at all?" he asked.

"No, I would not," she said strongly. "It's just that – well, it makes me feel good – murder is a mess… and I'm a tidy person."

"Then why do you usually feel you need the services of a round-the-clock nurse afterward?" Dr. Gregson asked gently.

Georgina flushed slightly, and said "I take to my bed for a little while, and I suppose I enjoy having someone look after me every now and again. She keeps track of my medication, and brings me what I need so I don't have to do anything I don't want to. It usually doesn't last long."

"No, I know that." Dr. Gregson moved off of the familiarly touchy subject. "So, you've determined you're going to look for a job?"

"Yes," she said, sitting up a bit straighter.

"Do you already have something in mind?" he asked.

She glanced over at him, sometimes surprised by his insights, "Yes, there's something I'm interested in. I'm fairly certain Konig is going to get called in, if they haven't already. I thought I might ask for it."

"Is this someone you know?" he asked.

"It's someone who I have met, yes. I wouldn't even say it's an acquaintance. I would say we travel in similar circles."

"I see," he said.

"I really don't want to go into it any further than that just yet," she said.

"I understand," he said, looking at the clock. "I guess if I can't talk you into taking a little break, I think in our weekly sessions we should keep very close tabs on how the case is proceeding, and how you're feeling about it," he said.

"That's fine."

"Well, our time is nearly up. Is there anything else you'd like to talk about today? It seems you've got things fairly well worked out."

"I think so."

"How is your medication?" he asked.

"I'm taking the Xanax situationally," she said. "I haven't actually taken any since last week."

"And you're still off the Paxil CR?" he asked.

"Yes," she said, strongly.

"I do think we should revisit the idea of trying that again. I think you might find yourself feeling much more comfortable with an SSRI. Perhaps we could try Pristiq. It's fairly new, but it's having good results."

"I don't think so. I don't feel as sharp, or as acute, when I'm taking those types of medications. And when I'm working outside, I don't take anything at all. I need to be working on all gears. I can't be fuzzy at all."

"Alright," he said, "Well, we'll keep thinking about that." He took a deep breath. Georgina Adams was one of his most difficult patients, but by far his most interesting. Dealing with her was like walking a very thin tightrope. "I will see you again next week," he said, smiling and rising.

"Yes," she said, also standing, shaking his hand, and pulling her sheared brown mink coat off the back of one of his chairs.

Georgina turned, threw on her coat and walked out of the doctor's back door, tying her multi-colored Hermès scarf around her neck. She sometimes wondered why she bothered talking to Dr. Gregson. She had a Ph.D. in Psychology of her own, and had done some very extensive and groundbreaking research in methodology and analysis. She felt she knew already what was wrong with her – that her parents had been killed when she was less than three years old, and that she had been raised by a great-aunt who barely knew she existed. "I have attachment issues. I have trust issues. I have control issues, and a slight case of OCD," she thought to herself. "Duh."

She also felt that the systems she had put in place in her own life had made her very comfortable, and shouldn't be messed with. By anyone's standards, she was very productive. She had five university degrees, had been published in countless psychological journals, and had personally solved (officially or unofficially) over 50 murders.

All of this ran through her mind as she took the elevator down to the lobby of her doctor's Art Deco office building. His office was on the Upper East Side, only six blocks away from her own apartment, and sometimes she walked there, but the March chill had her taking her car. She walked towards a black Lincoln Town Car, with a 6'4," 270-pound young black man in a black suit and tie leaning against it, arms crossed, glaring at and frightening passers-by. He noticed her, and moved to open the back door. "Jason," she said. Jason's head was shaved, and Georgina never knew whether he had done it because he had started to become bald, which she doubted because he was still so young, or just because it made him look meaner. She suspected the latter.

"Ms. Adams," he said, helping her into the car, and closing the door behind her. He moved around the car and got behind the wheel. "Home?" he asked, looking in the rear view mirror.

"Yes, please, Jason," she said.

Jason wasn't chatty, and Georgina appreciated it. When she did take her car out, she liked to either look out of the window, or quietly read. Sometimes she drove herself, if it was a great distance, but within the city limits itself, she liked riding with Jason. Certainly nobody was going to bother her with him at the wheel.

On impulse, she pulled out her Blackberry and called Daniel Levine. She almost wanted to do it before she changed her mind. Three Winds would have to exercise with the groom again today.

"Daniel?" she said, once she finally got through to him. "Do you have some time this morning?"

"For you? Always," he said.

"Thanks. I'll be there in about ten minutes," she said, punching the button on her phone. "Jason?" she said.

"Yes, Ms. Adams."

"I changed my mind. We're going to Konig's offices."

Without a word, Jason took a left at the next corner, and headed back in the other direction.

If it Could Happen to Her

Chapter Two

Georgina sat cross-legged on the floor of Daniel Levine's office at Konig Investigations. It was a particularly male sort-of place with an enormous mahogany desk, brass-studded brown leather furniture, and several photographs of him with his Green Beret buddies and a variety of politicians and businessmen. He sat in one of his own guest chairs, turned to face the center of room and Georgina, his legs comfortably crossed at the knee, his hands folded together neatly on his thigh. He was dressed impeccably in a dark navy suit which fit his tall, athletic frame, dark hair and eyes perfectly, a crisp white shirt, and a lighter blue patterned tie with a perfect Windsor knot at his throat. He watched appreciatively as Georgina went through his files. It reminded him of the first night he had met her, more than four years ago.

They had attended a dinner party in Manhattan at the home of mutual friends, and had gotten onto the subject of crime. He told her what he did for a living, and she grilled him on his procedures. If she hadn't been so drop-dead gorgeous, he might not have been as content to listen, but as he listened, their contentious conversation became more interesting, and he had to admit she had made many good points. The friendly argument had ended in a challenge. Georgina asked to look at some of his open files – the ones he hadn't been able to close to his satisfaction. She insisted she could solve them all, just by looking at the paperwork. Intoxicated with her good looks, and three glasses of Scotch, he took her up on the challenge. They went back to his offices, he had her sign a confidentiality agreement, and then she took up the same spot on the floor where she sat now – of course, that night, she was in an evening gown, and they had continued to drink Scotch as she methodically examined paper after paper for hours, until the sun came up.

She wasn't able to come through, completely, with what she had boasted. She did, however, close – right there on the floor of his office – around 20 percent of his open cases, with evidence to back them up, and solid corridors for his investigators to follow through with. And she had given him what he believed to be the right answers, based on solid reasoning, in at least another 25 percent of them – but with no evidence, he would be unable to close them completely. He had sat, mostly mute, as he watched her process. She quickly, but thoroughly, examined each piece of paper in the file, reorganizing each into various piles, and then re-reorganizing them as she worked, mostly in silence. He answered whatever questions she had, but otherwise sipped on his Scotch

If it Could Happen to Her

and observed.

At the end of her analysis of each file, she had sat back and told him what she thought. Sometimes she had some new avenues his investigators might try, sometimes she had the answer dead-to-rights. By far, she was the most frustrated when she had to admit the information they had was inadequate, that all alleys were dead-ends, and there was nothing to be done.

He had offered her a job then and there. She laughed at him, and told him what her net worth was. He had to admit he was impressed by the number, but she stopped laughing when he asked her what she did with her time, since she didn't have to work. She grudgingly admitted she spent most of her time studying psychology, reading, and obtaining university degrees, mostly online. They left that night in a polite stand-off, with Georgina considering his offer.

First thing the following morning, she called and offered to do some work for him, on a consulting basis, but only if she was allowed to take those dead files and work on them first. He agreed, and didn't hear from her for about four months, aside from an e-mail every week or two when she closed a file. She ended up closing another 15 files, which, to him, was remarkable. To her, however, it must have been terribly frustrating, because he didn't hear from her again for another two months, despite his telephone calls and e-mails.

Out of the blue, she called him again, and asked if he had anything interesting to work on. She came over and looked at a few things, and he let her have her choice. Since then, he had known Georgina Adams was an odd duck, but she was brilliant. She probably had the finest mind of any investigator he currently had on his payroll, and he was probably also half in love with her. And since some of the files she had closed had been extremely lucrative insurance contracts, payable on a contingency fee basis, her cut of the fees had already run into millions. Money she didn't need, and hardly even noticed when he gave it to her.

He thought of that now, as he watched her sit cross-legged, in her jeans this time, going through the files from the Musgrave murders.

"So," she said, looking at the gruesome photographs of the bodies of Ingrid Musgrave and Bartolomeo Molina, "it's the beneficiaries' position that the killings were just incident to a robbery?"

"Yes, and it's the position of the police, too – which turns a $10 million payout each, into a $20 million payout each, and Lloyd's doesn't like that."

"No, I imagine they wouldn't," Georgina said. "And it's just the kids, not the ex-husband?"

"No, in fact, the ex-husband's splitting our fee with Lloyd's," Daniel said.

"Really?" Georgina said, looking up at him.

"Mm-hmm," Daniel murmured, nodding his head and raising his eyebrows.

"Hmm," Georgina said, looking back down at the photos.

"What do you think?" Daniel said.

"Well, it's overkill, but it's not malicious," Georgina said. "Three shots to the head, each? Is that what you said?" she asked.

"That's what the Coroner said," Daniel murmured.

She looked at the photographs again. Ingrid Musgrave lay on her side on the rug in her front hallway, dressed in cream-colored silk pajamas, a plush white robe and slip-on fleece-lined slippers. In the closer photographs, what was left of her face registered surprise. Bartolomeo Molina was slumped backward over the arm of an upholstered chair with a floral pattern. There was a lot of blood, but their skulls were still mostly intact despite three rounds each. "Not that much damage, considering," Georgina said. "A .22 or nine millimeter?"

"Nine millimeter," he said.

"That's a very precise weapon to use. No wiggle room for mistakes." She paused. "And they didn't bother with the televisions or the stereos. It certainly wasn't a bunch of gang-bangers bursting in and holding their guns sideways," she said, looking at the other crime scene photos.

"Nope," Daniel said.

"Well, then, I doubt they ever felt any pain," she said, "maybe even no apprehension." She paused for a moment, considering. "It certainly looks as though it was incidental to a robbery, but that doesn't mean anything. It could have been incidental to a robbery, or someone might have gone to some considerable trouble to make it look that way." She looked up at him. "Can I have the list of the stolen items again?" she asked.

He turned around to his desk, picked it up and handed it to her.

"Very nice things," she said. "Total value, $70 million? Wow."

"Well, most of that was the art. There was some in the way of jewelry and cash, in the safe they removed," he said.

"I can see that for myself," Georgina said sharply. "Of course, we'll never know everything that was in that safe." She paused. "And the security system was off?"

If it Could Happen to Her

"Off," he said.

"Completely off? There's no back-up? It wasn't damaged, or tampered with?"

"Nope, just off," he said.

"Well, that seems inside," Georgina said. "It might have been a simple mistake if someone hadn't come along at just that particular time and killed everybody and stolen everything."

"Exactly," Daniel said.

"And the housekeeper was the last one to leave. Have the police talked to her?" she asked.

"Swears she left it on. Took a polygraph," he said. "Passed."

"Well, I wonder if I would have asked the same questions as our fine men in blue," she muttered. "I'm going to talk to her." She turned over another piece of paper. "Hmm… Why's the ex-husband hand-in-hand with Lloyd's on this one?"

"He's the executor of the estate."

"Still?"

"Still."

"What does the will say?" she asked.

"It leaves everything to the Metropolitan Museum of Art, for the introduction of an Ingrid Musgrave wing," he said, smiling crookedly, "including the art that's now gone."

"Nothing to the kids?" Georgina said, sitting back on her heels.

"Nope," he said.

"Wow."

"Yep."

"So, all the kids would be getting would be the $20 million each from Lloyd's, basically?"

"Basically."

Georgina ran all of this through her head. "So, the father is the executor, but he doesn't necessarily have to look into this if he doesn't want to."

"He does, actually. There's a recent codicil to the wife's will, specifically demanding an investigation if she were to die under suspicious circumstances."

"You're kidding," she said.

"Nope."

"Well," she said, pausing. "That's unusual."

"Yep. Plus," he added. "I get the feeling the ex-husband hates his kids."

"Oh, he does," Georgina said. "At least the ones from his first marriage."

"How do you know that?"

"I know," she said, not bothering to elaborate. "So, they might not be inheriting anything from him when he goes."

"I'd tend to doubt it," Daniel said.

"So, conceivably, this $20 million might be the last free money they're going to get for the rest of their lives?"

"Looks that way," he said.

"That's interesting," she said.

"I think so."

"People can get pretty desperate about that kind of money. Disagreements can come up about splitting it up, more people could get hurt. It rarely goes smoothly," she said.

"Nope," he agreed.

"So, why you? The police are content with calling it murder in the course of a robbery?"

"They are, unless we prove otherwise."

"Well, it only happened last week. They can't have that carved in stone yet. Do you have a copy of the will?" Georgina asked.

"I do," he said, turning around in his chair, picking that file off his desk and handing it to her.

She glanced it over quickly, flipping through the pages. "I thought so. I was pretty sure if you're disinheriting your children, you have to be fairly specific about it. It says, 'It is my intention to leave no money to my children, having adequately provided for them during their lifetimes, and wishing to fund, instead, the charity of my choice.'"

"Cold," he said.

"I've seen worse," she said, flipping through more pages. "And here's the codicil." She read, "'Should my death be of anything other than natural causes, it is my wish that a thorough investigation be undertaken by a private firm of my Executor's choosing.' Well," Georgina said, "it seems she wasn't worried about her ex killing her. Otherwise, he could have hired any rinky-dink P.I. service that would have given him whatever result he asked for. I wonder what else she was afraid of? The Metropolitan Museum of Art is usually content to let its donors die of natural causes."

"It's nearly $400 million," Daniel said. "Can we completely discount that?"

"Maybe not completely," she said, "but they've got that much hanging on just one wall in there. And they're not hurting. They're doing very well."

"So, the kids?" Daniel asked.

Georgina shrugged her shoulders. "I guess. Lloyd's would certainly like that. $70 million in trinkets is pretty powerful incentive, too. It could just be a robbery." She picked up the paperwork from Lloyd's. "Key man policies," she said, "all through the ex-husband's holding company. Apparently, she still sat on the Board of Directors."

Georgina sat thinking for a moment.

"Geoffrey Musgrave wants it handled as quietly as possible," Daniel said, intruding on her thoughts.

"Well, with the newspapers and magazines he owns, that should make the PR angle easier," she said, sniffing out a little laugh. "Can we get him on the phone?" she asked.

Daniel raised his eyebrows. "Sure," he said. "Why?"

"I just want to talk to him," she said, "to get a feel for him again. It's been awhile. Call him in Bedford."

Daniel knew better than to ignore Georgina's instincts. He got the telephone number out of the file and dialed, moving the telephone from his desk to the floor in between them, and turning on the speaker.

A maid picked up the telephone, but before Daniel had a chance to introduce himself, Georgina said, "Geoffrey Musgrave, please. Georgina Adams calling."

After a few minutes, they heard a loud, gruff voice say, "Georgina Adams? I hope you're not looking for more money for that Frick. It hasn't been a year yet. Do you think I don't keep track?"

"It's not the Frick this time, Mr. Musgrave," she said, "although I do appreciate your last donation. It was especially generous. Honestly, I don't know what we'd do without you."

"Well, I like to do what I can," he said.

"I'm sorry we didn't see you at the party last night," she said.

"Yes. Sorry about that. Couldn't make it, dear," he said, getting close to flirting with her, "You'll have to save me a dance for the next time."

"Oh, my pleasure," she said, smiling into the phone.

"What can I do for you today?"

"I'm calling because I'm working for Konig on Ingrid's murder."

If it Could Happen to Her

There was dead silence for close to a half a minute. Daniel and Georgina waited. "What the hell for?" he finally asked.

"I suppose you could call it a career," she said.

"What the hell is this?" Geoffrey Musgrave yelled, "Some kind of damn joke?"

"Oh, it's no joke, Mr. Musgrave," she said. "I've been working for Konig on a consulting basis for awhile."

"For money?" he asked.

"I get money, but I find the work interesting. I'm very good."

"Well, I guess you're smart. Weren't you Valedictorian or something when you graduated with Luanne?"

"Yes," she said.

"Well, at least you've got a decent job, unlike the wastes of space I've got," he growled.

"You're referring to your children from your first marriage?" she asked.

"You can quit fucking around, now, Adams," Mr. Musgrave growled.

Georgina smiled as Daniel leaned forward and spoke, "Mr. Musgrave, this is Daniel Levine. Georgina is the lead investigator on your wife's case. We wouldn't give it to her if we didn't feel she was the best one for it."

"Oh," Mr. Musgrave said, "Levine. Well," he paused for a moment, "What do you want, Adams? It's not easy to catch me off-guard."

"I just wanted to double-check a few things with you really quick. I'll probably also be coming out there for a visit to talk with you in the next few days," Georgina said.

"That's fine. Do what you need to do. I just want everything handled. I want it handled well. Somebody killed my wife, and I want to know who did it. People don't get away with just doing things like that to me."

"Certainly," Georgina said. "I understand. But, I have to ask you, what if it's one of your children who's done this thing?"

"Throw them under the bus," he said, without hesitation.

"Okay," Georgina said simply.

"Well," Mr. Musgrave said gruffly, "When are you coming out? I do have work to do, you know."

"Well, I want to drive down and look at Ingrid's house tomorrow, probably with the detective investigating it for the Cambridge department. You don't have a problem with that, I hope?" she asked.

"No, I don't have a problem with that. Levine should have the keys and

If it Could Happen to Her

the security system codes – a hell of a lot of good they are now," he said.

"How about we meet the day after tomorrow? After lunch?" Georgina asked.

"That's fine. I'll be working from out here. You know the way?" he asked.

"I do," she said.

"See you then," he said, hanging up the phone.

"Well, I guess you were right about the way he feels about his kids," Daniel said.

"Oh, yes," Georgina said. "I've found a man tends to love his children as much as he loves their mother. Once they move on to the next marriage, they usually move on to the next set of children, too. And his children *are* fairly worthless – probably through his lack of attention, though. They lost their oldest son, Geoffrey, Jr., in an accidental drowning when he was about 10 years old. Something like that can really change the family dynamic. Plus," she said, "I thought he needed to wrap his head around the fact that I was working on this."

"You clearly enjoyed throwing him for a loop. Do you know him socially?" Daniel asked.

"I went to Brown with Luanne, his daughter," she said. "And we've seen each other around. He's an asshole."

"He's also a billionaire, and he's the client," Daniel reminded her.

"I know," she said simply. She picked up the insurance policies again, and started making notes on a legal pad Daniel gave her. "The kids… Luanne, the oldest since Geoff Jr. died – she's a flake, and an undiagnosed dyslexic. Ingrid, Jr. comes next and then Matthew – they are *unusually* attached to one another," Georgina said, raising her eyebrows and looking at Daniel. "Frederick, a culture wannabe in San Francisco, and then little Magrit – a stoner. What about the old mistress, Marianne Daumier, and her bastard daughter, Olivia?"

Daniel sat up straighter. "Who are they?"

Georgina rolled her eyes. "For years," she said, "Mr. Musgrave was keeping Marianne on the side during his marriage to Ingrid. Everybody knew about it, including Ingrid. They even had a daughter together, Olivia. She's a little younger than me. Then, when Mr. Musgrave divorced the first Mrs. Musgrave, Marianne thought he was going to marry her. It came as something of an unhappy surprise when he married his personal trainer, who was about 20 years younger."

"Well, you certainly should talk to them," he said. "They didn't benefit from the insurance policies, but I'm sure they'd have a few things to tell you."

"I think it's strange, don't you, that he referred to Ingrid as his wife, not his ex-wife?" she asked.

"I also thought it was interesting that he considered something had been done to him, not her."

"Yes, he seemed almost *offended* by it," she said, trying to use exactly the right word. "He seems to have ownership issues about the people in his life," Georgina said, leaning back on the heels of her palms, and pushing the papers around with the toe of her ballet flat. "She was still on the Board of his company. They both seem to have little regard for their children. Maybe they were closer than they let on, even though poor Bartolomeo was in the picture," she said, while nudging an actual picture of poor, dead Bartolomeo with her toe. "And why the codicil? I don't think I've ever seen anything like that, and I've known some very paranoid rich people."

"I know. It's weird. You might talk to one of her friends, too," Daniel suggested. "maybe she had a best friend?"

"No," Georgina said, "not really. At least I don't think so. I can ask around, but I'm starting to think the ex-husband might still have been the best friend she had." She exhaled deeply. "I need some time to think." She looked up at Daniel. "Can I take these things with me?" she asked.

"They're yours," he said. "I'm giving you the originals, and I'm keeping the copies, so take good care of them, as usual." He reached down and started helping her to gather up the papers, and put them into the storage box. "I'll carry these down to Jason," he said.

Georgina got back to her apartment, and had Jason deposit the box of Musgrave materials and paperwork into the office, right next to her desk. She had cleared away her last research project, and her desk stood empty and ready to face the next task.

She pulled down a large scroll of magnetized plastic that rolled out of her ceiling to cover one-half of the wall of her study, and hooked the bottom of it to the baseboard. She pulled the box of papers over to the board, and got a box of small red-enameled magnets from her desk. She methodically pulled the pieces of paper from the file, including the photographs and other paper pieces of evidence, and affixed them to the board. She stepped back every few minutes, examining what she had done, reorganized, and began to add more. By the time she was done, nearly every relevant piece of paper, or a miniaturized photocopy of it, was affixed to the wall. She always called this her "murder board," and she liked to think it represented the contents of her head, in the file in her brain where she was slowly writing the story of Ingrid's Musgrave's untimely death. It was in constant flux, and she kept it constantly updated. Armeda knew never to go near it, or even so much as dust it, or she would deal with Georgina's firey temper. It would remain there until she was finished.

Georgina stepped back, and felt the board represented her current understanding and the information she had. She took a deep breath, and decided to now clear it all from her mind, and not look at it again until she could see it from a fresh perspective.

She called one of her personal trainers on the telephone, and had him come over. If she wasn't going to be able to ride Three Winds today, she needed a workout. She changed into a black tank top and black leggings. She stretched and warmed up while she waited. Once James got there, he found Georgina ready for a fight. She already had her own kickboxing equipment, so it wasn't long before they were into it. Georgina had transformed one of the extra bedrooms in her apartment into a spacious gym. It had little in the way of equipment, just an elliptical machine, and a Pilates reformer machine. It also had a large mat in the center of the room where Georgina liked to practice various forms of martial arts with private instructors. She found it centered her mind and relaxed her nerves almost as well as about 2 mg. of Xanax, with the added benefit of not making her tired, and keeping her fit and skinny.

Georgina worked up a sweat, and thought about the Musgrave family in one part of her brain, while the other part of her brain was strictly focused on not letting James kick her in the head. He was very, very good, and she had told him long ago not to hold back with her. She had also bloodied his nose more than once in a friendly reminder that she wasn't going to hold back, either. He knocked her on her ass for the second time, and she finally pushed the Musgrave murder completely away, and focused on the fight at hand. She matched him blow for blow, blocking and being blocked, and found herself, at the end of an hour, exhausted on her knees, breathing heavily.

"Thanks, James," she said, pulling herself up from the floor wearily.

"No problem, Ms. Adams. Same time next week?" he asked, breathing and sweating heavily himself.

"I'll call you," she said, heading off for the comfort of her shower.

If it Could Happen to Her

She let the shower heads pummel her body, using the strongest setting for water pressure, leaning into it. She wrapped her robe about her, and strode back into her office. She hefted what remained in the box from Konig onto the desk, and flipped off the top. She took out the folder of crime scene photographs again, and flipped through them, allowing her brain to absorb all of the details. She placed them one-by-one onto the board, too. She pulled out the various legal papers, the insurance policies, and the police reports, neatly sorting each pile, and moving papers from one file to another as she read and re-read the material. Then she sat quietly looking at the various tidy piles, and up at the board, until the sound of the front doorbell, and Armeda's quick footsteps, alerted her that her hairdresser was there to blow out her hair.

If it Could Happen to Her

Chapter Three

Georgina called around and located all of the grieving children. Frederick was in town from San Francisco with his lovely blond wife. They were staying at his father's Fifth Avenue apartment, along with his younger sister Magrit, in from London with her three year-old son. "That explains why the old man's in Bedford," Georgina thought to herself. She could imagine the scene there, smiled, and shook her head. Frederick fancied himself an art historian, and a collector, and his wife had social pretensions which knew no bounds. Also, they were sharing the apartment at the moment with Magrit, whose little boy was the product of a brief fling with a British rock star who had since died of an overdose of heroin. Magrit, a hippie and stoner of long standing, could barely take care of herself, let alone properly raise a child. Georgina could imagine how they were getting along with the two San Franciscans who, after seven years of marriage, had still not seen fit to produce offspring. Not well, was her guess.

She needed to speak to all of them, and time was of the essence. They might scatter to the ends of the Earth at any moment, but she hoped their greed would keep them in New York City, while they waited to find out how their mother's death would affect, or benefit, them financially. The other three lived in NYC, so she had fewer worries about them.

First, however, she needed to see the crime scene itself, and talk to the housekeeper, Ms. Greta Larson. The police might be satisfied with a polygraph. They usually were. But she thought it was just too much of a coincidence the alarm system was turned off when the murderers arrived. It was too tidy.

Georgina made a call over to her garage to make sure her Range Rover was gassed up and ready to go. She hadn't used it in ages, and whenever it wasn't used regularly, she had it professionally garaged and maintained. She had a drive to Connecticut ahead of her. She put together a map of everywhere she wanted to go, with detailed driving instructions, and went over it several times. She hated to admit it, but staying in her apartment for so long had made her nervous about being far away from it for any length of time. Dr. Gregson would love for her to admit that at their next session. She memorized her driving plan, and printed it out. She also had a state-of-the art navigation system in her Rover, so she felt as comfortable as she possibly could. She thought of taking a sedative to steady her nerves before going, but decided against it. She knew that once she was interacting with people, her interest in them would take her sufficiently out of herself to calm down, and she needed to be sharp to read them properly. Until then, she would have to tolerate a few butterflies in her stomach as she drove.

Jason dropped her at the garage, and she generously tipped the attendant as he handed her the keys. She slipped into the cream-colored leather interior, and glanced around, checking each of the systems in turn. She rubbed the smooth leather and burled wood of the steering wheel, and adjusted her Cartier Balon Bleu watch, and then the amethyst and peridot Verdura three-stone ring that she wore on her right hand. The car appeared to be functioning perfectly, and she took a deep breath as she slowly moved it out of Park, and into Drive. She tried to keep her face without affect, in case the attendant was still looking at her. Men invariably stared at her, because she was so breathtakingly beautiful, but she didn't really want a witness to how nervous she was at the moment. She eased her foot off the brake, and drifted out of the parking garage onto a busy New York City street.

She gripped the wheel tightly as she eased into traffic, and paid attention to everything on every side. It didn't take long for her to relax behind the wheel, though, and, indeed, before she was even leaving the complicated and taxi-glutted streets of Manhattan, she was already piloting in and out of lanes with a confident expertise. She felt herself exhale deeply. Once she got onto the I-95, she really relaxed, and enjoyed the feel of the luxurious interior, and the control of the car underneath her. It was a powerful black Range Rover, a suggestion of Walter's. He had arranged for its purchase, although she wouldn't allow him to pay for it. It was reinforced with many options like specialized hearty bumpers in front and back, and a sophisticated and brutish suspension system that could go off-road quite deeply with perfect ease. He felt she would appreciate not only the superb performance, but also the confidence of knowing she was driving something designed for far more rough stuff than she was ever likely to need it for.

She had already programmed her first destination, the Cambridge, Connecticut Police Station headquarters, into her car's navigation system, and was able to enjoy listening to her audio lecture series on game theory from The Great Courses while she drove. After about an hour, she pulled into the parking lot of the police station, and straight into a clearly-marked Handicapped spot right next to the front door. She put her large tortoiseshell sunglasses on, checked her lipstick, and fluffed up her hair in the car's rear view mirror before exiting. She jumped out, and deliberately dropped her keys onto the parking lot cement. She bent over to pick them up, giving a perfect view of her derrière to anyone who might be looking from inside the police station. From her extensive study of, and experience with, police, she knew for certain they were. She retrieved the keys, and tucked them away into her purse as she strode purposefully into the police station. She opened the door with a flourish, and looked around, deliberately not connecting eyes with anyone, knowing they would all be on her. She took her sunglasses off, and swept them up off her face, pulling her hair back with them, and revealing her unusual blue-green eyes.

The desk sergeant came around his desk, looking stern, and she turned to face him. "Hi," she said, giving him her most dazzling smile.

He attempted to look unaffected, but the bob up and down of his Adam's apple as he swallowed betrayed him. "Ma'am, you've parked in a Handicapped spot. Can you please move your car?"

She laughed, and reached out to touch his forearm. "I'm completely helpless," she said, "does that count as handicapped?"

A smile flickered at the corners of his lips. "Not in this county, it doesn't."

"Well," she said, "why don't you just tell me where to find…" she fished for a few long moments in her large tote bag, "Detective Trigilio," she finally said, seemingly reading from a cocktail napkin, "and I'll get out of your hair." She looked him full in the eye, then, and he had trouble looking away.

"Alright, but then you're going to have to move that Rover, or it's going to get towed," he said.

"Okay," she said. "That's a deal." She sat down on one of the benches against the front window, and turned to her left to bestow her haughtiest smile at a portly middle-aged woman who had been watching the entire exchange, but who now looked away. Georgina examined her manicure until she saw a pair of brown size 12 worn Hush Puppies appear near her feet.

Georgina looked up and saw a man who matched those shoes more perfectly than she could ever have imagined. She smiled, this time quite honestly, as she saw a 50-ish man, about 6'3" tall, weighing close to 300 pounds, dark brown hair cut poorly and starting to show some grey around the temples, wearing a boring brown tie and a brown tweed jacket that didn't match either the tie or the season, and a world-weary, bored air that didn't for a moment seem to notice her good looks. Immediately, Georgina knew she had met someone she could talk to.

She got up, and extended her hand. "Detective Trigilio?" she asked.

"That's me," he said. "You're from Konig?"

"Yes, Daniel Levine sent me."

"Alright, well, that's fine," he said, pulling out a notebook from his back pocket. "I talked to him earlier today." He looked up at her, "I guess you've got the keys and the security codes? We've got them, but you're really supposed to have them yourself."

"Yep, I've got them," she said, patting her purse.

"Have you got any identification in there?" he asked, pointing at her Louis Vuitton Neverfull totebag.

Georgina pulled out her wallet, and showed Trigilio her New York State driver's license, and her photo identification from Konig. He made notes of the identification numbers on his pad, and made sure he had the spelling of her name correct. "Adams," he said. "I just read a book about John Adams."

"He's my great-great-great-great-great grandfather," Georgina said.

"Do you know the book I mean? Won the Pulitzer?" he said, ignoring the reference to her famous forebear that made most people drool.

"I do," she said.

"Good book. I like a guy who isn't flashy. A guy you don't see coming."

"Me, too."

"Must be nice to say you're related to a president."

"It is," she said.

"Maybe in about two hundred years, my great-great-great-great-great grandkids will like to brag that I was a cop." He swept his left hand out toward the door, indicating to her he was ready to leave. She followed him out.

"We can both go in my car," he said.

"Okay, then I'd better move mine, or it won't be here when I get back."

He saw she was parked in the Handicapped space, and said, "What are you, some kind of a jerk? All of these spaces all over here, and you've got to park where the folks with wheelchairs need to go?"

"Sorry, Detective," she said, honestly meaning it. "I did it to get attention. If I hadn't, I'd still be sitting there on that bench with everybody else, waiting for somebody to notice me."

"Well," he said, "maybe that's true, but get it out of there now. Handicapped people don't call ahead for reservations, you know."

"Yes, Sir," she said, and moved the Rover quickly into a proper spot.

She followed Trigilio to his blue Chevy Impala, and got into the passenger seat. Clearly, he was not the type to hold a car door for a lady. As she snapped her seatbelt on, she asked, "could this car look any more like an unmarked police car?"

"I'm not out to fool anybody," he said, looking over his shoulder as he backed out of his spot.

They drove for about ten minutes, straight outside the village, with the countryside getting more and more rural. But, unlike most rural countrysides, this land had been groomed and planted with a symmetry God had never intended. The extremely wealthy people who had made this their country home had pulled up ancient trees, and planted new ancient trees, as it suited them. There were a few dairy farms, but with none of the sulfuric smell that usually heralded such places. Georgina sensed that they were more decorative than functional, and that only enough milk flowed, so locals could find it 'adorable' to be getting their milk from the local dairy.

They pulled into the driveway of Ingrid Musgrave's 210-acre estate, and drove about the length of two football fields on the cobblestone surface before arriving at the curve which turned right in front of the massive Colonial house. Georgina had noted the location of several cameras nestled in amongst the trees which lined the drive. She got out of the car, and buttoned up her barn jacket around her neck, tucking her hands into her pockets. The late March chill which hadn't been quite so noticeable in the city, was definitely felt here. A slight breeze carried dampness, and the gray sky hid any sunshine that might have warmed things up, or changed the somber mood of the scene. The house had a stone exterior, slate roof, and copper trim, with black enamel shutters on each of the fourteen windows, eight on the top floor, and three on either side of the front door, each with a flower box filled with pink and white flowers. Georgina walked slowly back and forth in front of the house, looking at the electrical hookups, the wires and cables for telephone and television, observing the security cameras, some of them trained back down the driveway, and some trained at the entrance to the house. She walked over to the right side of the house, and looked back at the lawn. "Is it alright if I walk on the lawn?" she asked Trigilio, who had been watching her every move.

"Sure," he said, following her. Georgina walked slowly along the right side of building. She saw the deep triangular indentation in the lawn. "I guess this is where the safe landed. If you've got the right equipment, it's smart to just take it with you."

His eyebrows raised. "We expect that's right."

She looked up at the windows. "It's hard to tell with these colonials," she said. "They're so lovely and symmetrical. If this were a typical McMansion, there would be no doubt where the master bedroom was. But I'll bet it's up there," she said, pointing.

"You'd win your bet," Trigilio said, "but I would have said Federalist."

Georgina smiled at him. "You could be right." She was really starting to enjoy his company.

They continued on a walk about the perimeter of the house, and then walked up and down the driveway again, taking note of the position of the security cameras. "That's unusual, isn't it?" Georgina said. "Why wouldn't Ingrid just have these running all of the time on a looping recording?"

"I've seen all kinds," Trigilio said, "motion control – turn it on, turn it off. It's hard to say. We're looking into it with her security company, a local place. If it was installed more than three years ago, it might still be running on videotape. If it's recent, then it should have been digital, with practically unlimited storage, and could, and should, run all the time. If she was extremely security-minded, I would also say they should always be running. She's got quite a few of them, but I'm looking around, and there are plenty of blind spots. Who's to say? Maybe she wanted to have the best security possible, but got a little bit cheap when she got the quote from the contractor."

Georgina nodded, "That's exactly what she would do. But she didn't spend all of her time here, either. I think she was in Florida most of the time, or in the city. And out here –" she said, gesturing at the rolling hills, "one might feel safe." She stood and thought for a moment, looking about her at the property, feeling another chill up her spine that was only partly caused by the gust of chill wind that swept her hair to the side. "Hmm. Well, shall we go in?"

They approached the front of the home, meant to be welcoming, with a flagstone walk flanked by black, iron, solar-powered spot lights and careful plantings of pink and white perennials, leading up to a large black enamel-painted double door, with two enormous brass door knockers, and a lively white and pink wildflower wreath hanging from each. The only thing marring the otherwise idyllic scene was the yellow crime scene tape which stretched across the door, secured on either side. "May I?" Georgina asked, gesturing to the tape, "or would you rather?"

"I'll take the tape down," Trigilio said, "but you're supposed to let yourself in. Do you have everything you need?"

"I should have," she said, reaching into her coat pocket for a small zippered leather wallet which contained a notepad, and the key to the front door. She put the key into the lock and turned it, pushing the door open at the same time. Instantly, a steady beeping told her she had 60 seconds to punch in the ten-digit security code. Trigilio looked on with appreciation as he watched her turn to her right, flip open the security panel and punch it in without referring to any notes, having clearly memorized it. The beeping stopped, and she said, "I wish it had been on that night."

"Yeah," he agreed. "She had a motion sensor that would have told her the minute somebody pulled into her driveway."

They both stood very still, very quietly for a moment, looking around them respectfully, knowing this was where Ingrid Musgrave had met her end. Georgina finally allowed her gaze to drop to the rectangular carpet which covered the center of the foyer, with long console tables and mirrors on either side. The stain from the pool of blood still covered almost the entire area of the 10' x 14' Samarkand Persian rug. Georgina never failed to be surprised when faced with the amount of blood the human body holds. Ingrid was fashionably thin, and her body would have held slightly more than 4 quarts of blood. "So," she said, "a nine millimeter shot as she opened the front door, from a distance of about three feet, and then two more shots to the head once she was down, both from about 6 inches."

"Seems professional," Trigilio said, "and confident. They didn't just take a .38 and blow her head off with one shot."

"And none of them were through-and-through?" Georgina asked.

"Nope," he said, looking down at the rug. "Mrs. Musgrave here had one that glanced off her skull, but stayed lodged in her scalp – but she was probably already dead when she got that one. The first shot most likely finished her off. Right between the eyes."

"And poor Bartolomeo," Georgina said, walking forward, past the formal living room and into a smaller television room. She looked at the flowered chintz-covered easy chair, the top half of which was now covered in Bartolomeo Molina's blood and brain matter.

"He was sitting over there," Trigilio said. "He got up, but not very far. They shot him, and put him straight away. He ended up sitting back down, and they got closer and put two more into his forehead. Those all stayed in." He paused for a moment. "And I wonder why she got the door? It's late at night. Why didn't the man get the door?"

"Hard to say," Georgina said. "And they weren't a bunch of goofballs, either. They took some quality stuff, and didn't bother with anything relatively inexpensive. Was there any trace?"

"None," Trigilio said, growling. "The rugs had been vacuumed before the housekeeper left, but they left nothing, not a hair, not a speck of mud, nothing. I almost see them wearing plastic booties and hair nets."

"Definitely not goofballs," Georgina agreed. She went back to the front door and started examining each room on the first floor, trying to look beyond the fingerprint powder scattered over everything, observing the places where pieces of art had been removed from its housings on the wall, and taking in whatever she could gather from this observation of what Ingrid Musgrave liked to have around her. At least in the public rooms of the house. The photographs which were displayed in the formal living room downstairs were exactly what she would have expected from Ingrid. Pics of Ingrid with two ex-Presidents, and the current President. Pics of Ingrid with the Governor. Pics of Ingrid with several celebrities. Pics of Ingrid with Bartolomeo on vacation were in the television room where he was murdered.

"So far no pictures of the kids... or the grandkid, either," Georgina said to herself, somewhat surprised by that. Although knowing what she knew of Magrit, the perma-stoner probably never was able to produce a photograph of the child sufficiently cleaned up to pass mustard with Ingrid. "Maybe upstairs in the bedroom."

Trigilio followed her around the house, keeping quiet unless she asked a question, but observing her observing. She started up the stairs to the second floor, and went, room-by-room, seeing Ingrid's bedroom, but leaving that for last. She looked at all of the guest bedrooms, one clearly fitted up for children, with two twin beds with rails and a crib. "Hmm," she thought, but moved breezily amongst these rooms, as they were clearly the product of the decorator's imagination.

When she finally went back to Ingrid's room, she stopped at the door, and slowly took it all in. It was nearly as large as the formal living room downstairs, which it was directly above. Bookshelves near the window told Georgina these books were favorites, too frequently consulted to be downstairs in the formal library. The writing desk, situated next to the bookshelves and square in front of the window showcasing her perfectly symmetrical backyard,

If it Could Happen to Her

was not merely for decorative purposes. There were shelves holding papers neatly stacked, and two sides of full-size drawers, which Georgina found held files, favorite writing implements, stationery, etc. Through a set of double doors opposite her, Georgina saw a glimpse of a marble and mahogany bathroom that rivaled her own in spa-like beauty. Ingrid clearly spent nearly as much time up here as she did downstairs. This was her lair.

Georgina drifted about, and slowly took in the measure of the room. It was lovely, without question. The color palette was an off-white toward the pink end of the spectrum, with highlights of salmon and other darker floral colors. The bed itself sat against the far wall, facing the fireplace, and a mediocre landscape in an elaborate gold frame that Georgina didn't recognize. She went over to the right side of the bed, furthest from the door, slid out the drawer of the bedside table and found the remote control. She pointed it at the painting and the canvas slowly rolled up to reveal a flat screen TV.

"Goddamn!" Trigilio said. "That's incredible."

"I have one just like it at home," Georgina said, smiling. She punched a few different buttons, and found the link into the security system. Once she was in there, she goofed around with it, and made a few mistakes, but finally was able to see how Ingrid could monitor her various security cameras (both inside and outside her home) from her bed. "I don't have this, though," she said. "Did you see any cameras downstairs, inside?" She looked over at Trigilio with amazement. "I was looking, and I didn't see any."

"I didn't either," he said. "And none are listed. We didn't have any idea this setup was here."

"It's meant to look just like a regular television remote control, so I can understand, but why didn't your guys wonder why there was a remote control without a television to control remotely?" Georgina asked, waving the remote control in her hand, her eyes showing anger briefly.

"I don't know," he said. "I was here, and I checked the inventory, but I didn't put two and two together."

Georgina sat down on the end of Ingrid's bed, and shrugged her arms out of her jacket. She said, sharply "TV plus remote equals 0. Remote minus TV equals negative 1."

"Understood," he said. Trigilio swallowed and watched Georgina work. She quickly scrolled through the various options of cameras in each of the rooms of the house and outdoors, and scanned through the recording options as well. The good news was she was able to pinpoint the location of the cameras

If it Could Happen to Her

in each of the rooms, including the guest bedrooms, Georgina didn't hesitate to notice with a frown. So Ingrid liked to watch.

The bad news was that the inside cameras didn't appear to have recorded anything, either.

"This is bullshit," she said, turning to Trigilio. "There is no fucking way this woman, who liked to watch the cameras in her house from her bed, as a form of entertainment," she bit the words out, "was going to have it just turned off by accident. No fucking way. Where's the housekeeper?" She stood up and tugged on her coat.

"She passed the polygraph," Trigilio said.

"She didn't pass any polygraph I administered," Georgina said, getting ready to charge past him.

He put out his arm and stopped her. At her look, he moved his arm back out of the way and raised both of his hands up, but said, "Just wait a minute. Now I'll admit we missed this monitor. But stop and think for a minute. Those things don't need to be taped to be enjoyed. They're clearly running, even now, with the system turned off. Maybe she just liked to watch what her guests were up to. Maybe she didn't tape it."

Georgina stood fuming for a moment. "Ask me about the polygraph," Trigilio said. "I wasn't happy with it, either."

"In a minute," she said, taking advantage of his guilt. She took a deep breath, and appeared to be thinking hard. "Do me a favor and go downstairs into the television room, and move that book that's blocking part of that camera." She reached over and picked up the remote again and sat down. When Trigilio went out of the room, she jumped up and hustled over to Ingrid's desk. She pulled out drawers, and reached her hands up and behind them, not finding anything until she reached the bottom of the right hand stack of drawers. She felt a crinkling of paper and smiled. She pulled very carefully and dislodged a soft package, wrapped in brown paper. She chuckled to herself, and quickly shut the drawer and shoved the package into her handbag.

She was proud of herself, but still pissed the police missed so much. "Idiots," she said. She picked up the remote again, and saw Trigilio had, indeed, moved the book, and was probably on his way back upstairs. Georgina took a deep breath, and tried to shake off the feeling she needed 10 milligrams of Librium. Goddamn it, but incompetence pissed her off. When he walked in, she flipped off the remote, put it back into the drawer, turned and sat down in one of Ingrid's chairs in front of the fireplace. "What did the housekeeper say?"

Trigilio joined her in the chair opposite. "They asked her about turning the system on and off. It was her job, her responsibility. She'd forgotten to do it once or twice several years ago, and got her ass handed to her, verbally. She said she'd never forgotten since, because she knew she'd be fired. She'd been told as much. She swears she left it on, and her pulse reflects that. That's what we've got."

"And that's it?" Georgina asked. "Maybe that was all for the polygraph, but I hope you interviewed her better than that."

"I did," he said. "The questions on the poly were all about the system. But the questions I asked were more about her associations, her family, her friends."

"What'd you find?"

"She's got next to nothing. She's got this job. Or she used to. She didn't get paid very much – figured it was an honor to work for 'such fine people,' she said. She's got no kids; she's got no husband. She was here six days out of every seven."

"But Ingrid wasn't," Georgina said. "Maybe that's why Greta liked it. Ingrid couldn't have spent more than four or five months here, total, here during the course of the year. She spent some time in New York City, but she had to spend half of her time in Florida, for income taxes."

"That's how the rich stay rich," Trigilio grumbled.

A smile pulled at the corners of Georgina's lips when she thought how much money she would save every year if she spent more of her time at her house in Wellington. "And all you've got is her say-so that she's got no kids, no husband."

"We're checking it out. It's the first avenue I'm going down."

"But if somebody she knows was involved, she wouldn't necessarily know about it herself," Georgina said.

"I know," Trigilio said, sounding annoyed.

"Okay," Georgina said. "I would like to talk to her, though. Where is she?"

Trigilio sat up straighter. "She lives in town, apartment above the drycleaner. You're welcome to go and question her, obviously, but I need to be there."

"You don't need to be there," Georgina said evenly. "It's not mandatory."

"Unless you're walking there, it is," he said, taking his car keys out of his pocket and getting up from the chair.

If it Could Happen to Her

<u>Chapter Four</u>

Georgina quickly determined that she could abide Trigilio's company, since her own car was over 20 miles away, and she was not disposed to walk to get it. Plus, she also knew her disappointment with the police investigation couldn't be entirely held against him. For a moment, as they drove together in silence, she wondered if perhaps she was so uncomfortable because, if somebody like Ingrid could get murdered, and somebody could get away with it, then somebody might be able to get that close to somebody like Georgina, too. If it could happen to her… she didn't like the thought.

They arrived in the charming village of Cambridge, with its rustic-looking painted signs, all seeming small-town, but hanging over entrances for shops like Lilly Pulitzer, Prada, Gucci. "There's a lot of money in this town," Trigilio said as he pulled into a space in front of the local drycleaner, a cheerful place called Village Clean.

"That's for sure," Georgina said, getting out of the car, and pulling her jacket up around her neck. She followed Trigilio around the side of the building, and up a flight of bright, white enamel-painted stairs. He pushed a button which warbled politely. They only had to wait a few seconds before a tall woman in her late 50s, with clear pale blue eyes, a trim figure and dignified bearing, blonde hair slightly graying and tucked neatly into a bun at the back of her neck, opened the door. Seeing Detective Trigilio, a shadow flashed over her face for a moment. Typical reaction, Georgina thought. Ms. Larson thought she was done with the police.

"Hello, Detective," she said, holding the door tightly with her right hand for a moment, before stepping to the side, and gesturing with her hand for them to come in.

"Thank you," Trigilio said. "Ms. Larson, this is Georgina Adams. She's looking into Mrs. Musgrave's murder."

"Well," Ms. Larson said, "what can I do to help you?" she asked, shutting the door behind them.

Georgina smiled at her, and walked around her small but bright and neatly-furnished living room. The walls were a sunny shade of yellow, and the furniture was all stark-white and slipcovered. The bookshelves held a very eclectic set of reference materials and religious books, and the knick-knacks were all first class. She even had a couple of Staffordshire figurines on her shelves. The room gave off to a small dining room, attached to a smaller kitchen, all equally neat as a pin, and, while seemingly simple, were furnished with very fine housewares and nice, quality furniture. There were a few pictures on the surfaces, all of different Pekingese dogs, with one exception. "This is lovely," Georgina said, picking up a framed photograph of Ingrid's house from a table beside a chair.

"Yes," Ms. Larson said, "I had it in my photo album, but I put it there now to remind me. I miss that house."

The current Pekingese came running out from a hallway that ran down to the back of the apartment. A fluffy little reddish poof of a dog, it came into the room and yapped twice at the visitors. "They're guests, Carina," Ms. Larson said, smiling at the dog.

Georgina smiled at the dog, too. "It's a gorgeous house," Georgina agreed, looking back at the picture. "And you kept it in great shape, too. It was still neat and tidy when we were there earlier, and probably would have hardly a speck of dust, if there weren't fingerprint powder everywhere." Ms. Larson visibly stiffened. "How did you manage to do it all by yourself?"

"I didn't," she said. "I had a couple of girls from the village high school who helped me every now and again, with the heavier cleaning, and polishing the silver, especially when Mrs. Musgrave was in residence." Mrs. Larson sat down, tucking her yellow gingham house coat around her knees.

"Different girls every year?" Georgina asked.

"Yes," Ms. Larson said, "I put an ad on the high school bulletin board, with the guidance counselor's permission." She seemed uncomfortable that Georgina continued to walk around and inspect her things. "Can I offer you something to drink?" she asked.

"No, thank you," Georgina said.

"Me, either, but thank you," Trigilio added.

"Why don't you sit down?" Mrs. Larson asked, gesturing to the couch.

"Because we hadn't yet been asked," Georgina said, smiling, moving over and taking a sit on the couch.

"Oh, forgive me. My manners," she said. "Please." The rims of her ears turned slightly pink.

Detective Trigilio sat down next to Georgina. "How did that work? Were the girls ever left alone in the house?"

"No, never," Ms. Larson said. "I would give them a specific job, and I would supervise them while they did it. While they vacuumed, I dusted the finer pieces on the shelves. While they cleaned the bathroom, I tidied the cosmetics, and wiped them off. I always stayed in the room with them. Mrs. Musgrave insisted. She said if one thing ever went missing, she would hold me to blame for it." She looked at the two of them, thinking how that sounded, and her ears got redder. "But she was absolutely right. Her things were beautiful, and needed to be treated with special care. She trusted me, and knew if I was in the room, nothing would get broken, or stolen. And then, four times a year, we'd have a cleaning crew come in, and scrub it from top to bottom."

"What did Ingrid do with her stuff, then?" Georgina asked, leaning forward, her elbow on her knee, and her chin in her hand, giving Ms. Larson her utmost attention.

"The most expensive things were stored when that happened," Ms. Larson said, looking back and forth between Georgina and Trigilio, evidently trying to figure out why this cultured young woman was here in the same capacity as Trigilio.

Georgina turned to Trigilio, "I assume the part-time help has been checked out, too?"

"It's in the works," he said.

She put her chin back into the curve of her hand and smiled at Ms. Larson. "What did she call you? Ms. Larson? Or Greta?"

"She called me Greta," she said.

"What did the kids call you?"

"The kids?" Ms. Larson asked.

"Ingrid's kids. What'd they call you?" Georgina asked, still smiling warmly.

"I guess they called me Greta, I really don't know. They weren't there very often."

"No?" Georgina asked. "I understood they were a close family."

"Well," Ms. Larson said, uncrossing her legs, and then crossing them the other way, "I don't think they were. I think her children were a great disappointment to her."

"Oh," Georgina said, looking stricken, "that's too bad. What makes you say that?"

"They didn't call very much, and they hardly ever came to stay. When they did, Mrs. Musgrave seemed tense. She was a very great lady, but all they wanted from her was her money. I felt sorry for her. I don't like to gossip," she said, taking a deep breath. Georgina loved hearing those words, because it meant a big, long gossip was just about to begin. "But when one of the kids invited themselves down – she never had the opportunity to ask them – they always asked themselves – she always said 'here they come with their hands out.' And it was true. I didn't eavesdrop, but you couldn't help it when they started begging. That son of hers from San Francisco, with his prissy wife, always ordering me around, asking her for this and that – telling her he was an art collector. All he did was collect money. They had quite a blowout the last time he was down – about two months ago."

"Really?" Georgina asked, raising her eyebrows.

"Oh, yes," Ms. Larson said, "he wanted her to buy them the townhouse they'd been renting. Their lease was up, and I guess all of their friends already thought they owned it. He said it would be an embarrassment for the family. She laughed right in his face. She said, 'it wouldn't be an embarrassment for me,' and she told him no." Ms. Larson took a deep breath, but sat back and continued, clearly warming to her subject, "And the same with the rest of them. Worthless, the whole lot. It's a heartbreak to a woman when she spends that much time bringing children into the world and providing for them, and then they can't fend for themselves. It's a terrible shame." This she said with fierce determination.

"What about little Ingrid, and Matthew?" Georgina asked.

"Oh, those two," Greta said, rolling her eyes. "The less said about those two, the better."

"Yes, I know them," Georgina said, smiling at Ms. Larson with understanding. "And Magrit's hardly ever here, is she?"

"No, and it would have been nice to have the child around – a decent, clean child, but that one's not even potty trained. They were there once and it was a great strain on Mrs. Musgrave's nerves."

"And Luanne?" Georgina asked, "how often did she come down?"

"Now, Luanne," Ms. Larson said, "she's a little different. She'd come down for the day, or for lunch, and she'd remember to bring something with her – candy, a bottle of wine, something. I know she asked for money like the rest of them, but it was usually for some charity or other, and she didn't impose herself the way the others did. She was polite to me, respectful of her mother, and always behaved. She wasn't so bad."

"No, I went to school with Luanne. I liked her," Georgina said. "Well, it's nice, though," she continued, "it's nice Ingrid had somebody like you she could trust, and who showed her respect." She paused for a moment as Greta nodded her head, and segued into the matter at hand, "Detective Trigilio already told me you passed the polygraph, and you definitely turned the security system on before you left."

"Yes, I did," she said firmly. "I certainly did. I never forgot that. I did the same thing every night." Ms. Larson put one hand out, and karate-chopped into it with the other, emphasizing her words as she spoke. "I walked one last time around the house, and tidied everything. I went into the kitchen, and picked up my purse and my coat. I went to the television room to tell her I was leaving. I said goodnight," she said, starting to tear up a bit, "for the last time, little did I know it. And then I went out the front door, and armed the security system when I left. I had to lock the front door behind me, jog to my car, get in, and get to the end of the driveway before 60 seconds went by, otherwise I'd set off the motion detector at the stone wall at the beginning of the driveway. So there's no way I forget that, ever." She sniffed, and wiped at her nose briefly. The dog jumped into her lap, and turned around once before settling itself in a little circle. She patted the dog as she breathed deeply and got herself under control.

"Would you like a tissue?" Georgina asked.

"No, I'm alright," Ms. Larson said, taking a handkerchief from the inside of her left sleeve, and wiping her nose.

"Well, I'm sorry if we've upset you," Georgina said, reaching forward to pat Ms. Larson on the knee. She turned and looked at Detective Trigilio. "I think we're all set here, don't you think?"

"I am if you are," Trigilio said, rising. He reached out his big paw, and shook hands with Ms. Larson. "It's good to see you again."

"That's fine," Ms. Larson said, setting the dog on the floor and seeing them to the door. "I don't like being questioned, but I'll do anything for Mrs. Musgrave," she said.

Georgina shook her hand as well, and waited until they got in the car before speaking to Trigilio. "She only got an annuity in the will. It's less than she was making working at the house. I don't think she'd kill for that."

"Nope. Me, either," Trigilio said, as he backed out and piloted them toward the main road.

"But she might be stupid and give somebody a tour of the house, or let somebody in innocently, who was smart enough to figure out how things worked around there," she said.

"Maybe," he said. "But why would they have to risk murder? They could have knocked the place over when nobody was there."

"True," she said. "What did Greta do before she worked for Mrs. Musgrave?" Georgina asked.

"She worked for her for about 10 years," Trigilio said. "Before that, she worked for another family down here for about 15 years. It was actually the family that owns that dry cleaner below where she lives, but the kids sold the big house, kept the business, and the father, in his will, gave her a right to live in that apartment until she dies."

"That's a long time to be in the domestic trade," Georgina thought out loud. "She's not dumb. Those books in her apartment took some brains to read. And some of those things in her apartment were really nice. Gifts, maybe? I wonder. She clearly isn't acquisitive, or she'd want more than that little apartment, although it's nice. But she doesn't pay any rent. You'd think she would find something less demanding to do to pay for her groceries and whatever else she needs. She didn't have to keep flogging away, cleaning somebody else's house."

"She got a decent salary. But she knew she didn't have any kind of pension. Just Social Security. Maybe she wanted to keep working because it's all she knew. She clearly liked Mrs. Musgrave," he said.

"Bordering on worship, I would say," Georgina said. "Ingrid would have liked that."

They drove in silence for a few more minutes, and as they neared police headquarters, he said, "Now, I'm willing to continue to let you know what's going on with us. Are you willing to keep me informed of what you're finding out?"

"Oh, absolutely," Georgina said, popping a piece of Trident gum into her mouth.

"That's fine, but the minute I find out I'm not getting something, your info here dries, up, too, understood?" he said, pulling into the parking lot.

"Understood," Georgina said, shaking his hand. She got out of his car, and strolled over to her own car. As she jumped in and backed out, Trigilio watched her, shaking his head.

Georgina drove back into the city, with visions of the bloody scene in her mind. Ingrid had been comfortably secluded in her vast kingdom, and her wealth, and someone had been able to come into that world and end it for her, very, very quickly. A shiver went down her spine as she thought about how easily it seems they had done it, and then disappeared into the night.

If it Could Happen to Her

She parked her car in the underground lot at her own building, to keep it handy for her trip to Bedford the following day. She called Jason, and had him pick her up in front of her building, all the easier for a quick trip to Fifth Avenue. She called Mr. Musgrave's apartment, to be sure Frederick and Magrit were both there, before she headed over. She didn't mention, and she didn't feel it was her responsibility to mention, that she was investigating the murder. She rather enjoyed the speed with which Frederick had come to the telephone, and thanked her profusely for her condolences. Frederick had always estimated people based on their net worth, so Georgina's acquaintance he valued very highly.

She walked into Geoffrey Musgrave's fabulous apartment, and though she'd never been there, she knew it by sight. She had seen it laid out on the pages of one of Mr. Musgrave's various shelter magazines. It stretched across the entire top of a building that Mr. Musgrave owned, and took up part of the unit below as well. It was stark and decorated almost completely in white, with large-scale colorful modernist paintings strategically located. "Typical," Georgina thought to herself, and bet that she could name the designer who had done it. A maid in uniform met her at the door, and relieved Georgina of her jacket. Frederick and his wife came around the corner together, arm-in-arm, "Georgina!" he said, holding her by the upper arms and kissing her on both cheeks. He was aging fairly well, she thought – hair thinning, but at least he wasn't running to fat. Georgina stood and received the same kiss-kiss treatment from his platinum blond skinnier-than-skinny wife, Rika. She noticed the wife's eyes momentarily narrow as she assessed Georgina's good looks, in order to determine if she were skinnier and more attractive than herself.

"Come in," Frederick said, gesturing toward the living room with its glorious views overlooking Central Park, as though he were in his own home. He didn't know yet that she knew he was, in fact, effectively homeless. "This is all terrible. We've all been in shock. We can't even imagine how to cope."

"Is Magrit here?" Georgina asked innocently, enjoying the shadow which flew across Frederick's face and quickly disappeared.

"She is," Frederick said, offering Georgina a seat, while his wife composed herself in a lovely manner in a bergere chair opposite her, from her Christian Louboutin high heels to her Chanel earrings, the picture of glorious, wealthy comportment, legs crossed at the ankles, wrists resting on her knees. "She's got her son here, too. I think he's taking a nap. Cute little guy," he said

If it Could Happen to Her

without any feeling whatsoever.

"Well, how are you?" Georgina said, reaching over and patting Frederick's knee. He had chosen to take the seat next to her on the sofa. She saw out of the corner of her eye the frown she had expected to see from the blond wife. "This is just unbelievable. How could something like this happen?"

"Honestly, I think it's a lesson to all of us," Frederick said. "We can never be too careful. One has to protect ones' self from the criminal element. Just being fortunate makes one a target."

"Mm, yes," his wife murmured, "that's so true."

"When was the last time you saw your mother?" Georgina asked.

"Oh, let's see," Frederick said, looking up at the ceiling, "it must have been only a month or two ago. We visited her so often down in Cambridge. It's all just so shocking. She was doing so well. She was as happy as I had ever seen her. She was happy in her friendship with my father, hard-won after the divorce, and so happy and proud of her children and their accomplishments. I think she was very, very fulfilled and satisfied. She even had that new boyfriend, who was also killed," he frowned, not quite knowing how to disapprove of Bartolomeo without speaking ill of the dead, "who must have brought some comfort and companionship to her. She deserved it. She deserved all of that happiness. And to see it all brought to a violent end, well," he said, reaching up to wipe away tears at the corners of his eyes that weren't there, "it's just almost too much."

At that moment, Magrit wandered in from a hallway to their right, and headed into the kitchen without noticing them. "Magrit?" Georgina called.

Magrit came back in and looked at Georgina. She was actually in pretty good shape, Georgina noticed. She had her blond hair parted in the center, with two braids at the front pinned back at either side behind her ears. The hair was clean, and the face looked clean, too. Georgina had definitely seen her look worse. "Magrit, how are you?" she said. "Do you remember me? Georgina?"

"Oh, right. Luanne's friend," Magrit said, coming over and sitting in between her brother and Georgina, pushing him to the side with her behind. She held both of Georgina's hands, and said, "are you here about Mother?"

"Yes," Georgina said, looking at Magrit's blue eyes, and trying to determine her level of sobriety – thinking she was doing very well, considering. Maybe a sedative or something, but, other than that, she wasn't exhibiting any symptoms of withdrawal, or being under the influence of anything stronger.

Her brain might look like Swiss cheese inside, but Georgina hoped, for the sake of her son, she wouldn't make it any worse.

"Somebody killed Mother," Magrit said, holding tightly to Georgina's hands, and looking into her eyes. "They shot her, and they shot Bart, too." She started to cry. "I liked Bart. He was nice to Mother. He was really cute, and she liked him." Georgina put her arm around Magrit and patted her gently on the shoulder, noticing Frederick's look of annoyance at this public display of grief.

Magrit sat up and wiped her eyes. "Can I get you something to drink, Georgina?" she asked.

"Oh, yes, sorry about that, Georgina, where are my manners? Can we offer you something?" Frederick said, getting up and heading for the kitchen.

"Just a Coke or something would be fine," she said.

"Bring me a Heineken, please, Fred," Magrit said.

"Nothing for me," Rika said.

"How is your boy?" Georgina asked.

"Tommy," Magrit smiled. "He's in having his nap with his nanny. He still likes the afternoon nap. The morning nap is long gone." She turned and accepted the beer glass from Frederick.

Georgina was impressed. Magrit had apparently cleaned up her act quite a bit. The last time she had set eyes on her, she was falling down drunk, and had visible track marks, which she had made no attempt to hide. She was wearing a sleeveless babydoll top right now, and Georgina could see barely noticeable faded scars when she snuck a look, but nothing fresh. "Good for you," she thought. She chatted for a few moments with Magrit until she excused herself to check on her son.

"Magrit's looking well," Georgina said.

"She ought to be, after what Father and Mother spent on cleaning her up," Frederick sneered. "Don't get me wrong, I'm glad she's doing better, but that scumbag boyfriend of hers nearly dragged her into the grave with him, and now the little kid," he said, gesturing toward the back hallway where Magrit had just gone, "is a bit of a monster. She's trying to rein him in now, but it's not easy. He's got some behavioral problems…"

"To say the least," huffed Rika.

Frederick frowned at his wife. "Sorry, Georgina, Rika's a bit upset…"

"He pissed in my Birkin bag," she said to Georgina.

Georgina suppressed the immediate tendency to laugh, but instead said,

If it Could Happen to Her

"Oh, my goodness, that's horrible. It's like a travesty."

"Tell me about it," Rika said, flipping her hair over her shoulder. "I don't care, Frederick, nephew or not, that's $16,000 she owes me." Rika got up to leave the room, but Georgina stopped her.

"Oh, just one quick thing before you go," she said, hooking Rika firmly with her eyes, "what was the fight with your mom about last month, Frederick?"

Rika's mouth flew open, astonished, and she looked over at Frederick, exhaling loudly. Georgina took in Rika's response fully before she turned to Frederick with a smile. He, too was looking at her with his mouth open. "Um, I'm not sure what you mean," he said. "I don't fight with Mother. I, I didn't fight with Mother." He put his own glass down on the table and looked away from Georgina's gaze. Blink.

"I heard you wanted her to buy your townhouse for you, because the lease is nearly up, and everybody thinks you already own it," Georgina said, turning toward him, taking her right hand, and sweeping her hair off her face, placing the back of her arm on the back of the couch, leaning her head against her hand.

"What? Who told you that, Magrit? Luanne?" Rika shouted.

"Blink, again," Georgina thought.

"Well, that certainly is none of their business," Frederick said. "And, I have to say, Georgina, it's in fairly poor taste to be bringing it up now."

Georgina didn't move or flinch. "Then you're definitely not going to like the fact that I'm going to ask you about the 10, or 20, million dollars that you hope to receive from the insurance company."

"What the fuck?" Frederick said, now clearly losing his cool, and getting up from the couch. "Georgina, really, this is too much. I'm going to have to ask you to leave."

"Even though I'm investigating this for Lloyd's, and my report will likely determine what, if anything, you receive?" she said, keeping her voice at the same level of modulation.

There was dead silence for a solid 30 seconds, before Rika broke the ice. "You're investigating," she spat the word out, "for Lloyd's? Aren't you Georgina Adams? Frederick, isn't this Georgina Adams?"

Georgina never moved her eyes away from Frederick's. "Just relax, Frederick," she said. "Sit down."

Frederick sat down, half angry and half intrigued. Rika still stood, her hands on her hips, now, wondering what was going on.

"I work for Konig sometimes, investigating things that have some bearing on the kind of work I do," she said.

"I think I heard you were a psychologist or something," Frederick said, trying to get all of the pieces to fall into place.

"I'm more of an academic, really," she said, "and sometimes I do work that interests me. When I heard this thing happened to your mother, I was interested. I knew Ingrid, and I knew you guys, and I wanted to find out what happened. That's all."

"Well... I don't..." Frederick sputtered.

Rika, still standing, asked, "but you're going to report to Lloyd's? You get to decide whether we get our money?"

"Shut up, Rika," Frederick said quietly. Rika sat down again.

"Don't pee your pants, Fred," Georgina said. "Wouldn't you rather have a family friend looking into this, than a stranger? I know I would if I were in the same position."

"Well, yes, of course," he said, sitting back, and trying to regain his composure.

"So why don't you tell me about the fight?" she asked again.

Rika crossed her arms in front of her and looked disgusted that her personal business was about to be divulged.

"Well, it's true," Frederick said, "we've got a wonderful townhouse, and we've been leasing it. My allowance is adequate for that, but it's inadequate to purchase it," his face grew slightly more pink as he went on. "Now that the lease is up, we've been given the option to buy it. And it's not a bad price. I wanted to buy it. But Mother wouldn't give me the money. It's as simple as that." He got up and went to the bar to fix himself a serious drink. He poured some good Scotch into a tumbler, and took a sip before he came back to the couch.

"And now that she's dead, you could afford to buy it with the money – that's what a small-minded, suspicious person might think," Georgina said, comfortingly.

"I'm going to kill my mother over a townhouse?" he laughed and showed his perfect white teeth. "I wanted it, but I certainly can get another place to live. I do still get an allowance, and I have company stock. I'm not independently wealthy, but I'm fine. It's wasn't that big of a deal."

Georgina found herself believing him. "Well, I did have to ask, Fred.

I'm sure you understand."

"Certainly," he said, not looking at her, and sipping his cocktail.

She asked them a few more questions about what they'd been up to, and slowly, the conversation turned into a typical catching-up session. The mood lightened slightly, and Georgina could sense them relaxing again.

Georgina figured she had done just about enough damage for one day, and wanted to leave on a high note. "Well," she said, "I'm going to get going." She stood and picked up her bag, slinging it over her shoulder.

Rika stood up, quickly realizing that having Georgina as a friend was in her best interest. "Well, feel free to come over anytime, Georgina," she said. "You'll have to excuse us for being shocked, but, you're right, it's better to have a friend of the family looking into this, than some stranger."

"Yes," Frederick said, standing and readily agreeing. "We're grateful for anything you could find out," he said, "whatever you can do for Mother."

Exiting with a quick kiss-kiss for each of them, Georgina stepped into the elevator and called Jason. By the time she got to the lobby, he was waiting right outside the front door for her. She swept inside and went back to her apartment to revise her murder board, and get a good night's sleep before starting out again the following morning, this time for Bedford.

If it Could Happen to Her

Chapter Five

Georgina got up the following morning, and got ready with her usual care and attention to her appearance. She was again dressed casually, in jeans and flats, but she made sure she wore one of her lower-cut tank tops underneath a deep V-necked cashmere sweater. She knew Geoffrey Musgrave, Sr., and she knew he could hear a woman better if he could see some cleavage.

She took the elevator down to the basement level, and walked to the left, seeing her shiny black Rover just where she left it, in the spot she rarely used. She pressed the button which, with a boop-boop, turned off the alarm system, and reached for the driver's side door handle.

She caught a movement out of the corner of her right eye, and was able to dodge to the left just barely fast enough to avoid the pipe aimed at her head, hearing it shatter the glass of her driver's side window instead. She fell off balance, down to the left, and rolled away toward the wall quickly, but not quickly enough. She saw the dark hulking figure swing the pipe again, missing her head, but connecting with her upper arm hard enough for her to hear as well as feel the breaking bones. She screamed at the pain, but managed to lean her back against the wall hard enough to give extra force to a hard kick directed at the man's groin. He howled, too, and fell to his knees, momentarily incapacitated.

She forced herself up, her left arm completely useless to her and already excruciating. She got her first look at her attacker. He was easily 6'4" tall, and close to 300 pounds. More blubber than muscle, she thought quickly, or she would easily have her head bashed in by now. He wore a black ski mask, obviously to conceal himself from the security cameras that ran 24-7 in the posh garage. She didn't bother to get a much closer look, as he growled like a bear and launched himself toward her again. She aimed a kick at his midsection, but wasn't quite fast enough, as he tackled her rearwards against the wall. She felt the back of her head smack hard against the cement, and saw stars, momentarily disoriented.

Her attacker had clearly dropped his pipe when she crushed his testicles, but he improvised with his bare hands, grabbing her around the throat from behind. Before he could get a good hold, though, she used his own weight against him to duck from under him, and shift him to the right, against her car. Using her good right arm, she drove her elbow up and under his ribs, feeling at least one of them crack. Her attacker again howled, and in that moment, she was able to sweep his legs out from underneath him, and deposit him on his side, with his back against her Rover's tire, and Georgina on top of him, her back to him. One of his arms was pinned underneath him, and before he could extricate it, Georgina planted both of her legs on the column beside her Rover, and used all of her leg strength to hold him in place and drive her elbow into his windpipe. He thrashed and clawed with the left arm he had free, punching her several times in the back and side of the head, but with his one arm pinned, he couldn't move out of his vulnerable position. His blows connected, though, and Georgina began to see far more stars than garage as she continued to lean on him. She tried hard to maintain her consciousness, but eventually the stars obliterated everything and it all turned to black.

Georgina woke up slowly, trying to make sense of a white suspended ceiling above her, and a pale blue curtain beside her. It took a few moments for her to realize she was in the hospital. It took a few more moments for her to remember why she was there. Once she did, she tried to sit up. She found herself hooked up to an intravenous drip through a stint in her right hand. Her left arm was tied to her side with a sling that seemingly went all the way around, because she was unable to move it at all. When she did try, though, a thumping dull ache told her she had broken her humerus. She wished she could have a look, to see if it was a compound fracture. She shivered for a moment, when she thought of the impact of the pipe. Then her eyes flipped wide open, and she thought of the man who had wielded the pipe. She looked around her, but saw no one in the room she was in, which was very comfortable as hospital rooms go. She had to know if someone from her building had found her, and if they had found the man who did this, too.

The button to summon the nurse lay on the table on her bedstand, about two feet away, and up to the right. She groaned, but determined to reach up and find it. She got it with two fingers, and dragged it toward her, and punched the button hard. She waited a few seconds, and looked at the drip bag, seeing that she was being dosed with Fentanyl. "Oh, Jesus," she thought. She was post-surgical. They must have already set her arm, if they were treating with something as strong as that. Having not received a response yet, she punched the button again twice, and finally heard, "can I help you?"

"Yes," Georgina said, her voice sounding thick and unusual to her own ear, because her throat was so dry, "I'm conscious. Can I see my attending right now?"

If it Could Happen to Her

"I'll be right in," was the response.

"That would be great, dear, but bring the doctor with you," Georgina said.

"O-kay," was the steely-sounding response. The nurse did come in without the doctor, to check Georgina's vitals, and her drip, and told Georgina, with a fake smile, that Dr. Han would be in to see her in a moment.

"That's great," Georgina said. "Bring me the telephone, and put it over here by my right hand."

The nurse did as Georgina asked, giving her a dirty look which Georgina ignored. She began punching numbers even before the nurse exited the room. Her first call was to her private general practitioner, Dr. Westfall. She received his answering service and told them it was an emergency, and she expected to hear from Dr. Westfall sometime in the next five minutes.

Two minutes later, the phone rang. "Andrew?" Georgina asked.

"Georgina, you don't even need to tell me. Dr. Han is taking care of you there at the Hospital for Special Surgery."

"How did I get here, and how soon can I get out of this foul place?"

"Georgina, I believe your room has leather furniture and a view of the East River," Dr. Westfall said.

"I didn't ask you who the decorator was," she said, raising her voice, and feeling her head start to throb. "Ouch," she said.

"Yes, Georgina. You're in pain. You've not only got a fractured humerus..."

"Compound?"

"No," he said. "You've sustained several blows to the head which have caused your loss of consciousness, and have caused simple concussion. You should recover completely from that in just a few days."

"About that," she said, "what happened to the guy who beat me up? Did they get him?"

"He's not quite as lucky as you," Dr. Westfall said. "He's at New York Downtown, and he's in a coma. A Mrs. Jacobs from your building apparently found you both unconscious."

Georgina breathed deeply. She wasn't quite sure how to feel. Should she be happy she hadn't killed someone, or should she be disappointed, because he had clearly been trying to kill her?

"Alright, well..." she paused, briefly, collecting her thoughts, "Andrew, I want to get out of here. Do whatever you need to do, hire whomever you need to hire, but get me moved back to my apartment immediately, and get me whatever medical care I'll be needing over there. I want to be home before two hours go by, or I'll be ripping this stint out of my hand and taking a cab." She hung up the phone before he had a chance to argue with her, and dialed another number she'd used recently and had memorized.

"Geoffrey Musgrave," she said, "Georgina Adams calling."

She waited only about thirty seconds before she heard his voice. "Adams," he said, "I've been waiting for you, damn it..."

He started to say something else, but she interrupted him. "Geoffrey, I'm in the hospital. I just got the shit kicked out of me in the parking garage under my apartment. The man who did it is in a coma. I do not want to hear about it in any one of your newspapers, and I'd like you to lean on your friends for favors, and keep it out of the other two, too."

"What the..." he began.

"Geoffrey, I've got a broken arm, a concussion, and I put a guy in a coma," she shouted, "and it's probably all your fucking fault because I'm investigating what happened to your wife. Keep it the hell out of the papers, do you understand?"

She heard nothing but deep breathing for a moment, and then heard, "I'll take care of it." He hung up.

Georgina laid back, letting the Fentanyl do its work, because the time she'd spent on the phone had both given her a headache, and strained her injured arm. And she felt like she could finally relax and concentrating on healing, quickly.

Once Georgina was settled in comfortably at home, she had to get through the obligatory paperwork and details of having been physically assaulted. She sat through an annoying interview with a uniformed female police officer from the NYPD, in which the woman filled in the blanks on a form, and asked very few questions other than those that were printed there. She was shown a photograph of the man, eyes closed, tubes in his mouth. "No," she said, "I've never seen him before." The photo depicted a pudgy white man, so white he must have rarely seen the sun, with a shaved head showing a fringe of reddish hair and a brownish-red untidy goatee on his chin. His head seemed to sit on his shoulders without connection, except for the three chins Georgina could count.

"Can you think of any reason he might attack you?"

If it Could Happen to Her

"I don't know – robbery?" Georgina said, just waiting for the interview to be over with. She already knew from Daniel Levine, who was having Konig look into the attack, that the man had snuck in along the side of the building when another occupant of the building had driven their car in the night before. She had personally arranged to have a 24-hour guarded security presence in the garage, and the building Board of Trustees had been more than happy to pick up the tab, after being assured Georgina would not sue them.

Detective Trigilio came by shortly after the uniformed officer left. Georgina had called to let him know what had happened, but she hadn't expected him to drive into the City to see her. Armeda gave him a nasty look as he came in the front door, and tapped him a little harder than necessary on the shoulder, "You don't tire her out," she said, wagging her finger in his face.

Georgina smiled as she saw Detective Trigilio turn into an obedient little boy, "Oh, no, ma'am," he said, as he looked around, taking in the vast apartment with an indulgent grin on his face.

Georgina was perched on one of the sofas in her large living room. The room was so big that it easily accommodated two separate seating areas on opposite sides of the room, one with slightly more formal furniture, such as a newly upholstered and refurbished Chippendale suite of seating furniture which had been in Georgina's family for years, and which was centered around a fireplace with a large marble mantle. The other seating area was much more comfortable, consisting of a sofa with puffy down-filled cushions, chintz, silk and chenille fabrics, chosen more for their comfort than their provenance, and a chaise lounge that was nearly as large as a twin bed, where Georgina was now ensconced. This seating area faced the same kind of television setup that Georgina had found in Ingrid's bedroom. A middling sort-of painting that Georgina liked, but didn't mind wearing a bit, rolled up in its intricately-carved gold frame to reveal a 36-inch flat screen television.

She was dressed in a sleeveless t-shirt, pajama bottoms, and had a gray cashmere throw wrapped around her shoulders. In addition to her left arm in a sling, she had her left leg up to soothe a muscle she had also strained during the struggle. Her hair was tugged up into a ponytail, and a bunch of papers, magazines, books, and her laptop lay by her side. She also had a packet of letters Mr. Musgrave had written to Mrs. Musgrave, after their divorce – the contents of the brown paper-wrapped package she had found when Trigilio wasn't looking. She had been reading those when he stopped by, and she put a pillow over them now, hoping he wouldn't notice.

If it Could Happen to Her

"Well, you don't look so bad," Trigilio said, "considering." He sat down in one of the chairs opposite her without her invitation.

"You should see the other guy," Georgina said evenly.

"I have," he said. "I've asked NYPD if I can be of any assistance in identifying this bozo. They're running his fingerprints rights now. After a stunt like that, I would be very surprised if he didn't have some of record." He unbuttoned his jacket to make more room for his big belly. "But I don't think we'll be talking to him anytime soon. He's still in a coma, and he may have been without oxygen for some time," Trigilio said. "I'm hoping his jacket might turn up some known associates, and we can go from there. It's not a bad lead. How did you manage to get the jump on him?" he asked. "Big guy."

"I didn't," she said. "I just happened to see his reflection in the window before he hit me," Georgina said, "and he was a little too pudgy for his own good. It slowed him down."

"Oh, no doubt about that," Trigilio said, patting his belly. "I'm glad I don't have to chase anybody around anymore."

"Hmm," Georgina hummed, noncommittally.

"So, what's next for you?" he asked.

"I told you I'd let you know if I found anything out," Georgina said. "I didn't say you could have my itinerary."

"Just curious," he said, shrugging. "I thought you might like to know what I found out from the security company about the system, but if you're not interested..." He gestured with his hands open.

Georgina frowned, "I'm going out to Bedford to talk to Mrs. Musgrave's ex-husband, if he can manage to make some time for me. What did the security company say?"

"It was like I said, the system was put in about three years ago. They had recommended updates to get it recording onto digital, etc., but she never got around to it. The outside camera ran onto a videotape, but they were only on when the system was armed. The system on the inside of the house ran separately, and was pretty much always on, barring a complete loss of power."

"Well," Georgina said. "It pays to upgrade. And what about the high school girls who used to work there?"

"Went back for the last three years, since the system went in. Almost all of them are out of town at college. I've interviewed two that are still in town, and commute into the city. We'll eventually talk to all of them, but from the outside, they all seem like nice girls, and from what Ms. Larson's told us, they probably didn't get a look at the system if she was always breathing down their necks."

"If she was," Georgina muttered.

"Yeah, we're checking out the gardeners, too, although Mrs. Larson tells me it was the policy to never, never let them inside the house." he paused. "I keep thinking about her, too," Trigilio said. "Every time I go and see her, I just somehow get more interested."

"I agree," Georgina said, "I still think it's a long time for somebody to be in the domestic service if they don't necessarily have to be. And that apartment thing – the more I think about it – how normal would it be to give your housekeeper a place to live for the rest of her life? I'm sure the kids would like to have that space for themselves, to either rent out or use for office space. It seems too friendly – almost like family."

Georgina thought about how young Ms. Larson would have been at the time she worked for the drycleaner's family, and how it almost felt like the way one would take care of a mistress, not a housekeeper, but she kept her thoughts to herself. "Can you find out more about her?"

"I intend to," he said. "So, how long is this going to keep you on the couch?" he asked, gesturing at the little nest she had created for herself.

"Only one more day," she said. "I've got some lumps on the back and side of my head that need a little time to go down before I try to drive again, my doctor tells me." "If I ever decide to drive myself again," she thought, but didn't say to Trigilio.

"Concussion?" Trigilio asked.

"Slight," Georgina said.

"Yeah, you seemed smarter the other day."

"Very funny," she said.

"Alright, well, if I find out anything, I'll let you know," he said, getting up. "Do you need any magazines or takeout, or anything? It must be hell to have to recuperate in a dump like this."

"Thanks for stopping by, Detective," she said, picking up her computer and pretending to ignore him. "Don't feel as though you need to rush back."

"Unless I've got something else you want to know, right?" he said, smiling and walking toward the front door.

"Exactly," she said, looking up and smiling at his back as he strode toward the door and let himself out, with Armeda rushing behind him to shut the door and sweep the entryway.

If it Could Happen to Her

Georgina was able to get some work done, some journal reading and some research on her computer, but her mind kept drifting back to Mrs. Musgrave, and the image of her dead body lying sprawled on her carpet. She started on her laptop, going back through archived copies of party pictures taken by Patrick McMullen, and others who do the same thing, trying to remind herself who, exactly, it was Ingrid palled-around with. There were countless pictures to be gone through – Ingrid posing with literally hundreds of New York City's erstwhile socialites, from the truly accomplished to the truly desperate. A few caught her eye, and struck her memory. She started copying certain photos and making notes next to them on her computer, creating a photo album of sorts, with captions like, "Didn't she travel on their yacht during the winter last year? Didn't I see them having dinner together at Cipriani?" Georgina started a short list of ladies she thought might know Ingrid well – well enough to talk to about disinheriting her children, anyway.

This was delicate work, though. It wasn't like taking the legs out from under the Musgrave kids – these were serious people with money as old as hers, and people she really, really didn't want to piss off. The first lady she tried to reach was not in the country, so she left a message. The second lady she tried to reach was simply not at home. She left a message there as well. Georgina hit pay dirt, however, with her third call. She called Ingrid's co-chair on the Committee which organized the Costume Gala at the Met last year. She knew the ladies primarily attended lunches and chose themes and menus, went over guest lists, etc., and left the really tough work to people who were paid. But she also knew even that much was an enormous undertaking for an event like the Costume Gala. Georgina was a decent contributor to the Metropolitan Museum herself, and had originally thought the party was quite cool, but it had, over the past couple of years, gradually devolved into the Vanity Fair Oscars party of the East Coast. The 'temporarily famous' had never been invited in the party's heyday, but now the place reeked with tabloid flavor.

Georgina thought she would probably leave those observations out when she spoke to Charlotte Rumsey, though. "Charlotte!" Georgina gushed, when Mrs. Rumsey came to the phone.

"Georgina!" Charlotte gushed right back, "how are you? I haven't seen you in ages. What have you been up to? How's the riding?"

"Well, I haven't fallen off lately, so that's an improvement for me," Georgina laughed.

"Oh, now, I know you're one of the best," Charlotte said, "don't play coy with me."

"You're so sweet," Georgina said. "How have you been?" she asked gently. "I've been thinking about you a little bit ever since I heard about what happened to Ingrid Musgrave. I know you were her friend, and I just…" she paused, leaving the sentence unfinished, "well, it's just horrible."

"Oh, Georgina," Charlotte said, her voice getting a little lower and a bit thicker. "It's horrible. Did you know Ingrid very well? I didn't realize…"

"I graduated from Brown with Luanne," Georgina said, feeling badly that she had to parlay that tenuous link into a relationship that might get Mrs. Rumsey to open up, "and I spent a bit of time with Ingrid, just talking and… I found her to be just one of the most generous people… so cultured and witty… it's just such a loss."

"Oh, Georgina," she said, "there will never be another like her. Truly one of the grande dames of New York City, and the world, for that matter, certainly. And Bartolomeo… I'm just sick over it."

"I think she told me she spent some time with you and your husband last year. I think that meant a lot to her," Georgina said, gritting her teeth, and hoping she hadn't just pushed too far, with an outright lie.

When Charlotte Rumsey started crying softly, Georgina felt bad, but knew she had got it right. "Oh, Georgina. We had a wonderful time. It was so relaxing. We just sat on the deck of our boat and talked and talked and talked. My husband actually liked Bart, so the two of them would spend the whole day shooting skeet, or watching sports on the satellite television, but, honestly, Ingrid and I had some of the best conversations of our life."

"You had just finished the Costume Gala, hadn't you? A triumph," Georgina said.

"Oh, that's so nice of you to say, Georgina. And thank you, again, for sponsoring a table. It is so much work, though. Most people have no idea. We start about nine months ahead of time with our planning and work, work, work, and then it's over in a flash."

"But a lot of money gets raised for a great cause," Georgina said. "I know Ingrid wasn't afraid of hard work when it came to the Metropolitan."

"Oh, it meant the world to her," Charlotte said, "really, just the world. We were exhausted, and we were talking about everything that was important. You're still so young, Georgina, but once you reach our sort of age, you really only bother yourself about a few things you find very, very important. And the rest of it, you just let it go."

If it Could Happen to Her

"I haven't stayed in close touch with Luanne," Georgina said, again treading on thin ice, and hoping she was guessing correctly. "I think I knew Ingrid better than Luanne. And, honestly, I think I – well, I hate to say it, but I really liked Ingrid better than Luanne, or even Frederick, who I knew a little bit. She was just so much more substantial... I don't know. It probably wasn't their fault – Geoffrey their father was just so busy..." she left that hanging out in the air, hoping Charlotte would pick it up. She held her breath.

"Well it certainly wasn't Ingrid's fault the way they all turned out," Charlotte said, very pointedly, and the only thing that kept Georgina from bouncing up and down in her chair was her bad leg. She knew a woman on the verge of a colossal, glorious bitch on a subject when she heard one. "Ingrid spent so much time with those children, and gave them the very best of everything, the best schools, the best companions.... Ingrid worked and worked, and those ungrateful children – not completely embarrassing – at least not publicly, but they were just greedy, greedy, greedy, and had no idea how to take care of themselves. Ingrid had paid her dues – she worked her fingers to the bone when she was first married to Geoffrey, and he owes that media empire of his to her. There's not a doubt about it. She scrimped and saved and worked, and entertained, and did everything that was required. When they divorced, Geoffrey was good to her, very good to her, and she deserved it. But those kids, well, what did they know how to do except shop? How does one make a career out of that? The one who lives in San Francisco calling himself an important collector, always asking for more, more, more. Luanne always begging in that round-and-round way of hers about whatever her latest bleeding heart cause was. Magrit stoned and bringing bastard grandchildren into the world. And little Ingrid and Matthew – oh my Heavens! Can you even imagine a brother and sister running a bookshop together, and living together, and carrying on in public the way they have? Ingrid practically wanted to have them both committed! She wouldn't even talk to those two toward the end. She deserved better... far, far better than she got from those worthless cretins of hers." Charlotte started to cry again. "She deserved to enjoy her time. She deserved to enjoy Bart, and she should have had decent children, with decent occupations she could be proud of, and grandchildren she could be proud of, but all of them, worthless, worthless, worthless. She was even a little bit afraid of them, if you want to know the truth," Charlotte said, and Georgina's eyebrows went up.

"How so?" she asked, breathlessly.

"She actually thought they might just murder her to get her money. If they didn't want to wait until she died of natural causes. She said 'I'm a little too healthy for their preference.' She was joking, sort of, but I don't think she would have put it past them. Now they're getting all that money, and she's gone." Charlotte clearly didn't know about the will, the fact that the children had been disinherited, and the codicil, but it all made clear sense now to her. Ingrid did hate her children, and was honestly afraid of them. Maybe that's why she had the indoor cameras, not so much to be a voyeur, but because they made her nervous when they were in the house, and it's almost certainly why she added the codicil to the will about a mandatory investigation. "What a family," she thought.

Charlotte went on for several more minutes, being subtly egged on by Georgina, but she had already gotten everything she wanted. They agreed to see each other at the memorial service, and made plans to have lunch together, "real, real soon."

Chapter Six

After another full day spent lying on her couch, which even Georgina had to agree with Andrew Westfall she needed, tended to by a 24-hour round of nurses, and Armeda, who fussed over her unmercifully, she was ready to get back on the horse, figuratively, if not literally, and she made another appointment with Geoffrey Musgrave. He had sounded very caring and concerned, and had moved his schedule around to accommodate her, clearly feeling somewhat responsible for what happened. And, she had to admit, she hadn't seen a thing in the newspapers about it. Thank you, Geoffrey.

She took his fatherly-type concern into consideration, and didn't attempt to cover up the fading bruises on her face with makeup, which she could quite easily have done. But she also took his predatory sexuality into account as well as she again made her chest the focus of her otherwise casual outfit. She decorously covered her cast with an Hermès scarf, and threw a thick shawl around her shoulders. Late March had brought a lovely 60 degree day forward, and Georgina was tired of her sweaters and jackets.

She still wasn't quite ready to drive, however. She had called Max Gregson and told him what happened, but even her clearly invalid status hadn't gotten him to break his rule of not seeing her outside of the office. He had said, "If I make this one exception Georgina, next time it will just be something else. I really need to see you here." She decided to just keep her regular appointment, which was scheduled the next day, but she still felt vulnerable enough that she let Jason drive her all the way the Bedford, even though initially she had planned to drive herself. Walter had seen to the repairs on the Rover. It stood ready in her garage again, not only repaired, but polished and detailed – but she wasn't yet ready for it.

Walter had stopped by for dinner nearly every night, calling first to find out what she was in the mood for, and bringing her favorite dishes from the best restaurants in New York. He had been solicitous and kind, and ate and watched the NewsHour with Jim Lehrer with her, chatting for a while over wine, comfortably snuggling chastely on the sofa, and then going home. Georgina almost thought she could be married to him again if that would be the extent of their interaction. Occasional sex and dinner, and living in separate apartments. That could work. Perhaps she would propose it one day.

But this particular day she settled herself into the back of her Town Car with the New York Times and The Economist, and enjoyed the ride out to

Bedford. They encountered precious little traffic and made good time. Georgina put aside her reading materials as they entered the village of Bedford, enjoying the view. Bedford was a lot like Cambridge, Connecticut. It was one of those little hamlets that tried to pretend that they were still little hamlets, and not the playgrounds of the rich and famous. Bedford rivaled Greenwich and Cambridge for shear hedge fund money, but because the Bedford Village Board was so strict, it retained the class and charm Greenwich lacked. There were no 25,000 square-foot mansions with bowling alleys and three hair salons being built here. Here, by far the coolest thing to own was a large old house, meticulously restored.

Georgina knew Mr. Musgrave lived in just such a house, built in 1790, and had practically torn it down and put it back together in an awe-inspiring example of architectural wizardry. He had it taken apart, piece-by-piece, updated it with modern luxuries and amenities, but retained all of the original materials, and had the expansion pieces created by craftsmen who used strictly the exact same materials and techniques as the original house. It was now twice the original size, easily 9,000 square feet (about as large as a home was allowed to become in Bedford without being considered in poor taste), and equipped with a geothermal heating system and unobtrusive solar panels. She had read all about this home as well in one of Mr. Musgrave's shelter magazines. He had made most of the "green" additions in an effort to improve his public relations, after having been named as one of the humans on the planet with the largest carbon footprint. It hadn't stopped him from traveling in his private airplane everywhere he chose to go, and using his helicopter for everywhere that was local, but Georgina had to admit the press had been good.

"And you'd never know it had ever been touched," Georgina thought as they pulled through the gate, after Jason had announced her arrival to the PA system discretely embedded in one of the stone pillars flanking the gate. It looked as though it had been held in some sort of time warp since just after the American Revolution. "Good job, Geoffrey," she said appreciatively, as Jason came around and opened her door.

She shimmied to the side, unable to use her left arm, and took Jason's hand to help her up and out of the car. Jason reached in and picked up her Louis Vuitton totebag, which contained her reading materials, her tiny netbook computer, some parts of the file she had received from Konig, and some papers she thought Geoffrey might be interested in. She wondered if he had yet seen any of the crime photos, and was hoping she wouldn't have to show them to

If it Could Happen to Her

him today to make her point.

Jason walked to the front door with her, and rang the bell. Georgina found herself limping slightly, stiff from the long ride, and with the strained muscle in her left leg still bothering her. She took Jason's elbow as they waited at the door. A young Filipino woman in a white and pale blue uniform asked them in, and escorted them straight through the house, past the swooping marble staircase, and through the two-story great room, which had no fewer than three chandeliers and two fireplaces. The oversized furniture tended to minimize the overwhelming size of the room, but it still felt cavernous to Georgina, who was used to large rooms. Jason helped her all of the way out to the patio which lay just outside the French doors of the great room. A table for four was laid, and Georgina saw Mr. Musgrave jogging up the steps from the lawn to meet her. Jason helped her to sit down (she didn't need quite as much help as he was giving her, but it was having a nice effect on Mr. Musgrave, who swooped around the other side of her to guide her other elbow).

"I'll be outside, Ms. Adams," Jason said, and walked briskly back out to the front door. Georgina looked around her at the lavish rhododendrons planted all around the terrace, growing lushly, beginning to bloom in the bright sun and unusually warm temperatures, and spilling over the limestone, mixed with a Spanish ivy. The worked iron furniture had thick, richly-upholstered cushions, and Georgina was able to settle herself with some comfort.

"Good Lord, Adams," Mr. Musgrave said, as he looked more closely at her sling, and the bruises on the side of her face. "Are you alright?" he asked.

Georgina had tried not to stare at the bizarre transformation Mr. Musgrave had undergone. As he had hurried up the steps in his slightly-too-short shorts, and slightly-too-tight golf shirt, she saw the fit physique of a much younger man – cut abs, defined arms and legs, but which had a very unpleasant effect when coupled with the flabby gullet and neck of the nearly 70 year-old man that he was. She also observed what she was sure was evidence of an eye lift. "Oh, Jesus," she thought, wondering what she herself might feel inclined to do as her youth and her beauty waned. She hoped she would grow old gracefully.

"Oh, I'll be fine," she said, sounding brave.

"That's pretty amazing, I have to say," he said, sitting down next to her and waving to a tall Hispanic man in black pants and a white jacket, "I'm impressed. Kicking that guy's ass like that."

Georgina smiled.

If it Could Happen to Her

"I can't believe you won't let me put it in my papers," he said. "It would sell a lot of fucking papers." He gestured briskly at the white-jacketed servant, who came over and poured Georgina a generous glass of iced tea. Another man dressed identically, but who was somewhat shorter, came over with a tray of fruits, vegetables, and cheeses. Georgina reached forward for a strawberry, and sat back, happy to accept Mr. Musgrave's generosity, and make him feel generous.

"I'm sure there's a lot of things that go on in your life that would sell a lot of papers, too, Mr. Musgrave," Georgina said as she sipped her iced tea.

"Huh," he laughed. "That's why I own the fucking papers. Oh hey," he said, getting to his feet and looking over to his left.

Georgina looked, too, and observed Wifey Number 2 approaching. A tight-butted, big-bosomed blonde with deep blue eyes, wearing workout clothing she probably rarely changed out of. Georgina suspected the breasts weren't real, although they were probably expensive, and when she got closer, Georgina thought those eyes weren't her natural color, either. Colored contacts. How 80s.

"This is Heather," Mr. Musgrave said, sitting down again as Heather took a seat.

Georgina reached forward and shook the woman's hand. "Of course it is," she said. Heather poured herself a glass of iced tea and made herself comfortable. "Mr. Musgrave…"

"Geoff," he said. "Geoff is fine."

"Geoff," Georgina said, smiling. "I'm very pleased to meet Heather, and I wish we could have time to chat, but I had some serious questions for you, and I think you and I should probably talk in private."

"You can talk in front of Heather," Mr. Musgrave said, reaching over and patting Heather's hand.

"Well, that's fine," Georgina said, reaching down to her totebag. She pulled out the copy of the will she had brought with her, and slapped it down on the table in front of Mr. Musgrave, and reached down into her bag for the red-ribbon-bound packet of correspondence from Mr. Musgrave to the ex-Mrs. Musgrave that she had found concealed in Mrs. Musgrave's desk. She pulled the letters halfway out of her bag, and waggled them to get Mr. Musgrave's attention, but so that Heather couldn't see.

Mr. Musgrave took one look at the packet, and said, "You know what, honey?" he reached over and kissed Heather on the cheek, "why don't you run

If it Could Happen to Her

along and check on the twins. I'll bet they're done with their nap soon, and they might like some face time with the old man when I'm done talking with Georgina here."

Heather looked momentarily put out, but, clearly knowing on which side her bread was buttered, she shook Georgina's hand again and excused herself.

"Well," Mr. Musgrave said, tapping the packet of letters Georgina now put on the tabletop, "I guess I can assume you've had the temerity to read all of this rather personal correspondence between a husband and wife?"

"I've had the *responsibility*," she corrected, "to read this rather personal correspondence between an *ex*-husband and wife. This all dates after the divorce, Geoff – years after."

"Well, we were friends," he said gruffly, sitting back and sipping his iced tea. "In fact, if I had it to do over again, I never would have divorced her. I'm going to go ahead and assume everything we talk about here is off the record, except for whatever you can use to find out what happened to Ingrid. Otherwise, I'd be telling you it's none of your god-damned business."

"I understand," she said. "So, why did you get divorced? If you were still so close?" Georgina asked.

"She was sick of me fucking around. She had asked for a divorce countless times before, and then, one time, I told her she could have one. I think she was as surprised as I was. But, we went through with it, and then I had to marry Heather here, which hasn't been bad at all, don't get me wrong, and the boys are cute." He was referring to his two year-old twin boys he enjoyed being photographed with, and also referring to the fact that they arrived approximately six months after his wedding. "I was being careful, too. I don't know how I screwed that one up."

Georgina smiled at his frankness. "I'll bet Marianne was pretty surprised, too."

"Surprised, hell," he laughed. "She nearly cut my balls off – literally. Those French chicks," he chuckled, "they're as hot-blooded as Latins when somebody really pisses them off. Came at me with a meat cleaver. Nearly got me, too. I spent a lot of money making it up to her. A lot of jewelry, a lot of real estate, and a lot of money. And there's money in trust for Olivia, too, so she'll never want for anything. I wouldn't say we're friends, though. Not like me and Ingrid."

"I guess that explains why you were the executor of her estate, too," Georgina said.

If it Could Happen to Her

"Of course," he said, popping a piece of bread smeared with Boursin cheese into his mouth, "who did she know who had a better head for money than me?"

"Did she consult you about other things? Like about household matters, or anything like that? I found out her security system was just a little bit out of date. Just enough to let somebody get in."

"No," he said, growling a little bit. To the young Hispanic man still standing by the door with his hands folded, he said, "bring me a gin and tonic, light on the tonic." To Georgina, he said, "No, damn it. I run a tighter ship here, and if she had asked me to take care of it for her, I would have. She pinched pennies in weird places, I always noticed. Stupid. Dying of stupidity," he said, taking a big tug on the gin and tonic that had arrived nearly instantaneously.

"Did you have anything to gain from Ingrid's death?" she asked.

"A little bit," he said. "Not much. Something like $110,000 a month. It's an annuity I bought for her, and I was the beneficiary. But it was paid for, and I don't even notice that kind of money. And she got a *huge* settlement when she divorced me – and a bunch of stock. She was fine. She was more than fine. She didn't need me. We just had our friendship in common." He drank again, heavily, tipping his head back, and gestured with a twist of his finger that another one was to be brought. "If Heather was here, she'd be bitching about this," he said, taking his next drink.

"And your kids?" Georgina asked.

"Pff," he said, clearly feeling the warmth of the drink. "Those little shits. They're only now half amounting to something, and they're still all the time with their hands out. Wouldn't know what to do to take care of themselves. At least they're not the freakin' disasters they were about ten years ago, but I suppose even losers have to grow up sometime."

"What were they like ten years ago?" she asked.

"You remember," he said. "Luanne was in a mental institution, for Christ's sake. Had tried to kill herself for about the fifth time, after about the third marriage. Magrit was floating all over Europe, sticking needles into her arms and contracting STDs. Frederick was in San Francisco being half a fag with that society wife of his, and I'm not sure it's only half. And Matthew and Little Ingrid," he said, sitting up and turning to spit into the rhododendrons behind him, "living together like husband and wife. I can't stand them. I can't look at them. Those two I don't even talk to anymore. They're paid to stay

If it Could Happen to Her

away. Sick, twisted little fucks, both of them. Makes me sick."

Georgina stayed quiet and listened respectfully. "Luanne's pulled herself together, but she's still a sucker for the latest lost cause. Frederick still flits around at art galleries, but he doesn't make a spectacle of himself. After about 15 trips to rehab, it seems to have stuck with Magrit, and that little urchin of hers might just get brought up properly – we'll see. He paused for a moment, and looked out over his vast lawn. "I often wonder what would have happened if Geoffrey, Jr. had lived."

"He drowned, didn't he?" Georgina asked gently.

"Yeah," Geoffrey said, his voice sounding thick. But he sat up straighter, and said, "So, whatever. I don't know what to say. They're worse than some, and not as bad as others." He received his third drink, and said, "you sure you wouldn't like anything stronger than that iced tea?"

"I would, actually" she said, "gin and tonic, too – just not as strong. The regular mix for me." She paused as he sipped. "So what if one of them has something to do with what happened? The policies went from 10 million to 20 million when it was incident to a robbery. Ingrid wasn't planning on leaving them anything," she said, pulling the will to the top of the pile of letters, and leaving it there, "are you?"

"No," he said. "And they know it." Georgina was served her drink, and she took a sip. A perfect mix. The unseasonably warm weather, coupled with a nice G&T made it feel almost like summer. She wished she were enjoying the weather, the cocktail, and the view all by herself. "They'll get the key man policies on me, $10 million each. And I've bought them annuities," he continued, "paid for. They've got those for an allowance, and that's it. That's it forever. Nothing in my will. But they'll never have to work a day in their lives, and I doubt if they ever will."

"So, what's your gut tell you? Did any of them have something to do with it?"

"Honestly, no," he said. "I really can't say I thought of them at all, and I still really don't see it. First of all, none of them are that smart, and that took some smarts to pull off. And it took guts, and none of them have guts. They might like the money they would get at the end, but they wouldn't like doing any kind of work to get it. I'm sure they would have just chugged along until Ingrid and I died of natural causes, and collected their $10 million each, figured out a way to piss it away in a few years, and then gone back to living on Daddy's allowance again, forever. Pathetic."

If it Could Happen to Her

Georgina thought of Geoffrey Musgrave's rather unique story of pulling himself up by the bootstraps, being born in one of the rougher sections of the city of Detroit, writing at a paper, buying a small one, then another, then another, then buying buildings, and on and on, working like a madman, and being tough as nails with the competition. No, his children's lethargy would have been particularly galling to him. He was a man of action. She could see him, even now, having trouble sitting still, unable to enjoy the fruits of his labors, because of an inability to stop competing.

They chatted for a few more minutes, but she could tell that he was all talked out, that the extra-strength gin-and-tonics were kicking in, and that she had probably already gotten everything she needed. She said her goodbyes as he went off to spend some "face time" with his youngest children.

As she got back into her car, on an impulse, she asked Jason to drive her to Luanne Balin's apartment in Soho. Even though her cover was blown with the children, she thought she might try to manage some element of surprise by showing up unannounced.

Georgina found herself sipping a cup of tea, about 25 minutes later, sitting on Luanne Balin's chic, but slightly uncomfortable, couch, in her two-bedroom apartment. Luanne sat across from her, sipping her own cup of tea, and looking very concerned about Georgina's injuries. "I'm really sorry that happened to you, Georgina," she said. "Really."

Luanne Balin – her third husband's last name, clearly she had never changed it back – was a tidy, preppy sort of girl, tall and lean, with chin-length blond hair, cut clean and sharp. Her long nose and light touch with makeup added to the overall effect of effortless class. She wore a tailored white shirt, with the sleeves rolled up, and a pair of khaki Capri pants, worn with ballet slippers. They had already been through the preliminaries of why Georgina was there, and now sat, trying to trade up-to-date information, like any former classmates would, while also acknowledging there was a professional reason for Georgina's visit.

"I'm sorry about your mom," she said. "Really." Georgina said, mimicking Luanne's tone. "I liked Ingrid."

"I did, too," Luanne said. "Liked her. And loved her, of course. She was a wonderful person, not just as a mother, because she was a very good mother to us, but she was also a giver. Very important as a giver. And not just because others considered it important, but because she considered it important

If it Could Happen to Her

herself." She took another sip of her tea. "I like to think of myself as a giver. But I can't afford to be a giver on the scale, monetarily, that she was. I can only hope that I can give of myself, and what I do have, to work on what's important to me."

"And what's that?" Georgina said, quickly stopping herself from saying, "these days?"

"Oh, I've been working on a charter school project. Truly revolutionary. Based on creativity. Everything based on creativity, the curriculum, the materials, the textbooks, the students. Everything chosen for its creative value, and all of the curriculum based on creating itself as it goes along."

"A self-creating curriculum," Georgina said, "self-evolving."

"Exactly," Luanne said, leaning forward, smiling brightly, and obviously feeling very understood.

Georgina found herself wondering if Luanne was being medicated. She was clearly much better, and more organized, than when Georgina knew her in school. And clearly far better, also, than the years through which had self-destructively sailed, marrying frequently and unsuccessfully, and occasionally attempting suicide. Georgina found herself happy for her, but not quite sure what to make of her. She supposed the charter school concept came from the fact that Luanne had been an undiagnosed dyslexic. She had just barely managed to get a Bachelor's degree, mostly because of her father's influence, but Georgina remembered going out to eat with her, and having to help her with the menu. A child like her wouldn't slip through the cracks at this new school. Perhaps that's what she thought.

"It's what I'm putting all of my resources toward these days," she said. "I'm so attached to the idea. Children are so important. And their younger years are so impressionable. Did you know that a child's personality is almost completely formed by the time they're age 6?"

"I did know that," Georgina said. "It's very interesting." She paused. "Was your mother interested in your work? I understood that you had approached her to help with funding a new project. Was it this school?"

Luanne stopped with her tea cup midway between the saucer on her knee and her mouth. She actually froze for a moment, and Georgina was fascinated. She found herself holding her breath for the three seconds it took for Luanne to unfreeze, and bring the cup of tea to her lips. She took a delicate sip. "Mother was very generous, as I said, and she sometimes contributed to my endeavors. I know you're investigating for the insurance company, trying to make sure that

If it Could Happen to Her

we get $10 million, instead of $20 million. I understand where your motivation is. It's all about a job well done. And I agree with that, in principal. Absolutely. No argument here. But, honestly, when I think of the good that I can do with $20 million, it boggles my mind."

"Obviously, double," Georgina said.

"Don't be flip," Luanne said snappily. "I don't intend to benefit from my mother's death. That would be sick. Only a truly sick person would be happy at that prospect. But I won't be keeping a cent of that money," she said. "I'll be giving it all away. All of it."

"I didn't mean to be flip, Luanne," Georgina said, "I know how you feel about your work. You're obviously not living in a mansion."

Luanne smiled brightly, "Thank you, Georgina. I'm not living in a mansion. It's a very comfortable apartment. A lot of people would be happy to live here. Here in America, even the poorest people live better than almost the entire rest of the world. But I don't need a mansion. I don't need a lot. I just need to feel that I'm being useful, and that I'm spending my time here on this planet finding what I'm supposed to be doing, and doing that. I think that's really important. There would be a lot less unhappiness in the world, if everyone would spend time finding out how they can be useful."

"I agree," Georgina said. "So – I have to ask you – as far as you know, your mother was just killed during the course of a robbery at her home?"

"Of course she was," Luanne said. "No one who knew my mother would ever dream of hurting her. It's the only possible explanation." Luanne held Georgina with her eyes, very directly.

Georgina sat back in her car, and thought about Luanne. She certainly was doing better than Georgina had ever seen her, and compared to the rest of her brothers and sisters, she was functioning very well. But some of her behavior was just so off, responses taking just a microsecond too long, expressions of happiness a microsecond too quick. Something. Georgina was more convinced than ever she was being medicated. She supposed Luanne was probably one of the psychological medical miracles, considering how close she'd been to death so many times, but Georgina found herself hoping Luanne was in counseling, too.

If it Could Happen to Her

Chapter Seven

As Georgina sat at her granite kitchen counter, pushing scrambled eggs around a Flora Danica plate, the morning paper was scant comfort. She was getting sick of meeting with Ingrid Musgrave's kids. The ones she had seen already had made her uncomfortable at best, and the ones she was about to meet today, Matthew and Ingrid, Jr., had the hair at the back of her neck standing up. If it weren't Lloyd's specific contention that the kids had to be completely cleared before they'd pay up, she'd be much more inclined to go down other avenues that had opened.

Detective Trigilio had called her the night before, just after she had finished her dinner. "How are you getting along there?" he asked. "Is the head functioning normally?"

"If it weren't, I'd probably be the last one to know," Georgina said, beginning to enjoy his banter.

"Well, I found something interesting," he said. "I thought about the drycleaner some more, and about the kids, and the housekeeper being up there over the shop all of those years."

"And?" Georgina asked.

"And, they're a little dicey," he said.

"How dicey?" she asked.

"Unfortunately, not so dicey that you'd really notice," he said, almost disappointed.

"I had one of the cops here check out the kids who run the shop now, and the oldest one, a Jerry Stone, Jr., is running the business now. There's a ton of kids, six, to be exact, and all of them except Jerry has done time."

"Well, that's interesting," Georgina said.

"I thought so," Trigilio said, "so I drove over to talk to Mr. Stone. As soon as he found out that I wasn't there investigating him, or his taxes, he felt pretty free to talk to me. I told him that the lady who lived above him used to be his father's housekeeper, and her new employer was dead, and I just had some routine questions – we were running into dead ends, and I had to do something with my time – you know the drill."

"Mm-hmm," she said.

"Well, luckily, he was chatty," Trigilio said. "He had some choice things to say about his younger brothers, and his younger sister. Makes you wonder if there's any kind of thing as a happy family anymore."

"So, anyway..." Georgina huffed.

"Anyway," Trigilio said, "they're all losers. They're living off of their small share of the business. They got equal shares, but Jerry there bought them out, one-by-one. He let them each keep a small portion, which basically pays rent on the shitty apartments they live in. When they live in them – that is to say – when they're not living courtesy of the hospitality of the State of Connecticut. Mostly petty crap, check fraud, a few assaults, DWI – your typical low-lifes."

"And?" Georgina knew that Trigilio was probably leading up to something.

"And he thought an awful lot of Ms. Larson. He'd never kick her out, or try to buy out her portion of that apartment. He goes up to have lunch with her every now and again. It turns out she practically raised those kids."

"Really?" Georgina had sat up straighter. "That makes me think about what she said when she was talking about Ingrid's ungrateful children. She wasn't just talking about Ingrid, she was speaking theoretically. I think she said 'it's terrible when you raise them, and they can't take care of themselves.' She was talking about herself, too."

"Well, if you find that interesting, then I think you're going to love this. I know Jerry did."

"What?" she asked.

"Guess who's laying over there in New York Downtown?"

"Who?" she asked, raising her voice and practically jumping off of her couch.

"It's little Johnny Stone. The youngest of the crappy bunch. I guess their parents did that stupid 'J' thing. All of their names begin with Js. And, let me tell you, Jerry Stone almost crapped his britches when I told him where his brother was, and why."

"Did you keep me out of it?"

"Oh, sure. I said that he was there because he'd assaulted someone, probably even attempted to kill them, and they, in turn, put him in the hospital. I didn't need to mention your name."

"Holy shit," Georgina breathed.

"Yup," he said, "and I know that because he's got a record."

"What for?" Georgina said.

"Muscle," he said. "He's got a couple of assault raps, and..." he paused for emphasis, "a little bit of experience with robbery."

If it Could Happen to Her

"Well," Georgina said, sitting back and smiling, "that's a coincidence."

"Yeah," Trigilio said, "so's the fact that he tried to bash your head in because you're investigating a murder and a robbery."

"And they had the same housekeeper," she said.

"Co-inky-dinky – all over the place," he said. "I would say that we've got a clear connection."

"Me, too," Georgina said, "but did you just blow it by telling good old Jerry who still runs the drycleaner? Won't he run upstairs and tell his beloved former housekeeper?"

"I assumed that he would," Trigilio said, "and I was right." Georgina could almost hear him smiling over the telephone.

"What did you do?"

"I waited," he said, "all of about 15 minutes. Now, in that time he might have been telephoning anybody and everybody, including his beloved former housekeeper, but he definitely went up to see her 15 minutes after I left."

"What I wouldn't give to be a fly on the wall," Georgina said.

"Or a Pekingese in a picture frame?" he joked.

"Exactly," she laughed. "Wow. I'm loving this. But I don't think you should jump on her right away, do you? Did you go up right there to talk to her again?"

"Nope," he said. "I thought I'd let her stew. And I actually thought I'd see if she'd come to me… all of that 'I'd do anything for Mrs. Musgrave' crap. We'll see. I don't think she's going anywhere."

"Me, either," Georgina said.

"What about you? How is the ex-husband and the kids?"

She gave him a *nearly* completely frank run-through of her meeting with the ex-husband, leaving out her pilfering of the love letters from the crime scene, and let him know she fairly well considered him out of the running as a planner. She also ran him quickly through the meetings she'd had with the other kids.

"So, what's your gut? Did they hire little Johnny, and a few of the friends he made in prison, to make their mom dead?"

"I'm still not sure," she said. "It's certainly a possibility. Money means a lot more to them than family. I'd like to get another crack at Johnny in the hospital. Have you talked to his doctor? Do we know if he's going to come out of it anytime soon?"

"His doctor basically said, 'I don't know.'"

"Well, that's very helpful," Georgina said.

"They don't exactly have the best of Johns Hopkins and Harvard working on him over there," Trigilio said. "They've got him handcuffed to a cot, and if he wakes up, he wakes up."

"It's all there inside his little pointed head, and we can't get it out," she huffed.

"Well, anyway," Trigilio said, "my wife's got dinner on the table. I've got to go. I assume you'll be in touch?"

"You know I will," she said, smiling.

So, now, as she sat on a pedestal chair at the island in her kitchen, trying to enjoy Armeda's home cooking, she wanted to be down in Connecticut with Detective Trigilio, running down known associates, instead of getting ready to interview the first-class perverts she was about to see.

"You need to keep your strength up," Armeda said, grabbing the plate out from under Georgina's nose. She popped it into the microwave for about 15 seconds, and then put it back. Georgina made a few more attempts to eat, but finally faced Armeda's scowl, and said she was full. She took a Diet Pepsi from the refrigerator and went in to have her shower, made more difficult by the cast she had to keep dry. She turned three of the four shower heads off, and carefully kept one side of her body out of the water flow, using a wash cloth to get the rest of her body clean. She couldn't wait until she could again take advantage of the massage capabilities of her magnificent shower. It didn't help that she felt that she had been run over by a truck – she was very, very sore.

In between everything else she had to do, Georgina made sure she spent an hour with Dr. Gregson. She talked some of the case, some of the fight, some of the interaction with Walter. Dr. Gregson seemed most interested in the fact that she was able to function fairly normally after an extremely stressful experience. She wasn't very forthcoming during this session, being more preoccupied with her upcoming meeting with the two remaining Musgraves she hadn't met yet.

"You don't seem to be paying attention, Georgina," Dr. Gregson said. "What's distracting you?"

"It's normal," she said. "I'm working on a case, and I'm thinking about it. I have a meeting with a couple of potential deviants after I get out of here, followed by a memorial service, and I'm not looking forward to either."

"Deviants?" he asked, "In what way?"

If it Could Happen to Her

"I really can't talk about it yet," she said, "but when this is all over, I have a feeling I'm going to need several back-to-back sessions to try to get some visuals out of my head. I think I'm postponing a very decent nervous breakdown."

"You've told me a little bit about the children of your murder victim with whom you've already met," he said quietly, then pausing, "you seem contemptuous."

"They're a pretty contemptible bunch," she said.

"But don't you feel any sympathy for them because they've lost a parent, especially lost them to murder?" He watched for her response.

She quickly looked over at him with a glare, "I know what you're getting at, and one thing's got nothing to do with the other," she said sharply.

"But your parents…" he ventured briefly.

"One thing's got nothing to do with the other," she said again, more firmly.

They moved on to other topics.

Georgina arrived for her meeting with Matthew and Ingrid, Jr. in a black turtleneck and black pair of pants. The only gesture toward color, if you could call it that, was the grey cashmere wrap she was using both for warmth, and to conceal her cast. She tapped on the doorbell of the townhouse in Brooklyn which they shared. She had skillfully used makeup to hide the bruises on the side of her face.

Little Ingrid answered the door. "Hello, Georgina," she said, stepping aside, and gesturing with her right arm, inviting Georgina in. "Please, come in. We've already talked to Fred and to Luanne, so we know that you're interviewing everybody about mother." She reached to take Georgina's shawl and hung it from a hook on a coat tree which stood in the brownstone's long hallway. It was darkly paneled, but the staircase to the left, leading to the second floor, was covered with a blue and pink floral carpet, and cheerful framed miniatures covered the wall up the staircase.

"Come on in here," she said, striding back past the stairway, and taking Georgina into the kitchen. She was struck by the sheer homey-ness that the house exuded. "Matt knew you were coming, but he's in the shower. He always runs late," Little Ingrid said, rolling her eyes. "Can I get you something to drink?" she asked, pulling open their refrigerator. She showed Georgina the contents, and said, "juice, milk, water, soda. I've got tea. I've also got some espresso going if you'd like some. It's the only thing that officially starts my day." Georgina looked around the kitchen, and took in the thick hand towels with drawings and flowers and leaves draped casually over the oven handle, and the few dishes that were stacked in the sink. It made Georgina think that Little Ingrid probably did the housework herself.

"I think I could go for some espresso," Georgina said, watching as Ingrid deftly and expertly operated the large, top-of-the-line semi-automatic espresso machine. As she observed her profile, she was surprised by how much she looked like her mother. Moreso than any of the other children. Perhaps it was because Little Ingrid was carrying around about thirty extra pounds, looked a little bit more matronly than her smarter-looking, skinnier sisters, and had that softness of the cheeks and jaw line, and fullness under the chin which went along with it.

As she prepared Georgina's drink, Matthew Musgrave sauntered into the kitchen in his bathrobe. He went around behind Ingrid, gave her a quick hug and kissed her on the cheek. She smiled, and went about what she was doing. "Georgina's here," she said, and Matthew swung around. He had also run a little bit to fat, with a bit of a chin, and a belly.

"Oh, hello," he said, reaching across the island, and shaking her hand, seemingly unembarrassed by being caught in his bathrobe. "I'm not sure we've ever met before. I know we run in somewhat similar circles, but I don't think we've crossed paths." Ingrid handed him a cup of espresso. "I believe I just mixed my metaphors. You'll have to forgive me. I haven't had my coffee yet, and I stayed up too late last night."

"He's trying to make it sound like he was partying," Ingrid said, sliding Georgina's cup across the counter, "but he was just playing backgammon with a friend of his."

"Um, excuse me," he said, "a friend of mine from Istanbul. Those people are vicious backgammon players, and we were also playing for $100 a game."

"What did you lose?" Ingrid asked, sitting down opposite Georgina on one of the kitchen stools.

"A little more than $2,000, I think. I've lost more." He sat down next to Ingrid, and focused his attention on Georgina. "So you've turned into an investigator? I thought you were a doctor or something."

"I have a doctorate in psychology," she said, "but I don't practice."

"No, you'd almost have to like people, wouldn't you?" he said, sipping from his cup.

Georgina was surprised. "What makes you think I don't like people?"

"Oh, I'm sorry," he said, looking honestly sorry. "I thought it was obvious. Forgive me. I don't know when to keep my mouth shut."

"Maybe you should be a psychologist," Georgina said, smiling.

He laughed. "Oh, no. I just like running my little shop. I enjoy the little things in life."

"So, you know why I'm here. I don't suppose we need to beat around the bush. How were things with your mom – between the two of you?" Georgina asked.

"They were nothing at all," Ingrid said. "Nothing. The same with our father. We don't see them, didn't see them – her, we don't talk to them. It's like we don't exist."

Matthew didn't say anything.

"I hate to sound like a psychologist," Georgina said, "but how did that make you feel?"

Ingrid said, "I don't really have many feelings about it. I mean, Matthew is my family."

Matthew still kept his lips tightly pursed. "Matthew?" Georgina asked.

He cleared his throat, and then said gruffly, "It hurts when your mother thinks poorly of you. Perhaps Ingrid here is a little tougher than I am."

There was silence for a moment. Ingrid said, "May be we should talk about the elephant in the room."

Matthew exhaled deeply, got up, and left the room.

Ingrid looked after him with sympathy in her eyes. "It's really tough on him, Georgina. I mean, frankly, people think that we're perverts. We're not. We live here together. We have separate rooms." She began to blush. "We had a childhood in which we basically raised ourselves. We had nannies, but our parents didn't give a shit about us. We had nothing except each other. We went to school together. We went to college together." Her voice gradually rose, and became louder as she went on. "And we've never met anyone to trust more than each other. Yes, we're insular, but it's not gross. It's not perverted. We just neither have any intention to marry. So why not live together? Why not? What's so weird?" She began rapping her hand gently against the counter, punctuating her words as she went on. "In the olden days, families used to always stay together, unmarried brothers and sisters, and nobody thought anything was going on."

"It's okay, Ingrid," Georgina said. "I understand." She took a sip of her espresso to inject a moment of peace and quiet into the conversation. "The only reason I'm asking these questions is because it's my job. I take it seriously. Someone put three bullets into your mother's head," she watched for Ingrid's reaction – and there was none, "and I'm supposed to, ideally, find out who did it, but, at the very least, ensure that none of you had anything to do with it. It's the difference between –"

"10 or 20 million," Ingrid said, "I know. Well, we're not greedy," she said, gesturing with her hand up above her. "We have this house. We own it. We live on our allowance, and the income from our shop, and it's fine. So, you can probably pretty well exclude us for that reason."

"Hmm," Georgina smiled. "Are you going to be attending the memorial service?" she asked.

Ingrid's entire face flushed then. "I don't know," she said. "I've been back and forth about it. Back and forth and back and forth. Matt definitely doesn't want to go, and if he doesn't go, then I won't. But I've tried to convince him a few times that we might regret it if we don't. A simple showing of respect, and a sort of closure."

"Sure," Georgina said. "Well," she said, getting up, "I'll be going, so perhaps I'll see you there."

"Perhaps," Ingrid said, looking into her coffee cup and holding it with both hands. She didn't get up to show Georgina to the door, but rather let her find her own way out.

On her way back to her apartment Georgina scanned her Blackberry and saw several e-mails from Daniel Levine. She scanned through them briefly, and they all said the same thing. He wanted a report. She deleted those, until she came to one that said he had a report for her about little Johnny Stone, her would-be murderer. "Damn," she said, punching his number.

"Georgina," he said sternly, "I've been trying to reach you for several days."

"Well, I've been very, very busy," she said, "and I've been recovering from a horrific attack, if you'll recall."

"I know. That was the other reason I was calling. How are you?" he asked.

"Fine," she said, in a tone that signaled the end of that subject.

He dropped it. "Have you seen all of the Musgraves?" he asked.

"I just ran out of Musgraves a few minutes ago," she said, looking out over the bridge on her way back into Manhattan.

"And?" he said.

"And what?" she asked. "None of them confessed."

She heard him exhale deeply. "Any gut instincts?"

"Yes."

"Care to share?" he asked.

"Not at the moment. What are you finding out about the pudgy bastard who beat me up?"

"Well, we're running down known associates, hand-in-hand with the police down there. You seem to have made quite an impression on a Detective Trigilio, who tells me that he's been able to track down most of Mr. Stone's friends, but that most of them are either still in jail, or back in jail, and have been for longer than Mrs. Musgrave has been dead."

"Any other leads?" she moaned.

"There are a few," he said, "but it will take time. These people aren't usually registered voters."

"Well, that's where the story's hot, Daniel," she said. "One of these idiots may have done the hiring, but we'll never find out until we know who they hired."

"Well, this is all knocking on doors and cold-calling, Georgina. You don't want to do it," he said, "so we're doing it, but it takes time. What's next for you?"

"I have a memorial service to go to," she said, hanging up.

Georgina wore a black Armani suit to Ingrid Musgrave's memorial service at St. Thomas Episcopal Church at 53rd and Fifth. The limousines and Town Cars out front were parked three deep, and Georgina added hers to the mix. Jason helped her out, and then scooted the car around the corner. She walked into the church practically unmolested, but in this crowd where she knew so many, it was difficult not to be accosted by well-meaning socialites. They either simply kindly wondered how she was doing, wanted an explanation for her cast – which she blamed on a riding accident – or wanted to obtain either her assistance, or her cash, for their pet projects. She saw Frederick and Rika standing at the door shaking hands, with Luanne, just beyond, exchanging supportive words with friends of her mother. Georgina shook hands with them each briefly, murmuring words of consolation, Frederick thanking her profusely, and Luanne touching her hand as though it contained poop, and pointedly looking over her shoulder, to see whom else she might talk to. Georgina couldn't remember offending Luanne that much, and found her affect interesting.

Once inside the glorious church, Georgina glanced up front to see Magrit and her small son, wonder of wonders, sitting next to her father and his new wife. And there, right behind them, in the second row, sat Ingrid and Matthew. Every now and again, Magrit turned around to say something to them, but their father pointedly ignored them. Georgina found a seat further back, but right on the aisle, so that she could observe. Several people came up to her inside the church as well, people she knew from the Maidstone Club, and a few young ladies she even liked and respected, from Wellington, and the riding circuit, which she immediately felt she'd been off for far too long. "I have to get out for a ride," she told herself.

Georgina allowed her mind to drift as she waited for the service to begin. Walter had also been trying to get her back in the saddle, literally. "As soon as this cast comes off," she told herself, but was brought back to the present as she watched Frederick, Rika and Luanne walk to the front and take their seats in the front row.

After a hymn, she listened to a benediction, and then the first speaker was actually the recently-appointed Director of the Metropolitan Museum. She enjoyed watching the stiffness in the back of the necks of the Musgrave children as he spoke about their mother's "extraordinary and unparalleled generosity." Then Frederick got up to speak, to tell everyone what a wonderful mother she was. "It's hard to think of mother at a time when she wasn't giving something," he said, "whether it was giving of her resources to her chosen charities, giving of her time and talent to the cultural and educational institutions which she held in such high esteem, or just giving of her presence to all of those of us who were lucky enough to know her. I just wish that she were still here, so that we could all make an attempt to give back just some of what she so freely gave to others." Georgina nearly laughed out loud. "Unfortunately, we will never have that chance. I take great comfort in the fact that my mother died quickly, at the height of her health and happiness, and I hope that Heaven is prepared to receive such a remarkable woman into the company of the angels." Good one, Georgina thought.

The rest of the service consisted of a couple more hymns, followed by a slow exodus, led by the Musgrave family from the front of the church, which emptied in proper reverse order. Georgina was smack in the middle, so it was

If it Could Happen to Her

hell trying to find Jason amongst a sea of black cars. Once she did, he took her over to Park Avenue, and The Colony Club, where Mr. Musgrave had invited her for a luncheon in his ex-wife's honor.

Georgina's car pulled up at the red brick Neo-Georgian building, and as she got out, she stepped back to look at it with appreciation. She had been approached so many times to join the club, she finally had done it. But, not being much of a joiner, and not one for bridge, or social lunches, or the spa treatments that she would rather enjoy in the privacy of her own home, she had seldom ever gone there.

Ingrid Musgrave's funeral luncheon was held in the larger of the two dining rooms of the club. A seating chart had been arranged, and Georgina immediately noticed people moving their cards around as they arrived. She absolutely hated it when people did that, but she knew it was a fact of life. She went to where they had seated her, and found her card was still there. She was surrounded by other young people, people who had been friends of the Musgrave children in one form or another. She knew most of them personally, and all of them by reputation, so she was able to enjoy a lively conversation, as well as hear speculation about what had happened to "poor Ingrid," and scuttlebutt about Little Ingrid and Matthew showing up at the funeral, but not being invited to the luncheon.

They almost looked like a happy family, Georgina thought. Geoffrey Musgrave sat with his new wife, his daughter Magrit, and her little son, Tommy. Mr. Musgrave was even tickling and playing with the little boy. Frederick Jr. and Rika walked around the room, saying hello to everyone, and thanking them for coming. Luanne sat quietly at her father's table, smiling serenely, and watching the little boy. Georgina wondered if Luanne was thinking about the many marriages which had never produced a child. Perhaps that's why she was so interested in children, now. Georgina hoped that was some comfort to her.

In glancing around the room, Georgina was very, very surprised to see Ms. Larson, seated at a bad table, but present nonetheless. Georgina smiled, thinking about how Detective Trigilio would probably tackle her if he knew she was about to strike up a conversation with their only connection. She got up from her seat, and strolled over to Ms. Larson's table. Ms. Larson saw her coming from across the room, because, not knowing anyone else at her table, she hadn't been talking to anyone. She looked stricken, as though she wished she could be almost anywhere else. She was able to remove that expression from her face by the time Georgina reached her, and was able to muster up a look of concern, and a questioning glance toward Georgina's arm, wrapped in yet another of her vast collection of Hermès scarves.

"How are you feeling?" she asked, looking almost embarrassed.

"I'll be alright," Georgina said, taking a chair from the neighboring table, and pulling it over next to Ms. Larson. She arranged herself comfortably, with her legs neatly crossed at the ankles, before saying, "but I wish I'd never met little Johnny Stone."

Ms. Larsen's ears grew immediately red, and her cheeks flushed. She swallowed, and looked as though she were about to cry.

"So, how often was little Johnny at Mrs. Musgrave's house?" Georgina asked.

Ms. Larson lost it then, putting her face into her hands and sobbing, her shoulders shaking. A few people at her table and the neighboring tables noticed, looking momentarily surprised by what appeared to be an honest expression of grief, but quickly returned to their chicken.

Georgina sat quietly for a few moments, and allowed Ms. Larson to collect herself. Ms. Larson sat up straighter and sniffed. She took her napkin from the side of her plate, and used it to wipe her face and dab at her eyes. "How often?" she said again, softly.

"Only a couple of times," she said. Her eyes were red, and she looked like she might lose it again. "I just can't believe that I'm sitting here, and it's probably my fault that Mrs. Musgrave's dead."

Georgina stayed very quiet, knowing that if she did, Mrs. Larson would continue. "I thought that because I knew, because I was positive I had set that alarm, that there was no way it was my fault. I even volunteered for a lie detector test. But it looks like it's my fault, anyway."

"It's not your fault," Georgina said. "If you didn't pull the trigger, then it wasn't your fault."

"But I knew what he was like," she said. "I knew he was worthless, and stupid, and couldn't be trusted, but I still let him come to the house and help me move some of the big things when she was having spring cleaning. I gave him a few bucks to help me to do it. She wasn't there. It never occurred to me that he would be able to figure out the security system. The alarm is there to keep people like him out."

"He must have teamed up with some people that understood it a little better than he did," Georgina said.

If it Could Happen to Her

"But there's no doubt, is there?" she said, looking at Georgina with red eyes. She glanced down at Georgina's arm. "Look at your arm. Look at your eye." Georgina had thought she had covered her bruises sufficiently, but apparently not. "There's no way he wasn't involved." She reached down for her handbag and fished out a tissue. She blew her nose loudly, and said, "I'm sorry, Ms. Adams. I'm very, very sorry. I'm sorry to you, and I'm sorry to Mrs. Musgrave."

Georgina put her hand on the woman's shoulder, and let her cry.

If it Could Happen to Her

<u>Chapter Eight</u>

Georgina brought Ms. Larson to a restaurant around the corner from The Colony. She had begun to make such a scene, Georgina suggested they leave, and finish talking elsewhere.

Neither one ordered alcohol, although Georgina had a feeling if she had ordered a cocktail, Ms. Larson would have been happy to join her. "So tell me about when they were young," Georgina said softly, hoping that by moving Ms. Larson back to perhaps a happier period of time, she might get her talking. She knew the strategy worked when she saw Ms. Larson smile through her tears. "Oh, they were lovely children," she said. "Their mother died when Jerry was about 12. All of the rest of them were just too young to understand what happened, and it scarred them all. I did the best I could, and their father did the best he could, but it was hard. He worked hard, and I wasn't their mother, so half of the time, they wouldn't listen to me."

"I'm sure you did what you could," Georgina said. "I understand Jerry is a good guy."

"He is," she said, smiling. "He takes good care of things. He also takes care of his brothers and sisters, too. He wouldn't have to. They sold him their shares of the business a long time ago. They go through money like water. But he's got them set up so they can at least survive."

"I guess surviving wasn't good enough for Johnny," Georgina said.

"No," Ms. Larson said sternly, sniffing and straightening her back. "It wasn't good enough. And he could never figure out how to earn a living, either. He felt like it was beneath him. Would never even work at the drycleaner – nothing. But he always had these get rich quick schemes. He was always looking for the big pay day. Now it looks like he's killed Mrs. Musgrave, and he tried to kill you," she said, reaching up to touch Georgina's broken arm gently. "I just never thought it would turn into that. He'd always done stupid things, gambling, wasting money, and he tried robbery a few times, and went to jail every time."

"He was stupid, too?" Georgina said, smiling, and trying to get Ms. Larson to smile.

She did. She smiled for a moment, but quickly became serious again. "I suppose we shouldn't be speaking of him in the past tense. He's not dead."

"No, he's not," Georgina said. "And, although I might not hold him in very high esteem, I do hope he gets better. At least well enough to tell us who

If it Could Happen to Her

he planned this with. He doesn't strike me as somebody who could have put that intricate robbery together. I'd like to know who he worked with, and I'd like to know who did the planning," she said, looking very sternly at Ms. Larson.

"You," Ms. Larson sputtered, "You don't think I could have anything to do with this, do you? Are you mad?"

"No," Georgina said. "I'm not. I know you passed the polygraph test, and you didn't leave the system off for them. But you're the connection. You might not like it, but there's only one thing Johnny Stone and Ingrid Musgrave had in common, and that's you for a housekeeper."

Ms. Larson stood up and grabbed her purse, throwing it over her shoulder, and fishing in it for some money. She threw a few bills on the table, and said, "I'd like to say that it's been nice to talk to you. But it hasn't." She put her wallet back in her purse, collected herself for a moment, and said, "I'm sorry you got hurt. I really am. I still feel responsible for those children. But I didn't have anything to do with this." She turned on her heel and walked out of the restaurant.

A few hours later, Georgina found herself slumped at her desk, her back to her murder board. She had just gotten her ass kicked verbally by Detective Trigilio, when she told him she'd confronted Ms. Larson. "What was I supposed to do?" she had said. "She was sitting right there. I'm sitting there with my arm in a cast – there was just no way we were going to be able to pretend we didn't both know what was going on. I actually think it was the perfect time to talk to her."

"Oh, you do?" he yelled. "Well, that's great. I guess I can just sit back and let you handle this one. What do I know?"

"Don't get so mad," she said. "I wasn't going behind your back. It just happened. I'll be happy to write it up in a report for you, if you want me to."

"A report," he snorted. "A report is going to tell me whether her temperature rose? Whether she had any tells? Whether she was holding anything back?"

"I am perfectly qualified to tell you all of those things. Nothing slipped past me," she snapped.

"You might be as smart as fucking Einstein, but you're a baby. I've been doing this for longer than you've been alive. There's no way you know people better than I do. You can read all of the books you want, but it won't substitute for spending time reading people. I'll never know what I missed. I can never have that opportunity back."

"Like I said," Georgina said, getting tired of arguing, "I'll write it up, thoroughly, including her physical responses and verbal tics, everything. I'll fax it to you first thing in the morning."

"Well, thank you very much. I'll tell you what? How'd you like me to send you a fax in the morning with a list I've accumulated of buddies of little Johnny Stone – guys who are smarter than he is, and are still on the outside?"

"I'd love that," she said.

"Fuck you," he said, and hung up.

Georgina sat now at her desk, knowing some sort of act of contrition would be required. She could probably find out what she wanted about Johnny Stone's contacts from Daniel Levine, and was, in fact, just about to call him to get that information. And what Daniel Levine knew might very well turn out to be more than Detective Trigilio knew. However, nothing would repair the fact that he now considered her to be a hindrance to his investigation. And she could tell he would not give it up, unless she made a gesture. Of course, she hated making gestures.

She picked up the telephone on her desk and placed a call to Daniel Levine. For once, he wasn't available to her, but his very trusted and able associate, Greg Jeffers, was able to give her a very good briefing on what they had discovered. She thanked him kindly, and asked him to fax over a copy of the report. She waited by her fax machine until she received it, and then made another copy of it on her photocopier. She put a tidy staple into it, perfectly horizontal, and directly in the upper right-hand corner, and placed the report into a manila folder. Then she took a deep breath, and prepared herself for something she hadn't thought she'd have to face so quickly. She felt she needed to drive down to Connecticut to see Detective Trigilio in person, and it would be impossible to make the right impression if she got out of a chauffer-driven Lincoln Town Car.

She took a deep breath, and worked on some of the anxiety-controlling measures she had been taught during her therapeutic training. She had certainly been taught them so they could apply to potential patients, but they benefited her as well. She had, luckily, never had to use them with actual patients, other than those she encountered during her training. Even then, with the training they gave her to remain emotionally detached from her patients, she found it difficult. It was yet another reason why she never practiced, and

If it Could Happen to Her

rather more enjoyed the academic part of the field.

She slowly took herself through her preparations, once she had made the decision to do what she was going to do. She went up to her room, polished up her makeup, but not so it hid the bruises, brushed her hair, and carefully packed her handbag with everything she thought she might need. When she told Armeda she was leaving, she tried hard to keep her voice steady. Armeda came out into the foyer, "Where do you think you're going?" she asked, her hands on her hips.

"I'm driving out to Connecticut to see Detective Trigilio," she said, not prepared to argue with Armeda, but not sure how much strength she had for a fight.

"You're driving," Armeda said. She still had her hands on her hips, but her voice had softened a little. "Jason's not taking you?"

"No," Georgina said, gingerly placing her bag on her shoulder, and walking toward the door.

"Do you want me to have Jason follow you in the Town Car?" Armeda asked.

Georgina turned and smiled at Armeda briefly, "No, Armeda," she said, "that won't be necessary." She turned back toward her front door and grasped the doorknob.

"Do you want me to come down to the garage with you?" Armeda asked.

Georgina actually considered that for a moment, but said, "No, I'll be fine." She turned around and gave Armeda another brief smile, before turning and opening the door to her private elevator lobby.

Georgina practiced deep breathing as the elevator went down to the basement garage level. When the doors opened, her pulse shot up, and she looked immediately to her right, to make sure the new security guard was in the booth which had just been installed the previous week. He was reading, which she didn't appreciate. But he did look up immediately at the opening of the elevator doors. He put his magazine down. "Newsweek," she was happy to see. At least it wasn't "Playboy."

"Hi," he said, coming over to her. "I'm Rafael. Can I help you with your car?"

"Yes, please," she said, handing him the keys to her Rover, and telling him which spot to find it in. She felt a little bit better, but couldn't help looking around into corners as she waited for Rafael to bring her car. He brought it straight to her, left the driver's side door opened, and jogged back to his booth to open the door to the side street. Georgina got into the car, glanced into the back, punched the door locks a little faster than she would have liked, and took another deep breath. She slowly worked her way through the preparation process. Her GPS device still had the driving directions to Detective Trigilio's office. She moved the car into drive, and slowly drove out.

It took her longer this time to relax into the feeling of driving. She didn't put on any CD, or anything else to listen to. She sat and enjoyed the silence, and finally felt something like relaxation once she got out of the city. When she got into Cambridge, she went to the nicest bakery in the village, which she had seen when she was driving around with Detective Trigilio. She saw the drycleaner across the street, and resisted the temptation of making a friendly drop-in on either Jerry Stone, or Ms. Larson. She was already in enough trouble. She hoped that her pathetic appearance, the report from Konig, and three dozen krullers, might get her out of the trouble she was already in.

As much as she gave him shit, she knew Detective Trigilio was the real deal. He might choose to do his work in this lovely haven where ordinarily the worst thing to deal with might be a stolen bicycle, or sticky-fingered household help, but he knew what he was doing. He had worked Queens for more than 20 years, Daniel Levine had told her. He could have taken his time out, then, and retired. But he moved to a nicer place, stayed in the job, and stayed working. He didn't have to work very hard, but every now and again a real crime took place that he had to deal with. And once he had one, he wasn't going to let any kooky heiress from the City tell him how to run it, or fuck it up for him. She owed him an apology, she needed him as a helpmate, and she thought, quite honestly, perhaps she even wanted him for a friend.

She had overstepped her bounds, and now she had to pay the price. She wasn't a complete fool. She had let the bruises show, and didn't cover her cast with a scarf, either. But she showed up at the front desk at the Cambridge Police Department, krullers in hand, and was told she'd have to wait. So she did. For a three-quarters of an hour. She sat there, like a good girl, and took her medicine. She knew he was probably wondering how long it would take for her to blow out of there, but she was determined to wait as long as it took, politely, with the box of krullers on her lap, not even reading to pass the time.

When Detective Trigilio finally deigned to walk out and see if she was still there, he found her just like that. Politely waiting. He went over, and Georgina had to admit she made a bit of a show of having trouble picking up her handbag and managing the enormous box of krullers with her injured arm.

When he rushed forward to take the box from her, she knew she had him.

She gave him a big smile. He tried to look like he was still pissed. She said, "these are for you. I hope you like them."

"Well," he said gruffly, "I probably don't need too many of these, but I'm sure some of the guys will be grateful."

"This," she said, "is also for you." She handed him the manila folder, and he put the box of krullers on the floor to open it. He perused it for a second, grunted with satisfaction, looked at her with what *might* have been considered a grin, and picked up the box of krullers. "Follow me," he said.

Georgina went back, through a door that buzzed before Detective Trigilio opened it, past several desks, where other detectives and uniformed officers stopped what they were doing to watch her walk by, and down to an interview room. "This isn't as nice as a conference room," he said, "but we can have a little privacy. None of the younger guys will get any work done if you're out there."

He put the box on the desk, opened it, took out a kruller, and sat back to read the report Georgina had brought. Since krullers weren't her thing, she waited politely again. "See," she thought to herself, "I can be good." As proud as she was of herself for going back into the parking garage, getting back in her Rover and driving, she was doubly proud of herself for how she was behaving herself now.

Once Detective Trigilio finished reading the file, thoroughly, he put it down on the table, and said, "that's interesting. That's about what we got."

"What did you get?" Georgina said evenly.

He sat back in his chair, thought for a moment, looked up at her, reached in and grabbed another kruller, got up and walked out of the interview room. In about two minutes, he was back with a folder of his own. He didn't hand his over, though, but opened it and read from it. Georgina felt like a perp, sitting there and waiting for him to dole out whatever information he had.

"Shouldn't you be reading me my rights at this point, Detective?" she asked.

He looked up innocently. "Oh, sorry. I guess it's the ambience," he said, looking back down at the file. "I did a little closer looking into some of Johnny's brothers and sisters. It turns out the sister's living downtown in a shitty apartment with the father of the three kids she's not even trying to raise. But the boys... there's three of them besides Jerry. Jimmy, Jason and Jacob. And they're all gone," he said, opening up his hand and blowing it like the wind on a dandelion.

"Gone where?" Georgina asked.

"Well, what the hell do you think I mean by gone?" he asked. "I mean I don't know where they are."

"They're not where they should be?" Georgina asked, being very patient.

"They should be at the nasty apartments Jerry keeps them in, working crappy jobs every now and again, but they're not. All three of them. Neighbors say, 'haven't seen 'em.' Rinky-dink sometime-employers say, 'haven't seen 'em.' Gone."

Georgina sat still for a moment. "Well, unless they have an unusual genetic component, none of them can be very smart, either. Do you really think they're the doers?"

"No," he said, seriously, "to be perfectly honest, I don't. But maybe somebody wants it to look that way. Maybe somebody paid them to take a long vacation. Maybe they just all happen to be out of town at the same time. I don't know."

"And you got the same thing I did with the known associates, right?" Georgina said.

"Same exact guys," Trigilio said, "most of them in jail. There's two we can't find – you couldn't, either. Robert Lanier and Matthew Ellston. So, we're looking. We'd appreciate it if you and your rich friends over there at Konig would keep looking for them, too."

"Consider it done," Georgina said, standing up. She put her handbag on her shoulder, and walked over to Trigilio, who stood. "So, are we good?" she asked.

"We are, as long as we're working together," he said. "You do any questioning, then I want to be there. That's the end of the story. I can tell when people are lying. I'm sure you've got training, but I've got the nose."

"Okay," she said. "I'm not going to ask your permission for every step I take, but I'll honestly try not to do any questioning without you. If I feel something is going to turn into that, then I'll let you know, and I'll give you a good faith opportunity to make yourself present. That's it. That's the best I can do. I'll let you know, and if you can get there, then that's fine."

"I guess that's the best we can ask for," he said.

"And you'll do the same for me?" she said.

"What? No," he said, smiling. "I won't give you a promise. I have a job to do."

If it Could Happen to Her

"Me, too," she said.

"My job isn't a hobby," he said.

"A hobby?" she said. "This is a hobby for me?" she said. "She couldn't believe her ears. "Who's standing here with a broken arm, you lardass? Agreement over. Shithead." She reached for the doorhandle.

"Hold up," he said, putting a hand on her good arm, "bad choice of words." She looked down at his hand on her arm, and he moved it, "Seriously. Bad choice of words. Maybe you don't need the money…"

"From what I've found out about you, Trigilio, you don't need the money, either," she said.

He leaned back. "Okay, maybe." He paused. "Okay. I see what you're saying. It's a thing with me. It's what I do. Maybe it's what you do, too. I'll shut up. I saw your place, and I made some assumptions. I should know better by now. I'm gonna' apologize, and that doesn't happen all the time, believe me. I apologize. And I'll tell you what. A broken arm goes a long way with me. You didn't let it slow you down. If it was a hobby, you'd still be laying on that $35,000 couch in your frickin' penthouse. Okay? Poor choice of words." He paused again, and looked down at his shoes, "I'll let you know what I find out. I'll keep you in the loop. Okay. It's done. What? Okay?"

"Okay," Georgina said.

He extended his hand, and she shook it. He reached to his left and opened up the interview room door for her. As she stepped through it, he said, "but I'll tell you, you could really use one of those krullers. You're too skinny."

She smiled as she walked out of the station, especially because he held each door for her. She sensed that he was a symbolic kind of guy, and that she had been placed in a different, better category in his estimation.

On her way back to the city, Georgina suddenly felt like visiting Johnny Stone in New York Downtown Hospital. She called Detective Trigilio and said, "Just so you know, I'm going over to New York Downtown to take a look at little Johnny Stone. I assume you wouldn't care to join me?"

"Not unless he wakes up," Triglio laughed.

Georgina hung up her phone and smiled.

She drove straight to the hospital, and entered, immediately hating the antiseptic smell. It wasn't like one of the hospitals she was used to, either.

If it Could Happen to Her

This hospital was purely functional, taking the poorest cases, those with no insurance, and comatose criminals like little Johnny Stone. She asked some nasty black nurse in a hideous blue-patterned smock, who did everything she could to be unhelpful, where she might find Johnny Stone's room. Georgina made her way up there, after "accidentally" knocking over the woman's tub of pencils.

She found little Johnny Stone lying in a sterile hospital bed, with one police officer on a chair outside the door, reading an issue of Car & Driver. She took one look through the door at his enormous bulk, and wondered why in the world she had taken to calling him "little Johnny Stone." She couldn't remember for the life of her who said it first. Was it Trigilio? Maybe he heard it from Ms. Larson. Either way, "little Johnny Stone" was fat, and comatose, and useless to her. Before going in search of his attending physician, she asked the cop at the door, "Many visitors for our little head-basher?"

"Just the girlfriend," the uniformed officer said, putting down his magazine once he'd gotten a look at Georgina.

"Girlfriend?" Georgina asked. "Who's the girlfriend?"

"Typical skanky type you'd imagine," he said, smoothing his hair, and sucking in his gut, "visits about once a day, though. Loyal, I guess you'd say."

"Has she been here today yet?" Georgina asked.

"Not that I've seen, and I've been here for about five hours," he said, "she usually comes while I'm here."

"Well, listen," she said, leaning in and sharing a whiff of her Shalimar with him, "I'm going to go and find his doctor, but if the girlfriend turns up while I'm here, ring me, will you?"

"Oh, sure," he said, "that's no problem." He clearly thought he was about to get the cell phone number of a woman who clearly outranked him on the 1-10 scale by at least 4. Luckily for Georgina, she carried around a pay-as-you-play mobile telephone that she disposed of whenever the minutes ran out. She'd learned that trick from many of the criminals she'd met. Not everything they did was stupid.

She was lucky to find the attending physician, Dr. Arani, and agreed to follow him around on his rounds so he could get his work done, and get back home for about six hours of sleep before he had to be back. "So who are you, again?" he asked, "Family?" He looked her over, as though he thought that was very, very unlikely.

"No," she said, "I'm the one who did that to him."

If it Could Happen to Her

The doctor took one step backwards, with a question in his eyes. He'd seen a lot at New York Downtown, and he didn't know for sure this woman wasn't going to beat him up, too.

"No, Doctor," she said, smiling, "he was trying to beat me up, and I got the better of him."

He looked at her blankly. "Okay. There's a cop sitting right outside his room, so if you're trying to finish the job…"

"No," she said. "I'm an investigator," she fished in her purse with her good arm. "He's the one who broke my arm, by the way," she said, pulling out her wallet, with her Konig identification.

He looked at it, and then he looked at her. "Alright," he said, clearly too busy to analyze the situation. "If you can keep up, I'll tell you what I can."

"Well, what's his prognosis?" she asked. "Is he coming out of it? And, if so, when? I have a few questions I'd like to ask him."

"Slow down. Unless you've got his signed HIPAA release, or a badge, I'm not telling you very much. He was without oxygen for a while, and he came in blue."

"Hypoxia?" she asked.

"Major," he said, going into a patient's room. Georgina waited. He came out again in a few moments. "And he might have trouble talking if he does wake up, because you crushed his trachea. Anyway, lady, I don't know how much that little ID of yours entitles you to, so…" he walked away into another room.

Her phone started ringing. She reached for it and put her bag down on the floor, and fished for it. It was the no-name phone, and she felt her pulse increase. "Hello," she said, trying to sound sexy while she tried to manage the bag and the phone with one arm.

"Hello, Ms. Adams," the officer said, "are you still in the hospital? Because the girlfriend just showed up."

"I am," she said, "thanks so much. I'll be right there." She threw the phone in her bag, and fairly flew up the stairs.

If it Could Happen to Her

<u>Chapter Nine</u>

Georgina called Trigilio and left him a voicemail message as she hurried back to little Johnny's room. She ignored the elevator and jogged up the stairs, glad that she stayed fit, because after four flights, she was barely breathing heavily as she rung off. She wanted to be sure Trigilio knew she was about to talk to the girlfriend, and she wasn't about to let the chance go by because he wasn't there.

She slowed her pace as she got closer to the hospital room. She didn't want to appear as interested as she was. "Play it cool," she said to herself. She saved a special smile for the officer who had alerted her to the girlfriend's presence. He managed to blush, and look very pleased with himself. Georgina reminded herself that she would need a new throw-away phone. "She just got here when I called you," he said conspiratorially. "Still in there," he said, whispering and gesturing with this thumb.

Georgina gave his arm a friendly little squeeze as she went around him and into the room. She winked at him as she reached to shut the door behind her. He looked surprised for a moment, but smiled again at her, and didn't seem to mind.

Georgina went over to the bed, and now saw a chubby young woman in a shapeless white tee shirt and faded red sweatpants, slightly greasy brown hair in a ponytail, sitting in the plastic chair next to little Johnny. She was reading to him out loud from a copy of a tabloid magazine. Georgina felt badly for a moment, but forced it into the back of her consciousness. "Everybody's got somebody to love," she thought, "even if he tried to knock my head off."

"Excuse me," she said, quietly, not wanting to surprise the young woman.

The woman didn't look surprised by the intrusion. She must have been used to nurses coming in and out by now, but she did look surprised when she turned to look at Georgina, who clearly was not a nurse. She started to rise, before Georgina said, "Oh, sit, sit, please. I don't want to interrupt. I'm Georgina," she said, reaching out to shake the woman's hand.

"I'm Betsy," the woman said. Georgina tried to guess her age, but it was difficult with women like that – she'd already adopted a look and a style that would probably take her all the way to the grave, but Georgina could ballpark her at slightly less than 30.

"Are you Johnny's wife?" Georgina asked.

"No," the woman said, blushing, "no. He's just my boyfriend. We kind of lived together."

"Oh," Georgina said, "I'm sorry about what happened." She paused for a moment, seemingly gravely considering the lumbering bulk of Little Johnny, "what are they telling you?"

"Not much of anything," Betsy said, muttering. "He's a Medicare case, and he's got a cop out there, too, so he's not too high on their list," she said. "They're telling me to hope for the best. Whatever the hell that means."

"That's not too easy," Georgina said soothingly.

"Are you a social worker or something?" Betsy asked hesitantly. She seemed exactly the type that a lowlife like Johnny Stone would go for. Somebody who wasn't too terribly in demand by the opposite sex, was grateful for the attention, and who was meek and easily intimidated.

"No, actually," Georgina said, "I'm the one who did this to your boyfriend."

Stunned silence, for a moment, and a blank face from Betsy. "I'm sorry?" she finally said.

"Your boyfriend attacked me in my parking garage, and I ended up coming out on top. He broke this arm of mine, though."

Betsy stood up. "So what are you here for?" She stood sort-of protectively between Johnny and Georgina, as though Georgina was there to finish him off or something.

"It's hard to say," Georgina said, making sure not to step any further forward, but rather leaning back on her heels. "I know he can't tell me why he did what he did. I guess I'm hoping for the best, too. I just don't know what that is. I want to know who persuaded him to try to kill me."

Tears brimmed in Betsy's eyes, accompanied by confusion. She obviously wasn't sure whether she should be angry or sad, or sorry, or what.

"I've heard from far too many people that he wasn't really a bad person," Georgina went on. "He'd gotten involved with a bad crowd when he was younger, and he'd gotten himself into a lot of trouble that wasn't his fault." Georgina didn't believe a word of that crap, but she hoped it would warm Betsy up.

It worked. "He's not bad," Betsy said. She looked again at Georgina's arm, and looked at her boyfriend in the bed, trying to put the two things together. "He's always been a little confused, I think. I've known him for about two years, and I know growing up without his mama was real tough on him. He missed her something awful. But he wasn't bad. When I met him, he

If it Could Happen to Her

had a job. He tried hard to keep it, too. But he drank too much sometimes. 'Made it tough to get up in the morning and get to work on time."

Betsy fished in her purse, and Georgina quickly grabbed a tissue from a box on the unused bedstand beside little Johnny, and handed it to her. She wiped her eyes, and looked at Georgina. "But something was going on lately. He had more money. He was happy to be able to buy me stuff. He took me out to eat, and took me shopping. He wouldn't say what it was, just said stuff like, his ship was finally coming in. That he was finally going to get to show what he was made of. Stuff like that. I kept asking him why he couldn't tell me what it is, and why he had the money before he did anything… stuff like that, but he just laughed. He said I was going to be proud of him. There's no way he was talking about hurting you. He wouldn't hurt a fly." Betsy broke down and wept heavily into her cheap hospital tissue. "Somebody must have forced him to do it," she said, wailing.

Georgina patted her on the shoulder while she thought, "Bullshit. This little fly is standing here with a broken wing." She also knew little Johnny had many such violent priors in his past. He didn't mind bringing a loaded gun along with him to a robbery every now and again, either. Little Johnny wasn't as sweet as Betsy thought he was. "Who's he been hanging out with lately?" she asked. "Any new friends? Anybody you didn't like?"

"No, not really," she said. And then she paused for a moment, thinking. "Well, nobody I met, but he was going out at night sometimes without me." She quickly looked at Georgina as though she needed to defend him. "That was okay with me. I didn't really like to go out. I liked staying in and watching television. He usually stayed with me, and drank some beer, or …" he voice drifted out. "But he'd been going out, and kind-of not telling me where he was going. He said it was business. 'Mixing business with pleasure,' is what he said. So I thought maybe it had something to do with this big deal he had going on. Maybe he had to wine and dine people, you know, like a big shot."

"He dressed up to go out?" Georgina asked.

"Well, no," Betsy said, thinking again, "not really. He didn't wear his knocking-around clothes, but he just wore jeans and a sweatshirt, you know, nothing special. Maybe the people he was working with were really casual. That would make sense. Johnny was really casual. Laid-back."

"Drunks usually are," Georgina thought, "until they get mad." Out loud, she said. "Usually you guys would just get a little stoned and hang out?"

If it Could Happen to Her

Betsy looked very worried at that. "Oh, no," she stuttered, "I mean…"

Georgina laughed. "I'm not a cop," she said, putting her hand on Betsy's shoulder, "I don't care. I think if more people smoked pot there would be a lot less violence in the world." She patted Betsy's arm. "And fewer potato chips," she thought, but didn't say out loud.

Betsy smiled, but didn't exactly say yes. "He was laid-back like that. We'd just hang out and he liked to drink beer, too. We'd play video games, or we'd rent movies or something."

"Are you living there alone now?" Georgina asked.

"It's actually my place," Betsy said. Georgina wasn't surprised. She knew little Johnny had had some difficulty keeping a permanent address, even with the subsidizing of his life by his big brother Jerry.

"Nice place?" Georgina asked.

Betsy sniffed and wiped her nose. "Yeah. I kept it pretty nice for him. He liked staying there with me. I think we were going to get married," she said, and her face dissolved in tears, and she wailed again into her tissue. Georgina handed her a few more, to replace the ones that were already soaked.

"Oh, sure," Georgina thought. Married. More than likely, Betsy would have wound up with a bun in the oven and years in Family Court fighting for child support, but that's probably the best she was going to do by little Johnny.

"Whereabouts?" she said out loud.

"Oh, I'm out in Brooklyn," she said, "but it's real nice." She gave Georgina the name of the street, and she knew it. Or rather knew of it. Not a great neighborhood. A lot of shitty apartment buildings, crappy duplexes and no-tell motels.

"That's nice," Georgina said, making a mental note to check the place out. Maybe have one of her friends at Konig check the place out, and do a quick drop-by when Betsy was home, but wasn't expecting company.

"Anyway…" Betsy said, clearly feeling a little uncomfortable.

"Listen," Georgina said, "I'll leave you alone. I just…" she turned aside for a moment and reached for a tissue herself. "You know… I don't know why he did what he did, but I never meant to hurt him this badly. I really hope he's okay." She tried very hard to see if she could muster up some tears, but she had never been able to do that. She hoped her fake was convincing enough. "I hope you don't mind if I keep visiting him every once in awhile. It's not like I feel responsible, it's just…" she sniffed, "I just hope he comes out of it okay."

Betsy turned around at that and reached and grabbed Georgina in a bearhug. It was everything Georgina could do not to flinch and stiffen at the pudgy woman's touch. She smelled like marijuana and French fries, and while some people might find that delightful, Georgina was not one of them. She grabbed Betsy's upper arms and pulled her off, gently gave her a supportive shake and a smile, and turned around, trying to calculate how long it would take her to get back to her home for a shower.

As she walked toward the door, her real cell phone rang. She reached into her bag to pull it out as she walked past the cop at the door, who stood as she walked by, and looked crushed when she didn't bother to acknowledge him. "Hello?" she said.

"You're supposed to have that turned off," said a tall, skinny white nurse in SpongeBob scrubs, who happened to be walking by.

Georgina ignored her as she heard Detective Trigilio's familiar voice, "Where are you?" he asked.

"I'm still at the hospital," Georgina said, preparing to defend herself. "I just got done talking with the girlfriend, and I was, literally, just about to call you…"

Detective Trigilio cut her off. "Guess who's dead?" he asked.

Georgina's heart beat faster as she stopped still in the hospital corridor. "Who?"

"Ms. Larson seem like the kind of lady who'd hang herself to you?" he asked.

Georgina's stomach flipped over. "No. I'd say definitely not."

"Me either," he said. "So explain to me why I'm standing in her bathroom while they get ready to cut her down from her showerhead?"

"I can be there in 20 minutes," Georgina said, starting to jog down the corridor. "Please, please wait for me."

"We'll be here for a while," he said. "But don't take your time. I can't get them to hold things for more than about that."

"I'll be there," she said, setting into a flat run on the way to her car.

Georgina's Rover screeched into a spot down the street from the drycleaners. Several police squad cars had blocked off most of the avenue, and there were a couple of other now-useless rescue trucks still there. Georgina could only imagine an incident of this nature was so rare in Cambridge that it was the most interesting thing these people had done all day – perhaps all month. She had broken several speed laws to find herself in Cambridge within

25 minutes of receiving Detective Trigilio's telephone call. She was grateful for the illegal state-of-the-art radar detector she had installed.

Georgina jogged up the sidewalk, her strained thigh muscles causing her pain, with all of the unexpected physical activity, and headed toward the steps on the side of the drycleaners building that led up to Ms. Larson's apartment. A couple of uniformed police officers were standing at the base of the staircase, along with five or six men who were a variety of fire, rescue and ambulance personnel. They were chatting and killing time, discussing what was probably the high point of their day, and avoiding any other kind of work that might await them back at their respective headquarters.

Georgina moved past them quickly. They were too stunned by what she looked like, and also by the air of authority she adopted. Georgina had done a portion of her dissertation work on the psychology of influence, and, she felt, had proven that if one simply acts as though they belong, and looks like they belong, then they simply belong, and everyone else who belongs will come to accept it without question.

She breezed past the two uniforms with a quick "Afternoon, Officers," and went up the stairs. One of them half-heartedly said, "Hey," and turned to his partner, who just shrugged his shoulders, and followed her up the stairs. Georgina walked through the door and the entryway, and saw Detective Trigilio seated at Ms. Larson's kitchen table, making notes onto a yellow legal pad. "Detective?" she said, breathing heavier than usual, for his benefit, to show that she had hurried.

He looked up at her from over his reading glasses. "You sure can move when you want to," he said, putting his pen back into his shirt pocket, and turning his notepad back to the front page. "Drew, give her some booties and gloves," he said. Another officer, who had been on his knees examining a portion of the rug, threw her a pair of blue plastic elasticized booties to cover her shoes with, and a pair of latex medical gloves. "You allergic to latex?" he asked briefly.

"No," she said, putting on the booties, and then accepting the gloves. Trigilio got up from the table, and put his arm out, allowing Georgina to move toward the back of the apartment. There was only one other officer in the apartment, obviously the ID officer, who was taking photographs at the moment, but who also had a large box open with jars of fingerprint dust and plastic evidence bags, etc. He also had a vacuum cleaner, standing ready to suck up all of the trace evidence that any intruders might have left behind. The

If it Could Happen to Her

officer who had followed Georgina up the stairs turned and went back down when he saw Trigilio welcome her.

"Is she still back there?" Georgina asked.

"Nope," he said. "They took her about a half-hour after they found her. Officer Drew got lots of pictures, but they had to get her down to do some of the tests, and they wanted to get her into autopsy. Luckily, I heard the call. I immediately told them they might be dealing with a murder, and not a suicide. They didn't mind. We don't have much to do here in the way of murder, and when I told them it was more than likely also connected with the Musgrave case, they were happy to oblige, and bring out everything."

"Yeah," Georgina said, "I noticed you had everybody cooling their heels downstairs."

"Well, it was almost too late," Trigilio grumbled. "The dumb fucks had already tramped all over the place. Officer Drew had to take samples from about ten pair of department shoes for purposes of elimination, and he wasn't happy about it."

Detective Trigilio showed Georgina the bathroom from the doorway. It was approximately 15 feet long by about 8 feet wide, with the tub at the far end equipped with a shower curtain. It was a very nice bathroom, with expensive fixtures, real ceramic tile, a granite countertop and lush, expensive towels. Trigilio pointed at the shower head. "She was hanging from that. She, or somebody, used one of her bathrobe ties. It matched the robe she was wearing at the time."

"She was tall," Georgina said, "and not that skinny. That thing could hold her?" she asked.

"It did. I saw it with my own eyes."

"But didn't her feet touch the bottom?" Georgina asked.

"Yep," he said. "They did. If this was a suicide, it shows she was determined to do it – no second thoughts."

"But you don't believe that, do you?" she asked, looking only a bit worried.

"Nope," he said simply.

"Where's the dog?" Georgina asked.

"The dog's in the bedroom," Trigilio said.

"Oh, shit," Georgina said.

"Yeah," agreed Trigilio.

They walked further down the back hall and into Ms. Larson's pristine bedroom, decorated in shades of yellow and cream, with delicate patterns, and expensive fabrics Georgina recognized as to-the-trade only. The only sign of disruption in this soothing sleep haven was a doggie bed tucked in the corner. Stuffed with down, and covered in a thick damask cotton that matched the balloon shades, it was the final resting place of Carina. The dog's throat had been cut, but there was very little evidence of blood.

"Where was the dog done?" Georgina asked.

"Over the kitchen sink, or in the tub," Trigilio said, shrugging his shoulders. "We'll find out when we run some tests in and around the drains. They cleaned up really well. If she did it, she didn't want to leave the dog with anybody else. If somebody else did it, maybe they did it to try to get her to tell them something, or just to keep the doggie quiet while they took care of her. Either way, it fits with suicide. That's in their favor."

The dog had been positioned in the doggie bed as though sleeping. "Poor little Carina."

Trigilio looked around to make sure the ID cop was out of earshot. "What's your gut?" Trigilio asked.

"I think somebody came in. There was nothing wrong with the door, right?"

"Right."

"So, somebody came in, ostensibly admitted by Ms. Larson. Once they got in, she was fairly quickly subdued. The dog had to be fairly quickly subdued as well, because it was a yapper that didn't like guests, if you'll remember."

"I remember," he said.

"So, they probably killed the dog in front of her, either because they had some questions to ask, or just because they had to anyway to keep it quiet. So, then, one of them held her while the other one strangled her, and hung her from the showerhead."

"You're assuming there were two?" Trigilio said.

"I guess I am," Georgina said. "Why am I?" she said, looking out into the hallway, and walking into the kitchen. "Well, one of them had to kill the dog. She would have fought about that. If they took care of her first, the dog would have been yapping the whole time, and that would have been too dangerous. And she was big. She was fit. She cleaned a big house, and did a lot of the dirty work herself. I think it would have taken more than one guy to control the situation, her, the dog, and keep it all so quiet hat everything is still in place." Georgina looked around. "There's not a knick-knack out of place or broken."

"I know," Trigilio said. "That's why some of the guys are rolling their eyes when I talk about murder."

"Have you talked to Jerry Stone downstairs?" Georgina said.

"Nope. It's his day off," Trigilio said. "I went down there right at first, and talked to the assistant manager. It's Jerry's regular day off."

"Well, what's Jerry doing with his day off?" Georgina smiled.

Detective Trigilio led the way downstairs to Pat Monroe, the Stone's assistant manager. He walked right past the counter, winking at the middle-aged woman who barely looked up from her folding duties, and pushed open the door to the back office. Pat Monroe sat up quickly. His feet had been up on the desk, and he had been reading a magazine. From the speed with which he stashed it in his left-hand top drawer, it was probably something dirty, Georgina thought.

"Detective," he said. "Any news about what's going on upstairs?" He stood up, obviously not feeling comfortable sitting down while the large Detective remained standing.

"Nothing concrete. Not yet. But we appreciate your help. Did you call your boss and tell him what happened? I told you I'd let him know myself, so I'm just curious."

Georgina could almost see the vein in Pat Monroe's neck start to throb faster. "It's his regular afternoon off, so…"

"I don't think he answered my question," Trigilio said to Georgina. "Did he answer my question?"

"That wasn't the question I heard you ask," Georgina said.

"Did you hear the question I asked you?" Trigilio said.

"Yes," Pat Monroe mumbled.

"Did you understand it?" Trigilio smiled and moved a little closer.

"Yes," Pat Monroe said. "Yes, I called him. That's alright, isn't it? Why wouldn't I? Somebody kills themselves upstairs on his property, of course I called him. He used to know her, too. They were friends," he trailed off.

"So, yes. You called him," Trigilio said.

"Yes," he said.

"When?" Trigilio asked.

"Just after you told me," he said, "probably about an hour ago, maybe less."

"Where did you catch him?"

"I'm sorry?"

"What number did you dial?" Trigilio asked, moving close enough now to look into the still-open top drawer, and smile a knowing smile at Pat Monroe.

His face now beet-red, Monroe said, "I got him on his cell phone, so I don't know where he is. He didn't say where he was."

"Where does he live?" Trigilio asked.

"Just outside the village, not more than ten minutes from here," Monroe said. "On Compton, 115 Compton."

"That's a nice neighborhood," Trigilio said to Georgina. "Not as nice as Mrs. Musgrave's neighborhood, but it's pretty nice."

"Well, Mrs. Musgrave purchased the entire neighborhood, and made it her own," Georgina said, turning without saying goodbye to Mr. Monroe. Trigilio reached into the top drawer and pulled out the copy of Penthouse Monroe had been reading. "I'll let you get back to work," he said, winking, and throwing it on the desk.

"That's my fault," Trigilio said to Georgina, as they walked together out of the drycleaner's shop. "I should have brought him upstairs with me, or had somebody sit here with him to make sure he didn't pick up a phone. Stupid. I should have known he'd call."

"Well, we don't know what it means," Georgina said. "Even if somebody ran, it would help us know what's going on. We'd be headed in the right direction." She was trying to make Trigilio feel better.

"Yeah, but a hell of a lot farther away," he growled, moving faster toward his car, and shouting at all of the other police cars to make a hole so he could get out quickly. Georgina gauged his clout at the Department by the speed with which all of the other officers ran to comply.

If it Could Happen to Her

Chapter Ten

Georgina hopped into Detective Trigilio's car, and rode along the Main Street of Cambridge, Connecticut. None of the houses were the palatial mansions Ingrid Musgrave had, but the entire town was a lovely example of tough zoning, coupled with enough money to make even the most humble of the abodes charming. The houses were large, old, and set well back from the street, all with big, welcoming front porches, and Victorian details. Most properties had stone borders along the front and sides. Delightful. They drove off onto a secondary street with houses not quite as old, and not quite as charming, as on Main Street, and then into a starkly-new housing development, with a green and gold-embossed sign heralding a welcome to "Independence Heights."

They drove into a perfectly-manicured small subdivision with large, 6,000 to 7,000 square foot houses built side-by-side on no more than half-acre lots. In fact, the only cars parked on the streets they passed were lawn maintenance vans and trucks with lawn maintenance equipment. Gardeners tended lawns, and Lexus', Mercedes' and Lincoln's all sat parked in driveways. "McMansions," Detective Trigilio said, "you either love them, or you hate them."

"I must say, I hate them," Georgina said. "The lots are so small. These people live practically on top of one another. I don't know how they can stand to go outside, with their neighbors about ten feet away."

"They don't go outside," Trigilio said. "With houses as big as that, they probably have fenced-in, tiny little yards, and try to pretend their neighbors aren't there."

"Which one's Jerry's?" she asked.

"Right here," he said, turning into a stone-front French Provincial Revival monstrosity.

"He was doing a lot better than his brothers and sisters," Georgina said. "Little Johnny was bunking with a recent girlfriend, because he didn't have anywhere to live." She made another cursory examination of the elaborate stone façade of the house, complete with shutters and window boxes filled with flowers, before getting out of the car. "Twenty bucks says the back is white siding, no shutters," Georgina said.

"What?" Trigilio said.

"These houses – all that matters is the front. There's usually nothing in the back. It's the weirdest thing. People will spend the money on the front, or even three-quarters of their house, but they leave the back almost completely undone, because nobody can see it," she laughed.

"That sounds about right," Trigilio said, turning the key off, and seeing only a Toyota Camry in the parking lot. "It looks like somebody's at home," he said.

"Toyota. If there's a fabric interior, it's the housekeeper," she said, getting out of the car.

Trigilio glanced in quickly, "fabric." He walked up and rapped at the door. The housekeeper, a sturdy medium-brown haired woman with her hair in loose messy curls around her face, a plain t-shirt and mom-front pleated jeans, came to the door. Detective Trigilio pulled out his badge right away, and said, "Is Jerry Stone at home?"

"No," she said, reaching to shut the door.

"Hey," Trigilio said, stiff-arming the door with a loud smack. "I wouldn't try to do that again if I were you," he said sternly.

"I told you, he's not home," she said gruffly, not intimidated by Trigilio.

He sniffed the air. "Is that marijuana, I smell?" He turned to Georgina. "Do you smell marijuana?"

"It's hard to say," Georgina said, sniffing the air herself. "I don't have much experience with those kinds of things, but there is definitely a pungent, sort-of smoky smell I can't identify. If you say it's marijuana, I would certainly bow to your superior experience."

The housekeeper's shoulders sagged, but she rolled her eyes, and exhaled deeply. She opened the door further, and put her arm out, indicating Detective Trigilio and Georgina could come inside. They stepped into an entryway with very nice ceramic tile, cut to look like marble, a large staircase sweeping up to the left, and two Doric columns seemingly holding up the entryways of the formal dining room on their left, and the formal living room, on their right. "Yuck," Georgina said to herself quietly, thinking how insane it was that someone would spend so much money to have something so cookie-cutter and boring. "Custom builders," she thought, "a contradiction in terms."

"He's not here," the woman said, leaving the door open, and her hand on it, "and what you smell is Lemon Pledge."

"You're the housekeeper?" Trigilio asked.

"Yes," she said.

"What's your name?"

If it Could Happen to Her

"Kathy," she said.

"Where is he?" Trigilio asked.

"I don't know," she said. "Nobody's home. Nobody was home when I got here."

"You've got your own key?" Trigilio asked.

"Yep, and the code to the alarm system," she said.

"Mom? Is somebody here?" Georgina and Trigilio both turned to see a younger version of the housekeeper emerge from around a corner, carrying a feather duster.

"That's my daughter," Kathy said.

"I thought you said nobody was here," Trigilio said.

"I said nobody was 'home,'" she said. "We don't live here."

Georgina smiled, and thought that, in another life, the woman would have made a fine litigator. "How are you doing?" she asked the girl.

"I'm fine," she said. Trigilio flashed his badge briefly, and Georgina asked her, "Do you know where Mr. Stone is?"

"No, but I think they're on vacation," she said.

"Cindy..." her mother said with a growl.

All of a sudden, Cindy looked nervous.

"What makes you think they're on vacation?" Trigilio asked.

Cindy looked at her mother, afraid to answer.

Moving to block the sight line between mother and daughter, Trigilio said, "You've already told us..." he said. "You may as well tell us why."

"Well, I just thought they were on vacation because their suitcases are gone," she said, after looking over Trigilio's shoulder and receiving a quick nod from her mother, "at least Mrs. Stone's are. She's got really nice Louis Vuitton suitcases, and they're gone. A lot of her clothes are gone, too. I noticed when I vacuumed her closet."

Trigilio turned to the mother, "Did they tell you they were going on vacation?"

"They don't check in with me," she said grudgingly.

"I'm getting a little tired of this attitude. Would you prefer to come downtown right now, and spend the rest of the day, and perhaps night, answering these questions in one of our interview rooms?"

Her eyes bugged out of her face, "What the hell would you take us in for?"

"We've just come from the scene of a murder, and we have some questions to ask Mr. Stone. He's not here, and for some reason, although you seem to suspect he's gone on vacation, you're giving me problems," Trigilio spread his hands out wide. "You tell me? What am I supposed to think?"

Kathy was quiet now, and pale, "What murder?" she asked.

"Just answer the questions I'm asking you," he said. "When your boss goes on vacation, does he usually tell you?"

"Yes," she said. "He usually tells me beforehand, or he leaves me a note to water the plants, set the timers on the lights, stop by in the evenings, stuff like that."

"Did he tell you beforehand this time?" Trigilio asked.

"No," she said.

"Did he leave you a note?" he asked.

"Yes," she said, turning and heading back past the grand staircase. Trigilio, her daughter, and Georgina all followed her back into a lavish kitchen, gleaming with granite surfaces and hardware, and elaborately-carved wood cabinetry, and stainless steel appliances. She reached and picked up a long narrow note, written on the sort of paper pad for making shopping lists. Georgina looked over and saw the corresponding pad magnetically attached to the side of the refrigerator.

She handed it to Trigilio, and he read it out loud, "Kathy, We're getting out of town for a few days to take advantage of the weather. Please take care of things. Thanks. Brenda." He looked up. "Who's Brenda?" he asked.

"Mrs. Stone," Kathy said.

Trigilio held the note up and shook it in the air, "A few days? That's a little vague. Is that common?"

"Yeah," she said. "They'd always do that," Kathy said. Cindy was hanging behind her mother, looking nervous, twisting the feather duster compulsively. "They'd go whenever they wanted. They owned their own business, so they didn't have to answer to anybody. They'd just go. They were back when they were back."

"Not bad," Trigilio said. "It sounds like a nice business to be in. Me, I've got a boss." He stepped closer to Kathy, "That boss is going to ask me why I shouldn't assume Jerry Stone and his wife have skipped town following a murder. What do you think?"

"No," Cindy said, from behind her mother, looking stricken.

"No way," Kathy said, too. "They're good people. Nice people. They've done well. They treat people good, take care of their family. No way."

Trigilio let the ladies off the hook, and took down their contact information, double-checking it against their driver's licenses. While he was there, he also took the information for the house, including the mobile phone numbers of both Mr. and Mrs. Stone, who were not answering at the moment, the code for the alarm system, and the placement of the hidden key to the side door. Kathy gave this information quite willingly, not asking for anything like a warrant, etc. She said she would continue to come by every day, as usual, and if she noticed anything strange, she would let him know. She had become far, far more happy to help.

"Remember," he said. "You hear from them, you call me," he had said, and they had both nodded meekly.

Back in the car, Georgina asked, "Innocent explanation? Coincidence? Or did the Stones just skip?" Georgina couldn't help smiling to herself.

"Skipping Stones?" he said, turning to her with raised eyebrows. "Did you just say that?"

"I'm sorry," she said, laughing. "This is clearly not a laughing matter."

Trigilio couldn't help chuckling. He drove her back to the station, and to her car.

Because she was still in Connecticut, she thought she might take a chance and go to visit Mr. Musgrave's old mistress, Marianne Daumier. Georgina knew she lived just less than an hour away in Darien, which was yet another expensive, charming hamlet in Connecticut, in a house Mr. Musgrave had purchased for her. She had lived in a house nearby for years, and raised their bastard daughter there. But she now had a brand new home very close to the old one, as well as an additional 3,500 square foot condominium in Palm Beach, received as a consolation present after Mr. Musgrave had dumped her, and she had nearly castrated him. Georgina said her farewells to Detective Trigilio after each extracted promises from one another, yet again, to keep each other informed.

Georgina called back to her apartment, and got the address information from Armeda, who didn't want her driving any more that day. "I like you to be out getting fresh air, but you've got a broken arm. You need to rest. You don't have to drive everywhere in the country today."

Georgina had to listen to the entire lecture, because Armeda was smart enough to know she could have her whole, uninterrupted, say if she waited

If it Could Happen to Her

until the end to give Georgina the information she wanted. Once Georgina finally had the address, and an earful from Armeda, she punched it into her GPS unit, and got the turn-by-turn directions, which showed her she only had about 45 minutes of driving ahead of her. Unfortunately, it was in the opposite direction from New York City, which meant she had yet another hour or more on the way back, some of which would be after sunset. She had some particular nervousness about driving after sunset, but she was comfortable with her eyesight, and her GPS unit. She sat for a few moments, going through the logical reasons why there was nothing to be worried about, and then a few deep breathing relaxation exercises which gave her the boost she needed.

Georgina called ahead, and spoke to Olivia, who answered the telephone. The two of them had met once or twice. She remembered the controversy when Olivia had wanted to go to Brown University. It was at the same time Georgina and Luanne Musgrave were attending Brown, and Geoffrey Musgrave had forbidden it. Olivia was more than qualified to attend the Ivy League school, but Geoffrey Musgrave didn't want his two families to intermingle. Each side was content to pretend the other didn't exist, and he was content with that, too. So, Olivia went to Princeton.

Georgina remembered Luanne talking to her about it at the time, though. Luanne talked when she wanted to. She had felt badly. She knew who Olivia was, and the controversy was a very poorly kept secret. "I wish they'd just let her come here," Luanne had said, "I'm going to be gone next year anyway. We'd hardly ever run into each other." But she shrugged it off, and accepted it as the typical behavior of a family which had very few corrective tendencies. Other families ran into difficulties with the law, or with finding success in general, if they didn't play by the rules. But if you were rich, the rules didn't apply. This was a difficult lesson to learn. Georgina remembered learning it when she was very young.

Olivia also knew who Georgina was, and, when Georgina explained what she had been doing, her Ph.D. in Psychology, and her current hands-on interest in crime, Olivia was fascinated. She had parlayed her education into a degree in Biochemistry, and was now working on her dissertation. She had also said that her mother was home, and that she wouldn't mind the visit, or the subject matter.

Georgina pulled up to a charming house, with an unassuming façade, looking exactly like a meticulously well cared-for small ranch house. Upon entering, with the assistance of a uniformed maid, Georgina discovered that the house was actually built into an escarpment, with each level built further out and down. Olivia took her by the arm as soon as she arrived, and, after Georgina expressed her interest in the unique layout, took her on a tour. She asked about Georgina's arm, but didn't pry after receiving a vague response about riding. Olivia didn't really look like her father, but she did resemble her half-sister Luanne, with her tall, blond, slim and willowy look. "I actually designed it myself," she said, in a very self-deprecating way. "I minored in architecture during undergrad," she said, by way of explanation. "My mother wanted something that wasn't obnoxious at the front, but which still had the space she wanted, because she likes a lot of space."

"It's gorgeous," Georgina said, and she really meant it. She respected the fact that they had abandoned their old house for a fresh start, and liked the fact that they wanted to have luxury, space and comfort, without having to advertise that fact to everyone who drove by. Even the stone that was used to cover the front of the house and mark out the driveway was similar to the stone of the escarpment itself. The entire house almost seemed to disappear into the ground it was built on.

Olivia led her down toward the back of the house, and the spot lowest on the escarpment, overlooking a drop of nearly 100 feet, which had been created as an elaborately tiled sunroom. Her mother sat there in a carved wooden chair with plush cushions, upholstered with lavish trimming and colorful tassels. She was dressed in a glamorous, colorful caftan, her silver-gray hair swept perfectly back from her lovely face. "Mother," Olivia said, "Georgina's here."

Marianne Daumier looked at Georgina over the top of her reading glasses. She had a copy of The Economist folded open in her left hand. Her right hand was adorned with an enormous rectangular emerald in an intricate setting with smaller stones in a rainbow of colors. Georgina could barely take her eyes off it, but wouldn't dare to avoid that gaze, either. Marianne's hair used to be blond, and her pale blue eyes were as lovely as ever. Her face was lovely, too, and she looked years younger than her nearly 65 years. Georgina was trying to guess who did her work, because, whoever it was, it was who Georgina wanted to see when the time came. Marianne managed to look older, but still lovely. She had resisted the temptation to try to stay frozen at age 25. It was probably her downfall with Geoffrey Musgrave, but that was all to her credit, and to his damnation. He didn't know class when he saw it.

Marianne placed the magazine down on a table which closely matched the chair, and which had an intricately-inlaid smattering of blue and white tile.

Beside it was a martini glass, about half-full.

Olivia walked briskly over to the bar which sat in the corner of the room, where a pitcher of martinis sat ready and chilling. She topped her mother's drink off, and said "Georgina, would you like a martini? Very dry," she said, smiling.

Actually, Georgina could think of nothing better after the day she'd had. "Yes, please," she said.

"Please, sit," Marianna said, gesturing gracefully with that bejeweled right hand to a seat by her side. Georgina sat down, and Olivia handed her a cocktail. She then went over to pour one for herself, and pulled a chair over from the wall to join their conversational circle. "We're having dinner in a half-hour," Marianne said, in her lightly French-accented English, "would you care to join us? I believe it's meatloaf tonight," she said, smiling, "Olivia's favorite."

Olivia sipped on her martini and smiled, too. "It is," she said, "our cook is amazing. If I didn't spend 20 minutes on the elliptical machine every day, I'd weigh 200 pounds."

"I'd love to," Georgina said, "honestly. But I've got a housekeeper back at home who's keeping my dinner warm for my return to the City, and if I don't eat it when I get there, the punishment will be severe."

"Good for you," Marianne said, reaching over to pat Georgina's knee. "Once you've found good help, and people you like to have around you, treat them with respect, and pay them whatever they want," she laughed.

"I agree," Georgina said.

"Mother, did you know Georgina got her doctorate in Psychology?" Olivia politely volunteered.

"Yes, I think I heard something like that," Marianne said. "Well done. Olivia's nearly finished. Half of the things she's working on I can't understand. I see her papers scattered all over her office, and can't make sense of anything."

"It's just boring old biochemistry," Olivia said, steering the conversation to the reason Georgina was there. "It's nothing as interesting or important as what Georgina's turned her attention to. She's using her talents to fight crime."

"That's a little dramatic, isn't it dear?" Marianne said, rolling her eyes. She looked over at Georgina, "but it is true, yes? Olivia tells me you've been looking into what happened to Ingrid."

Georgina was impressed that the woman's long-time rival's name could

If it Could Happen to Her

come so naturally out of her mouth. Perhaps the fact that she was dead made it easier. They had competed for years over the same man, with a dark horse coming in at the last minute and swooping to the finish line before either of them. Ingrid had divorced him, and Marianne had nearly killed him. But who could say little Heather was really the winner? Ingrid had lived for years as the queen in her own kingdom, funded by her divorce, with her handsome Bart to keep her company, and Marianne had received a lavish settlement, peace of mind, and a lovely daughter. In Georgina's mind, Heather certainly hadn't won, and they hadn't lost at all. "Well," she thought, "except Ingrid – now."

"Yes," she said. "I work for Konig Investigations occasionally, when a case interests me, and I was very interested in Ingrid's case."

"I hope you don't think I killed her," Marianne said evenly.

"Mother!" Olivia exclaimed. "Of course Georgina doesn't think that."

"No," Georgina said, taking another sip of her martini, "I never gave that a second thought. I'm sure the people who actually killed Ingrid, and Bartolomeo –"

"Bartolomeo?" Olivia asked.

"The polo player," Marianne said, wrinkling her nose.

"Oh," Olivia said, "oh, right."

Georgina smiled. "I'm sure the people who killed them were very talented robbers, who killed them because they were home, or may have been hired killers who then burgled the house to make a murder look like robbery."

"Luanne said the same thing," Olivia said, sipping her martini.

Georgina tried not to look surprised. "Maybe you talked to Luanne after I did," she said.

"Probably. We had lunch just a couple of days ago. She was torn up. Obviously, she was upset about her mother, and the memorial service, and everything, but she'd just come from Little Ingrid and Matthew's house, and had spent time with them, because they hadn't been invited to the luncheon. They were very upset as well. It was a terrible thing to do. Their father had made all of the arrangements, and just left them out."

Georgina noticed that Olivia was very comfortable referring to Geoffrey Musgrave as "their father," and she carefully broached what she found to be an even more fascinating subject, "I'm kind of surprised you and Luanne are in touch."

"Oh," Olivia said, "I guess it might seem funny, but we are half-sisters after all. And Luanne's always been the peace-maker. She's always the one who's trying to bring us together, and trying to make the other brothers and sisters be nicer to Little Ingrid and Matthew. I think now, she's probably the one who's holding everything together. It's marvelous."

"It is marvelous," Georgina said, and thought it was marvelous, indeed. And she hadn't known Luanne was in touch with Little Ingrid and Matthew. They had each given her the distinct impression there was a complete breach in the family. Why would they do that, she wondered?

"Luanne tried to convince the family to have them to the luncheon," Olivia said. "She even mentioned that they ought to invite Mother and me," she said, laughing out loud.

"Luanne is nice, dear," Marianne said, "but that's just ludicrous."

"Well, I wish she'd convinced them to have Little Ingrid and Matthew, whatever they think. They could all be completely wrong about... well... I suppose for appearances sake, they shouldn't... well, anyway. It's family. It wouldn't have harmed them to bury the hatchet," Olivia said.

Marianne rolled her eyes. "Olivia is extremely understanding," she said.

"Nobody know what goes on behind closed doors, Mother," Olivia lectured.

"Thank goodness," Marianne said, lifting her glass to her lips with a smile.

"So, you've kept in touch with Luanne," Georgina asked. "Any of the others?"

"No," Olivia said. "I, I don't know. I do what I can. I don't want to impose myself, but they are my half-brothers and sisters. When I was younger, I used to try to call them about once a year, on their birthdays or something. Now I just send Christmas cards. Luanne was the only one who ever reciprocated. Father and I talk occasionally, and meet at holidays, exchange gifts..." she shrugged her shoulders.

Marianne, who had been quiet throughout most of the conversation, said, "You know, Georgina, I think that's what I regret the most. Honestly, I regret spending so much time with that worthless man. It's terrible." Her eyes glowed with a certain pride for her daughter, mixed with contempt for her daughter's half-siblings. "Olivia's a fantastic child, and a wonderful woman, and all of them should be proud to be related to her. She turned out better than any one of them..."

"Mother," Olivia said.

"No, it's true. They're pathetic. All of them. And pretty soon they'll be calling you Doctor. But not Doctor Musgrave, no. Doctor Daumier. Because I chose so badly. I regret that I put you in a position you don't deserve."

"Doctor Daumier sounds better," Olivia said. "I like the ring of that. And, just think – if I get married, I might take his name, and end up Dr. Smith."

Marianne inhaled deeply, "I forbid it."

Olivia smiled at her mother, taking another small sip from her martini.

"Oh, you're having a little fun with me," Marianne said, smiling.

Georgina spent a few more minutes chatting with the ladies about mutual acquaintances, their summer plans, etc. She came away from it thinking that Geoffrey Musgrave had chosen very, very badly, and may yet come to regret some of his decisions.

As she climbed back into the soft leather upholstery of her Rover, Georgina thought again about Luanne and Little Ingrid and Matthew. Why should they be embarrassed they were in touch? Maybe they were just so used to keeping it from their father, that they instinctively lied, but Georgina wondered all the same. Strange behavior from strange people – who knew what to think?

If it Could Happen to Her

Chapter Eleven

Georgina got home without undue stress. She was actually rather proud of herself for the way she was coping, managing to maintain her cool as the unsavory aspects of the case took their toll on her peace of mind. Her arm was also killing her. She had been taking mild pain medication, but she hadn't taken any since that morning. When Little Johnny's fiancée had hugged her, she had also given Georgina's arm a squeeze it didn't need.

She had a moment of a rapid heartbeat when she pulled into the underground parking garage at her building, but she saw the guard on duty, and breathed deeply, and felt better. However, Georgina got upstairs and into her apartment in record time, moving quickly past Armeda, who met her at the door in a bathrobe, shedding her clothes on her way to her shower. Armeda picked them up one-by-one as she followed Georgina into her bedroom, and stuffed the clothes into the hamper in Georgina's bedroom. She turned away in a huff, and went back to bed, as Georgina grabbed a plastic bag to cover her cast, and jumped into the shower. She had been in a hospital, been hugged by a woman with questionable personal hygiene, been present at a homicide crime scene, and been in a police station. She wanted nothing more than to be clean, clean, clean.

Her thoughts were beginning to race, and she could feel her heart beating in her chest. The drive home in the dark had not done her any good. She got out of the shower and looked at the clock. It was already a little past 10:00, and close to her bedtime. She deeply disliked any deviation from her schedule, and she bit her lip. She tugged on her cashmere bathrobe and sat down at the vanity table in her bathroom, pausing for a moment before she pulled open the right-hand drawer. She took out the bottle of Librium and held it for a moment. She normally preferred to stay off any kind of medication while she was working outside, but her hands were shaking. She had put herself through a little more than even she could take for one day. She took a deep breath and shook out two 10 mg. pills. She took them and drank them down with a bottle of sparkling water she had taken from the refrigerator cleverly concealed among the bathroom cabinets. "I guess there's no pain pills tonight," she said to herself, although she was tempted to add them to the mix. She took a deep breath and began running a wide-tooth comb through her hair. She slowly blow-dried her hair, section-by-section, which was slow work with one good arm. But by the time she was done, she thought she could feel the Librium beginning to work. She knew it was probably too soon – perhaps it was actually the rhythmic movement of self-grooming, and the fact that she was clean, that was making her feel much more calm. She finished her hair and then covered herself from head-to-toe with Crème de la Mer lotion, feeling soft and silky as she walked into her closet and chose a long, dark gray tank-style cotton nightgown.

She opened up her safe, and put away the jewelry she had worn during the day, after taking it out of the professional ultrasonic jewelry cleaner she used to keep it meticulously clean. She then took out an enormous emerald-cut, 53-carat, D flawless white diamond ring that her father had given her mother, and his father had given to his mother before her. It was by far the most expensive piece of jewelry she owned, and should arguably be in a safe deposit box at her bank, but she kept it handy like a talisman, and wore it when she particularly needed comfort. The magnificent ring Marianne had worn reminded her of it.

She looked at herself in the full-length mirror in her closet. She ran her fingers through her silky brown hair, and looked at her face, lovely even without makeup, bruises beginning to fade, with those unusually blue-green eyes that were always commented on. "It would be nice if you could hold it together a little better than you do," she said to her reflection, tapping on the mirror with a perfectly French manicured finger. She walked barefoot back through her kitchen, and poured herself a glass of Pinot Noir. She knew she shouldn't be mixing alcohol with a near panic-attack level dose of Librium, but she did it anyway. She walked through the back door of her kitchen and into her study. She took a sip of her wine and put it down on her desk, sat down in her black leather chair, and spun around to face her murder board.

"It's been a busy day," she said to herself, rubbing her arm within its cast as she examined the murder board from top to bottom, looking at how many things had to be moved, things that had to be added, and things that had to be taken down. She got up, and the first thing she did was move the photograph she had of Ms. Larson up next to the photos of the murdered Ingrid and Bartolomeo. "Sorry to find you in that section of the board, Ms. Larson," she said quietly as she did it. She would have to get copies of the official crime scene photographs from Detective Trigilio sometime during the next couple of days, along with the autopsy report. Georgina was sure it wouldn't take long. There was a lot of money, and few priorities, in Cambridge, Connecticut. They were going to be working all night down there on this one.

If it Could Happen to Her

She patiently drew a caricature of Betsy, Little Johnny's girlfriend, and put her next to Little Johnny on the board. She got a photo of Jerry Stone from a local business journal website, printed it out and put it with Little Johnny. She turned her head to the side, took the picture off the board, thought again for a moment, and put it back. She took the pictures she had of Geoffrey, Jr., Luanne, Little Ingrid, Matthew and Magrit off of the board, and put them on the floor in front of her. She stared at them for a moment, got up and retrieved her glass of wine and her laptop computer. She sat there for the next hour and-a-half, drawing up extremely rough analyses of each of the children, and of Ingrid herself. She printed them out and put them down on the floor next to the pictures of the children. She began to write a narrative of why one of the children might have murdered their mother. For this, she used a plain yellow legal pad and a Mont Blanc pen. When she was done, she took a deep breath, rolled the legal pad back to the front page, and put it down with the rest of the stuff.

"Well, it's an idea," she said. "I am a woman, and women have intuition, don't they?"

The Librium had made her calm, and the wine had also helped to soothe her nerves. She would have a headache in the morning, but it was worth it if she was right. She put the pictures back onto the board, and tucked the psychological profiles and legal pad into a manila folder. She centered it perfectly in the middle of her desk, and took herself to bed.

After she had her breakfast and a painkiller, Georgina sat at the counter in her kitchen and read the five papers she usually read every morning, The New York Times, The New York Post, The New York Daily News, The Wall Street Journal and USA Today. Then she went back into her office, and sat down on the floor in front of her murder board, drinking a bottle of Diet Pepsi. She sat there for the better part of an hour, looking back and forth, from one photograph to another, from one document to another. Even after a good night's sleep, and the distraction of reading the world's news, she really thought she was right. She thought she had it. Of course, it was just a theory.

She knew she had another drive down to Cambridge ahead of her today, but she wanted to go alone. Trigilio would kill her if he found out, so she would have to make sure he didn't. There's no way she would run into him anyway. He would be at the Larson crime scene, if he wasn't at the police station, and she would drive there immediately after she did her search.

If it Could Happen to Her

She had Jason gas up her car while she got ready. She examined herself in the mirror, touching up her lip gloss and running her fingers through her hair, and thought about wearing the diamond ring she had slept in. She knew it would be too damn foolish, though. She didn't want it stolen. She put it back in the safe, and took another glance at the right-hand drawer of her vanity, thinking about the Librium inside. She thought about having just one, but decided against it, assuring herself she would be fine once she got down to work. She packed up her totebag and double-checked its contents, an assortment of Smythson notebooks and her planner, her netbook computer, her Kindle, and her Blackberry. She also took the manila file folder from the center of her desk, and stuffed that in.

Georgina drove straight down to Ingrid's house, glad that black Range Rovers were a common sight. She didn't want anyone to know she was in town just yet. She drove down the driveway, and tucked her car behind the garage, so it wouldn't be visible from the street. She knew she had to get to the keypad within two minutes from her entrance onto the driveway, or Detective Trigilio, and everybody else at the police station, would know she was there. She quickly moved the crime scene tape aside, opened the door with the key and punched in the key code. She reached out, refastened the tape and closed the door behind her. She stood in the entryway for a moment, listening. A large empty house always had a desolate feeling, and one that was a recent crime scene was downright creepy.

She took her jacket off and hung it on one of the chairs in the hallway. She put her shoes near the door, and put on latex gloves, and plastic booties. She went through the house quickly one time, room-by-room, opening doors and making sure she was alone. She certainly felt as though the house were empty, but she was also sure something was different, that someone had been there since the last time she was there. Detective Trigilio hadn't said he was coming back out here, but he didn't have to ask her permission. She certainly hadn't asked for his. But she got the feeling things had been moved around. Detective Trigilio wouldn't do that. She went down and stood in the TV room where Bart had died, and where she had the strongest feeling something was off. Then she knew what it was. She saw the photos had been moved. She had paid particular attention to them when she had first come to the house, because she had been trying to figure out where Ingrid's affections lay. Now, she knew they were in a different order. She also noticed one of them seemed crooked.

She picked up the picture of Bart and Ingrid on a boat, in the Caribbean, Georgina could guess from the pale blue water, and turned it around, seeing one corner peeking out of the black velvet backing now.

Somebody had taken each picture out and looked behind them. She couldn't be sure they were looking for the same thing she was, clearly, but it was strange. Somebody had painstakingly searched the house. She was fairly certain it wasn't the police, doubting that they would ever be so thorough. "Shit," she said to herself, hoping she was smarter than the person who was there before her. "God damn it," she said again, her hands on her hips. She thought of all of the things the person might have found that Georgina would never have access to now. She knew the safe, also, was long gone, and wondered what that might have contained.

"Well, the hell with it," she said, and started looking around the living room, knowing this was an informal room where Ingrid liked to hang out. She turned chairs over, looking along seams, and for false bottoms, carefully took books off shelves, leafed through them in case they held some pieces of paper, and looked for interior cabinets of any sort. Her heart jumped when she found one nook at the back of some books in the built-in bookcase, but it was already empty. Her heart then sank, but she kept on. "Why didn't I drag myself down here a few days ago?" she moaned.

She gave cursory attention to the other formal rooms on the first floor, including the kitchen, guessing Ingrid was the type of person who would want her secrets close to her. Georgina had left Ingrid's room for last for that very reason. She walked in and looked around again, admiring the lavishly decorated, yet comfortable and practical, master bedroom. She got the remote control from the table on the far side of the bed, threw back the covers, and climbed in. She propped the pillows comfortably behind her head, and threw the down comforter over her legs. She took the remote, rolled up the painting and turned on the television. She flicked through a few channels for a while, stopping for a moment on Law and Order: Criminal Intent, until it came to a commercial. Then she turned on the security system and scanned through the various rooms, experimenting with the recording functions, and observing the various vantage points Ingrid had to observe what was going on in her house.

She thought for a moment, got up, and went over to the television screen mounted over the mantle. She tried to look behind it, but was able to see only that it was fastened securely to the wall, with electrical wires installed through the wall itself. She pulled it out as far as she could without breaking its

If it Could Happen to Her

attachment, pushed her face flat against the wall to peer behind, and was able to count the cords, and observe the type of cords they were. There were six, one of which was the electrical cord, the other seemed thick enough to be a cable cord, and the other four seemed to be traditional AV-in, AV-out cords. "Four," she said to herself, stepping back and looking at the wall, the gold gilt-framed television screen and the marble mantle. "Where is your DVD player, Ingrid?" she asked the dead woman. "Where, as a matter of fact, are your DVDs?"

She stepped back again and scanned the molding which picked out the area above the mantle, with bookcases on either side. On the right, she observed an indentation about the size of a human hand behind the molding, which almost seemed to be part of the bookcase itself. She put her four fingers in there, and pulled. The middle four shelves of the bookcase tipped out towards her as though they were the door of a cupboard. She smiled, and saw the DVD player/recorder, and the VCR she expected to see, along with a fairly mainstream, slightly highbrow collection of movies and documentaries. "Clever," Georgina said, smiling now, "but still too obvious. What's over there?" She went over the left side of the bookcase, which, to all appearances, did not perform the same function. She could see no handhold on this side, and no spaces where the shelves could slide out from the others. "You put it back there, though, didn't you Ingrid?" she said, looking more carefully, and starting to remove books from the four shelves. "You thought if anyone was looking, they'd find the stuff over on the right and think they'd found whatever there was to find." She kept up a running commentary with the dead woman as she emptied the shelves. "But you liked symmetry, didn't you? You liked it when things balance out, just like I do."

Georgina examined the now-bare shelves, running her hands along their smooth surfaces. She felt slowly and carefully down the intricate molding which ran along each built-in shelf. Then she touched it, and smiled wide. She pushed on the round center of a carved acanthus leaf, and felt a soft mechanical click. The four shelves then moved out toward her just as the others had on the other side.

Situated in this spot was an area about three and-a-half feet high, two and-a-half feet wide, and about two feet deep. Here was yet another DVD and VCR recorder, and a cord left loose in case Ingrid had wanted to route anything else through the television screen. "That's four," she said to herself, looking at the fourth AV cord plugged into another laptop computer. And yet another collection of DVDs. "Oh, you were naughtier than I thought you were, Ingrid," she said, observing a fairly tame collection of heterosexual porn. She booted up the computer and cursed when she came across a password protection. She thought hard, and punched in "Geoffrey," and when that didn't work, she punched in "Bart," "Bartolomeo," and each one of Ingrid's kids, even though she didn't think she'd use their names. Then she got her netbook computer out of her totebag, and pulled open the files she had had scanned into it. She rummaged through the files, found what she wanted, and started checking birthdates. She got it when Geoffrey, Sr.'s birthday came up, backwards.

Once the computer was opened, Georgina unplugged it from its electrical cord, and put it on the floor. The computer could be viewed wirelessly on the television screen, too, Georgina was interested to find out. "Why would she do that?" she wondered. When she scanned the files it contained, she found innocuous software for music files and movies, but no content. She also found some software for editing recordings. All of the more mundane computer files, word processing, spreadsheets, e-mails, Internet, etc., had been found on the laptop which had sat on Ingrid's desk, out in the open, in the corner of the bedroom.

Georgina opened the editing software and goofed around with it for a few minutes. "Ingrid, what did you do?" she asked out loud. Georgina checked the drives of the laptop, the DVD and the VCR, and found they were empty. She hated to do it, but she was going to have to take all of those movies and old VCR tapes with her, to view them and see if they were what they seemed to be. That was definitely illegal, and it took her all of about 30 seconds to make up her mind. She went down to the kitchen, and got three plastic shopping bags. She filled them with all of the movies, the porn, and what appeared to be older home movies on videotape. She also took the laptop itself, and put it into her totebag. Then she closed everything back up, and placed the books where they were before.

She put her bags into the second floor hallway and went room-by-room, again checking to be sure she didn't miss anything, and didn't leave any evidence of her presence. Then she moved the bags down to the first floor entryway, and did the same thing there, and in the basement. She put on her coat and her shoes, took the bags one-by-one out to her car, stowing them in a closed storage bin behind the second row of seats, so they couldn't be seen from the outside, and moved her car right to the front door. Then she went back, punched the key code in to reactivate the system, locked the door, repositioned the crime scene tape, jumped in her car and hauled ass to the end of the driveway before 60 seconds had gone by.

Once she was off the property, she looked over at her totebag, and checked to make sure she had put the manila folder, with her theory, into the back. She didn't want Detective Trigilio to have that, not just yet. She could still be wrong, and she hated to look wrong.

She picked up krullers again and drove to police headquarters. Luckily, Detective Trigilio was there, and not at the Larson crime scene. "Well, I would say this is a lovely surprise, but I've got a hell of a lot of work to do," he said, taking the box of krullers and letting her follow him back into the station. "Why don't you call next time before you come down here?"

"You might have told me not to," she said.

"Damn right," he growled.

"Oh, Detective," she said, patting him on the back, "you knew I was nosey when you met me. And I want to know what you know about Ms. Larson."

He waived her into a conference room again after hearing a couple of wolf whistles directed at Georgina. "You'll have to forgive them," he said loudly, "most of their wives look like me," handed her a poisonous cup of coffee, and shut the door behind them. "Then maybe I could work at my desk." He left for a moment, and came back with a few files. He shuffled through them, and said, "Okay." He perched his reading glasses on the end of his nose.

"You don't wear glasses, or contacts, at your age?" Georgina asked with a smile.

"No," he said pointedly, looking at her over the top of his readers, clearly not enjoying the 'at your age' comment. "I used to be near-sighted," he said, "but I got that laser surgery. It's a fucking miracle," he said. Looking back down at his files, he said, "Okay. What do we have? Luckily, we've got a doctor here who doubles as the Medical Examiner. He doesn't have a whole hell of a lot to do, so he was happy to do the autopsy late yesterday afternoon, as soon as we got the body back to the funeral home, which is where he does it." He put that file aside, and looked through the others. "Okay, we don't have toxicology, but that's not a surprise. We go through a private place, so we get it quick, at least the presumptive part, but it's in the city, and we don't have it back yet," he said, leisurely flipping through the pages.

"The autopsy, though," Georgina said, trying to be patient, but knowing he was enjoying this. "What does it say?"

"It says," he said, sitting back in his chair, picking the file back up, and

If it Could Happen to Her

flipping through it again. "It says there was another, smaller, ligature mark underneath the mark made by the bathrobe. She was strangled with something about the size, shape and consistency of an electrical cord, and then strung up in the shower." He flipped through a few more pages, and then put the report down, "It's been officially declared a homicide."

"I knew it," Georgina said.

"Yeah," he said, "me, too. I'm trying not to enjoy being right while there's a woman layin' in the funeral home who might have gotten to enjoy her retirement."

"I suppose," Georgina said, silent for a moment.

"So," he said, taking his glasses off. "I haven't gotten any sleep. I've been looking over a doctor's shoulder and typing all night. What have you been up to?" he asked, looking her in the eye.

Luckily, Georgina was a practiced liar, even matched against somebody like Detective Trigilio. She controlled all of her tells, and knew the easiest way to tell a lie was to tell it in the form of the truth, "You don't want to know," she said simply.

"Oh, I actually do," he said.

"Last night, while you were working hard, I went home, took a shower and slept beautifully until I felt like getting up. I had a hot breakfast, read through my newspapers, and then worked on my murder board for a while. I had to do some rearranging to make room for Ms. Larson."

"You've got a murder board in your apartment?" he said, admiringly.

"Yep, it's in my office. I should have showed it to you when you were there."

"And you already moved Ms. Larson's picture? Did you put her with the murder victims?"

"Yes, I did," she said.

"Smart," he said.

"Well, I don't put them there with Krazy Glue. I could have always moved it back if I was wrong."

"Yeah, well, you weren't wrong this time," he said.

"Any sign of Jerry Stone yet?" she asked.

"Nope, and they're not answering their cell phones, or checking in at the business. They left that assistant manager a message that they'd be back in a few days. He says that's not unusual. But I think it fucking is. His dear friend and tenant gets croaked a few feet above his head, and he's gone," Trigilio said.

"But I've put out some feelers. I don't have enough to start looking seriously, and get other people involved, but I can stir the water a little bit."

"Can I get a copy of that report?" she asked.

"What for? I just told you what was in it," he said, gruffly.

"Why don't you get some sleep?" Georgina said. "Don't give me a problem. You know I'm going to need it."

"I just don't feel like running a fucking copy machine right now," he said.

She grabbed the file out of his hand. "Well why don't you stand there, looking like I'm your secretary, while I photocopy it for you?" she said.

"Oh," he said, smiling, "if you put it that way."

Georgina happily made a photocopy of the 15-page report. Detective Trigilio charged her 10 cents a page, and told her he would throw in the manila folder for free.

She shook his hand and took the file. She was anxious to get back to her apartment and start watching Ingrid Musgrave's old movies and porn, but she didn't want to appear anxious. This was supposedly where the crux of the investigation was happening, and she didn't want to seem in a rush to leave. "So," she said, "will you call me when you get the toxicology? Maybe you can even fax it to me?"

"Maybe," Trigilio said, "if I've got time." He took the box of krullers back to his desk, and waved the back of his hand at Georgina as his way of saying goodbye.

On the way back into the city, Georgina called Daniel Levine and asked to have Little Johnny's address with Betsy checked out, including Betsy herself. She thought she might stop by herself if her busy viewing didn't pan out.

If it Could Happen to Her

Chapter Twelve

"So," Georgina thought to herself, sitting cross-legged on the plush Berber carpeting of her bedroom floor, painstakingly sorting through shopping bags filled with DVDs and video cassettes, putting DVDs in one pile, and video cassettes in another, all stacked straight and tall, in alphabetical order and by genre as she talked to herself, "Jerry Stone has left town rather abruptly, it seems to me, and he and his wife aren't answering their cell phones. May be innocent, may be not. And Little Johnny Stone lies in New York Downtown Hospital where I put him. Unless we can track down Jerry Stone, I would say we probably know who took care of the robbery and murder of our poor Ingrid, Bart and Ms. Larson. The question is why? Simple robbery?" she asked herself, "could be. Bad luck for Lloyd's, and good luck for the kids. And, in that case, why am I about to spend the next several hours watching videos I don't want to see?"

She continued to sort through the collection of material she had taken from Ms. Musgrave's house. With more than 100 DVDs, and 30 videocassettes, she knew she was going to be viewing for quite awhile, on the off chance one of these recordings wasn't what it was packaged to be. Given the editing software Georgina found on the laptop computer, she knew it would have been easy for Ingrid to have copied a recording from her security system, and then edited it and placed it onto a DVD, printing a copy of a movie's logo onto it, and placing it into the appropriate movie box. "After all," Georgina thought, "that's what I'd do. The best place to hide a letter is in a letter holder. Someone once said that – who was it? Poe?" she tried to remember.

She heard a knock at the door, which she knew to be Armeda. "Just leave it outside the door, please," Georgina yelled.

"I don't know what you're doing in there, and I don't want to know," Armeda yelled back.

"You're darn right you don't," Georgina said to herself. When she had arrived home, she had asked Armeda go into the kitchen while she moved the bags into her bedroom. Armeda had been told to do such things before, and wasn't surprised, but rolled her eyes to convey her general disappointment. Georgina didn't want Armeda to be party to a crime, so she wanted her to have absolute deniability. "I'm committing a leetle beet of a crime, here, Armeda," Georgina said quietly to herself as she finished sorting the recordings. Then she went to her bedroom door and peeked out. Armeda was not there, but she had left a tray with a huge bowl of freshly-popped popcorn, and a six-pack of Heineken beer.

"Yummy," Georgina said, as she put the popcorn in front of the television, and put the bottles of Heineken into her bathroom refrigerator. Georgina pulled a Vicodin out of her drawer, thought about it, and put it back, instead pouring a Heineken into one of the Baccarat glasses kept in her bathroom. Her arm was throbbing, but manageable. It's not like she had never mixed painkillers with alcohol before, but if she was going to stay awake during the mind-numbing ordeal ahead of her, she couldn't risk it. As it was, she was probably going to have to switch to Diet Pepsi halfway through, just to stay awake.

She prepared a little nest in her king size bed, pulling the down comforter down to the end and folding it perfectly into thirds. Then she changed into a pair of soft cotton pajama bottoms and a white tank top. She propped the pillows behind her head, placed the Heineken on a coaster on her bedside table, placed the bowl of popcorn next to her, and hit "Play" on the first DVD. She had decided to go through the mainstream DVDs and videocassettes she had found on the right-hand side of Ingrid's cabinet first. She could roll through them fairly quickly at 8X speed, and would be able to tell easily if there was something she should pause to look at. Before she put the first into her DVD player, she had looked it over, and to all appearances it was a legitimate copy of "Amadeus."

Georgina put it in and started by fast-forwarding through all of the previews, fast-forwarded through the movie itself, and checked out all of the bonus features as well. There was nothing unusual on it. Then she picked up "Apocalypse Now," and did the same thing, pausing on some of her favorite scenes, and munching on popcorn.

She slowly worked her way through the stack of movies, sometimes watching when she knew there was a particularly interesting part. "I don't rent enough movies," she said to herself. Three hours had gone by, and she had gotten as far as "Reversal of Fortune." She watched far more of this than she should have, because it was such a damn great movie, and because her parents had socialized with Sunny Von Bulow, back when she was Sunny von Auersperg. She took a small break to stretch and to walk to the kitchen. Armeda walked in from the back of the apartment, where she had a small sitting room and her bedroom. "Are you done being a criminal? Are you ready to eat something decent?"

If it Could Happen to Her

"No and no," Georgina said, pulling open a drawer to the left of the refrigerator. She looked at Armeda out of the corner of her eye, took a menu, picked up the phone and ordered Lobster Ravioli and Calamari to be delivered from Bonifacio's as Armeda leaned against the counter with her arms crossed.

"Don't worry," she said as she hung up the phone, "I promise not to enjoy it as much as your food." She looked over at the grumpy Armeda, "Oh, for goodness' sake," she said, pulling open the refrigerator and taking out two 24 oz. bottles of Diet Pepsi, "take off your uniform and relax for the rest of the night. I won't be needing you."

"You'll be needing me to open the door and receive that garbage you just ordered," she barked back.

"Oh, yes," Georgina said, smiling, "after that." She placed a big kiss on Armeda's cheek, which the woman immediately wiped off, trying to hide her smile.

"And Jack is going to be stopping by to pick up... something," Georgina said, marching out of the kitchen. "Just send him back to my room, and have him rap on the door." Jack was Georgina's most favored tech genius. He took care of all of her equipment, and she wanted to give him Ingrid's laptop to look over tonight, to see if there was anything on it Georgina was looking for, that she couldn't find herself.

This time, Georgina curled up in the huge white chenille armchair and ottoman which sat next to her bed, with a cream cashmere Hermès blanket thrown over her knees. It was time for some caffeine to wake her up and brush away the Heineken cobwebs.

She finished going through the mainstream DVDs that had been on the right side of Ingrid's cabinet, and about 10 of the videotapes which were theatrical movies. She had saved the 10 or so videotapes that contained home movies, and went through them now, more slowly, watching parts of Ingrid and Geoffrey, Sr.'s ancient wedding video at actual speed, amazed people could look so hopeful, and end up screwing things up so badly. She watched as Geoffrey, Jr., and then Luanne, were baptized, then as they graduated from preschool, and saw the typical reduction in air time for the kids who came later. She saw family parties and barbecues, and, in the early years, they were absolutely charming. It was obviously before they had serious money, and Geoffrey was actually around, tossing the kids into the pool. Then, by the time Magrit came around, there was hardly anything. "That's sad," Georgina said. "You really blew it, guys."

If it Could Happen to Her

She got up once to meet Jack at the door of her bedroom with Ingrid's laptop. She explained in detail what she was looking for, and where she herself had already looked. He could find things that had been ostensibly deleted from the hard drive, and might be useful to her. He said he'd start working on it right away, and, based on the sweat on his upper lip caused by being so close to her in her bedroom, she suspected he wouldn't sleep until he had it done. She smiled as she shut her door behind him. "I love the geeks, and the geeks love me," she said to herself.

A few minutes later, as she was getting ready to view the materials from the left hand side of the cabinet, her food came. Armeda rapped on her door, and left the bag outside it. Georgina carefully prepared a carpet picnic, and popped in the first porno. She could barely contain her laughter, as she watched people committing sexually depraved acts in 8X speed. "So much for Viagra," she said. "Nobody wants to be called 'speedy' in a porno," she said. Those didn't take very long to go through, the DVDs and the videotapes. She paused every now and again, to make sure there wasn't anyone familiar in any of them, but there wasn't, and she looked closely at each and every actor. Even with big fake boobs and blond wigs, or toupees and furry mustaches, she knew she had never seen any of them before. She was finished with the pornos before she finished her meal.

She put in "Reversal of Fortune" again, in order to watch it all the way through, while she gave up, finished her meal and two more Heinekens, leaning against the tufted damask silk bench at the foot of her bed. "Fuck," she said to herself. She had been so convinced she was right. Was it possible it had already been removed? Or was she simply wrong? She would hate that. It was a pretty good guess, though. She wondered if it would be good enough for a bluff. "Hmm..." she thought about that as she watched the movie.

Georgina curled up and fell asleep as soon as the movie was over. She woke in the morning, a bit earlier than usual, and was already thinking. She peeked from under her sleeping mask to glance at the clock and saw it was only 6:30 a.m. She tried to roll over and go back to sleep, knowing Daniel Levine didn't get into his office until 8:00 at the earliest, and she really needed to talk to him – and Armeda wouldn't bring a breakfast tray until 8:00. She thought of perhaps calling Daniel at home, because she did have his home phone number – little did he know – but she didn't want to get that personal with him – she already suspected he had a crush, and she didn't want to encourage it.

If it Could Happen to Her

She rolled out of bed and had a lovely stretch, and a leisurely Pilates workout in her gym. She had some fattening pasta calories to burn off, but she still wanted one of Armeda's omelets for breakfast. She picked up the papers and read through them at the kitchen counter. She tried to make very little noise, because she knew at the slightest whisper, Armeda would be out here cooking, and she didn't want her to have to get up yet. She didn't even dare open the fridge.

About a half hour later, as Georgina was finishing up with the New York Times, Armeda came out and looked surprised. "You're up early," she said, pulling on her apron.

"Yes," Georgina said, "I'm as surprised as you are."

"What's in your omelet today, my dear?" Armeda asked.

"Let's have some mozzarella and bacon for naughty Georgina, and some tomatoes and mushrooms for good Georgina," she said, turning a page in the Times.

Once she'd eaten her full, Georgina went into her office and called Daniel. "Is anything interesting happening over at Betsy's house? Any visitors?" she asked. She put her pedicured feet up on the desk and used an enamel Chinese chopstick to reach an itch inside her cast. She had designated it specifically for that task, and planned on disposing of it once the cast was finally removed.

"No, but the Cambridge Police are clearly onto that idea, too, because their stakeout guys nodded to our stakeout guys every time there was a change in shift."

"Is it too obvious? It's a longshot," Georgina said.

"No, it's worth it, and we can afford it for the moment," he said. "Have you got anything else?" he asked.

"I think I do," she said, pausing.

He waited patiently for her to elaborate. "It's also a longshot – a bluff, really. I don't know." She brushed it out of her head for the moment. "Anyway – what I really can't ask you to do is have some of your more talented employees take a look around the apartment one of these days when Betsy goes to the hospital to visit Little Johnny."

"No, of course not," Daniel said. "That would be illegal. Besides, if we did have somebody go in and have a look around while she was at the hospital, all they'd find is a skuzzy apartment with stained shag carpeting, two bedrooms, one filled half-full with cardboard boxes stuffed with old clothes and junk, and nothing of use to us. They'd find another bedroom with a mattress on a simple metal bed frame, with dirty clothes, mostly hers, lying all over. They'd find that few of the things in the apartment actually belong to Little Johnny, aside from some XXL logo t-shirts, sweatshirts and jeans, and some longneck bottles of Budweiser in the refrigerator."

"So, he probably really lived somewhere else, even though Betsy was under the impression he lived with her."

"He either lived in another place, or kept his stuff in a car, van or storage unit somewhere. There's a 1999 blue Toyota Corolla registered in his name..."

"That guy fit his fat ass into a Corolla?" Georgina asked, amazed.

"It couldn't have been comfortable, but that's all we've got." He waited for a moment, "but I think you were going to say something else."

"Hmm," she said, "well, I have to tell you, I've been thinking about playing a little game, just to see if I can blow some dust off the shelves. But, can I ask you, what exactly does Lloyd's need? A conviction? Or would they be happy with an explanation, and a settlement for a reduced amount?" She bit her lip as she asked this question, hating the moral implications.

"I think they might be willing to settle," Daniel said. He paused for a moment. "I really hate to see rich people getting away with this kind of shit, but it wouldn't be the first time."

"Well, I'm not saying that, exactly," she said. "There are different kinds of punishment." She paused for a moment. "I just don't know if the courts are where this needs to go."

"We don't have any control over what the Cambridge Police Department does," he said. "They've got a lot of resources, a lot of time on their hands, and they've got two murders the folks around there are going to want their own explanation for. And they're *definitely* going to want it resolved in court."

"I know," Georgina said. "And the detective on it is good. He's smart, and he's been around for awhile."

"Trigilio," Daniel said. "He had a very, *very* good clearance rate when he was working out of New York City. There's no way he'd put it down."

"No," she said, biting her lip. "And I'm not saying I'd want him to, it's just..." she turned it over in her head in silence.

"What are you thinking, really?" Daniel asked.

"I don't know," she said. "I'm probably getting a little too clever for my own good. Let me give this some thought, and I'll be in touch," she said, putting down the receiver.

Georgina pulled her tote bag over to the desk, and pulled out the manila folder which held her theory. She read it through again, and then tossed it into the garbage. "It's pure bullshit conjecture," she told herself. "It's nothing like proof. And even if it's true, it only takes care of one side of it. We've got somebody, a group of somebody's, who did it. And we've got somebody who hired them to do it, maybe." She ran her fingers through her hair and looked at the folder in the garbage.

She picked up the telephone and called Jack. She leaned back in her leather chair and ran her fingers through her hair, gently rubbing her scalp as she did so. "Did you find anything I can use?" Georgina asked.

"I did," he said, his voice gravelly, and then yawned loudly. "There wasn't much on that computer, and I don't know who set it up for her. Whoever they were, they were simplistic – real straight-out-of-the-box stuff, for something that really should have been custom-designed. She might have even loaded it herself, if she had any kind of skill. She had some cool stuff. The editing software was *really* cool. I didn't even have that. But it was made so anybody who can handle e-mail can operate it. User-friendly."

"It basically takes a digital recording," Georgina said, "and lets you copy it onto another DVD, make a personal cover for it, and a logo for the DVD itself, right?"

"Well, that's a small part of it, but, yeah, and it's easy," Jack said. "And it should save a copy of whatever she worked on. But it's not out there, I mean, it's not among the hidden files, either. I didn't find anything. It looks like she never even used it. It's not 100%, I mean, you could definitely go in there into the hidden files, and, if you knew where to look, you could delete it, and then delete and re-load the software. That's about the only way I could think of. Was the owner that smart?" he asked.

"I really wouldn't think so," Georgina said, "but I've been surprised before. So, you're sure there's nothing left, no automatic backup, or anything?"

"No," he said, "that's what made it easy, and frustrating, at the same time. It's like the computer had never been used. It had all this cool stuff, but it was, like, clean, brand-new. I could do that to a laptop in a couple of hours, if I had all of the software in a box somewhere. I could reformat the hard drive, and just load everything again, and it's a brand new day. Poof."

"Yeah," Georgina said, "but I didn't find any of the software at her house. Damn it." She thought to herself that if Ingrid were going to hide the

If it Could Happen to Her

software, she would have hid it in the same place as the computer, especially if she planned to re-load at some point. Was Ingrid smarter than Georgina gave her credit for? She had seemed to just enjoy going to lunch, shopping, decorating and having Bart take care of her personal needs, but perhaps Georgina was underestimating her. She did, after all, help Geoffrey, Sr. to begin his little empire. It grew from a series of small town newspapers – where she used to help write the articles, run the printers and do the books – into the conglomerate it was today. It wouldn't have been completely out of line for her to have kept up with current technology, and know how to work a computer with the best of them. "Hmm," she said. "Well, listen, thanks Jack." She paused. "Do me a favor, though, do it all again, make sure you're 100% sure, and then bring it back to me."

"I'm already 100% sure," he said, sounding insulted, "but I'll do it all over again just to be 120% sure."

"Thanks, Jack," Georgina said, and hung up.

She sat back in her chair and thought, "How smart were you, Ingrid? And what did you do with the hard copy of that software?"

If it Could Happen to Her

Chapter Thirteen

Georgina telephoned Geoffrey Musgrave for his permission to search Ingrid's other two homes – the apartment around the corner from Georgina's, and the house in Hobe Sound. Discouraged by her questionable success at the murder scene in Connecticut, she wasn't looking forward to it. "Geoffrey, what do I need to do to get into the apartment?" she asked.

"Not much," he said. "Just tell the doorman who you are, and show him your driver's license. He'll let you in. I'll call him. What are you looking for?"

She knew exactly what she was looking for, but said, "Gosh, you know, I really won't know until I find it. Anything that helps me know more about Ingrid will help me know what happened. And I'm a pretty good searcher. The police didn't find those love letters of yours, did they?"

"No, they didn't," he said, gruffly. "Thank God for that." He paused. "I appreciate you giving those back, by the way. Who knows how much money they might have been worth to a crooked cop? I know how much I'd be willing to pay to get them back."

"Don't give it another thought," she said. "They belong with you. And what about the place in Hobe Sound? Is it closed up?"

"No, actually, it's not," he said. "Grace Heinman is staying down there. Has been for about seven months. At some point I'm going to have to ask her to get the hell out, but I'm not in a hurry."

"Why is she down there?" Georgina asked.

"She had all of her money with Harvey Mann," he said.

Georgina inhaled. "No," she said. "Not all of it."

"Every cent. The woman always was an idiot. Now she's a penniless idiot. She's sitting down in Ingrid's house, off-season, drinking all day long and gaining about five pounds a week."

"Wow. Talk about not putting all of your eggs in one basket," Georgina said quietly. They each had many friends who had found themselves in a similar situation when the "Miracle Mann," Harvey Mann, who had produced standard 12% returns for his clients for years had gone belly up in a huge Ponzi scheme. Most of Georgina's friends lost some money. But some poor fools – apparently Grace Heinman was one of them – lost everything. The scandal had produced an entire new social class of the formerly extremely wealthy, whose new status was tenuous and unsure among their old friends. Clearly Ingrid had

If it Could Happen to Her

taken Grace under her wing. "You weren't all bad, Ingrid," Georgina thought to herself.

But knowing that there had been a permanent houseguest for the past seven months made Georgina think twice about bothering to fly all the way down to Florida for a search. "Well, maybe I'll put that off, then," she said, going over the odds in her head.

"It's up to you," Geoffrey said. "Grace can let you in, if she's conscious. Ingrid's been paying for her housekeeper and groceries, so there'll be somebody there to help you."

"I think I'm going to put that on the back burner for now," she said. "When can I get into the apartment?"

"I'll call them right now," he said. "You can go over whenever you want. You know," he said, "seriously... thanks again for the letters, Adams. I won't forget it."

"No, problem," she said, smiling. She had photocopied them before she gave them to him anyway.

Jason drove her the three blocks it took to get to Ingrid's place. The doorman asked no questions, but had her upstairs in Ingrid's private elevator, and inside her apartment, in minutes. It was a duplex. Ingrid had purchased the apartment above hers when it had become available, and had doubled her square footage to slightly over 9,000, transforming a merely amazing home into something truly extraordinary. Georgina looked around admiringly at the high ceilings and elaborate crown molding, the lovingly-restored remains of the Rosario Candela original craftsmanship. She knew the architect who had undertaken the complicated remodel, and the designer Mark Hampton who had completed decorating it for her shortly before his death. It was an amazing job. She drifted from room to room, taking in the lush fabrics, ornate details, and, of course, Ingrid's amazing artwork. "It would have been more difficult to steal this art," Georgina thought out loud, standing in front of a magnificent but little-known Picasso which was soon to hang in the Metropolitan, "in a doorman building, with a private elevator. But why didn't they steal the art in Connecticut while you were here in New York? They wouldn't have had to kill you, then." Georgina had already come to the inevitable conclusion that that was the point.

After wandering through the sixteen rooms of the two-story apartment, Georgina was secure in the knowledge that her apartment was better, and that this home wasn't as lived-in as Ingrid's place in Connecticut. Georgina's interest had been piqued in the study, which, unlike its counterpart in the country, looked used and functional. Situated through double doors off the expansive living room, she went back down to it and examined things more carefully. She sat in Ingrid's chair and put her sore leg up on the desk. She sat there for a moment and examined the room from that perspective, looking about the room at the dark paneling, magnificent art and comfortable furniture, allowing her gaze to shift down to the drawers to her left. She opened the topmost drawer, and found the city version of Ingrid's appointment diary, with accepted invitations neatly tucked into their corresponding day. She also found the same blue monogrammed Smythson stationery that she had found in the country. In the second drawer from the top, she found a two-inch thick document bound in a firm black report cover, which at first glance appeared to be a legal brief of some sort. Intrigued, Georgina pulled it out, and flipped it open.

It turned out to be a draft of Ingrid's memoir. Georgina laughed out loud. "Good Lord, Ingrid... who would pay a dime for the story of your life?" The cover page gave her the ghost writer's name, and, as she flipped through, she saw Ingrid's meticulous notes on nearly every page, in small, tight, fine red print, making changes and revisions, and using some less-than-diplomatic language to do so. "Well, I've definitely got to talk to this guy," Georgina thought, as she tossed the manuscript over toward her totebag, where it landed on the floor with a smack. She examined the other papers in the desk, and found them fairly unremarkable, before turning around to look at the books behind her.

Some of the books were for show – erudite and thoughtful literary material that Georgina was sure Ingrid had never looked at, but there were some other books lining the lower shelves, behind the desk, that Georgina thought were more Ingrid's taste – crime novels, Jackie Collins steamy stories, celebrity biographies... and some photo albums.

"Hmm..." Georgina pulled out the first in a series of twelve identical navy leather-bound volumes. She flipped to the first page, and found photographs of Ingrid's childhood, Ingrid's parents in Stockholm, black-and-while shots of Ingrid as a child on Long Island. She looked through it, taking in the seemingly pleasant middle-class sort of upbringing, with Mom in an A-line dress and precisely lacquered hair, with Ingrid the child dressed and coiffed as a mini-version of her mother. Georgina put that one on the floor and picked up the second, which was Ingrid's school years, boarding school at

Dana Hall and college at Wellesley. The third and fourth held wedding photographs – charming photos of a young and hopeful couple, just starting out. The next two or three held photos of the children, with baptisms, birthdays, and finally graduations. Geoffrey Sr. was in them at the beginning, but gradually he disappeared. These homey photos gave way to a chronicle of Ingrid's social life, once she and Geoffrey were separated. Georgina flipped through those quickly, and with slight interest. She knew all of the players in this section of the social world, and they were all well-represented, from the has-beens who appeared in some of the earlier albums, to the nouveau riche who Ingrid clearly tolerated in the more recent volumes.

Georgina went back to the earlier albums of the children. Up to a point, she saw that they all seemed happy. Tall, lean, tanned and healthy, smiling and mugging for the camera. A happy family. Then, she noticed a change. Fewer smiles – the children got chubbier and more pale – and then Georgina realized that Geoffrey Jr. was gone. She flipped back to the last photos of him. He appeared in summer photos, tall, strong and full of promise, confidently smiling at the camera. It looked liked the family was at some kind of a campground in the woods, with tall trees. It seemed as though a season or two went missing, and then the photos resumed, with the children who remained changed and somber, and the photos far less frequent.

"That sucks," she said, taking a deep breath. She stacked all of the albums, and placed them by her tote bag, next to the manuscript of Ingrid's memoir. She did a cursory examination of the same typical hiding places where she had previously found Ingrid's things, but didn't find what she was looking for, and nothing remotely interesting, except – taped behind a drawer in her desk – a packet of photos of Bartolomeo in a Speedo bathing suit, posing for Ingrid on a sandy white beach, showing off the considerable attributes which had appealed to the newly single Ingrid. "Eeww," Georgina said, wrinkling her nose, "men should not wear Speedos."

Georgina called Jason downstairs, and had him come up. He carried the photo albums and manuscript down to the car. On the way to her own apartment, she flipped through the first few pages of the manuscript Trite and totally ass-kissing, it still wasn't flattering enough for Ingrid, who had written all over it, demanding changes. Georgina put it down beside her, knowing that the remainder of her day would entail reading the damn thing.

Several hours later, Georgina finally put the manuscript aside. She removed the reading glasses from her nose, and rubbed the bridge of it, where they had left a slight indentation. "That sucked," she said to herself, as she reached for the Heineken beer on her night table. She tilted her head back, downing the remainder of the bottle. She snuggled herself down further into her fluffy bed, and thought about what she had read. It was a clearly self-serving and self-congratulatory story that made Ingrid the heroine in the movie of her life, with all of the people around her as mere extras at best, and props at worst. Her children were props. She wrote with feeling about her early days, and chronicled her journey from the lower middle class community on Long Island, a scholarship to a good school, to her marriage, and partnership, with Geoffrey Musgrave, and how together they had collaborated in an attempt to conquer the world. At least the media world. She mentioned her children in passing, as she described the early years of her marriage, and only to the extent that her care of them held her back from participating in the business as much as she would have liked to. She mentioned Geoffrey Jr.'s death briefly, and seldom mentioned the children at all after that.

Far more interesting to Ingrid, and, she felt, to her readers, was her expedition from the mediocrity she was born into, to the upper strata of society and wealth that she felt was her due. "I liked you a lot better before I read that," Georgina said, opening her laptop computer, and tracking down the ghostwriter, Todd Casperson, who had written the marginally compelling draft before Ingrid got her hands on it. It turned out that he was a regular on the Town & Country magazine staff, who had done a story about the East Side apartment, and Ingrid, after the renovation.

Georgina found a photo online, and had Jason drive over to the magazine's offices. She sat outside and waited until ten minutes after 5:00, when she saw him stroll out – a tall young man, a little too tall for his weight, with large hands and feet, short brown hair, black-rimmed glasses and a grey turtleneck aiming for intellectual chic.

Georgina got out of the car, and with some discomfort, caught up with him mid-stride. Like most New Yorkers, he walked far too fast, and her leg was killing her. The painkiller she had taken before she left the apartment hadn't quite kicked in yet. "Excuse me, Mr. Casperson," she said, placing her hand lightly on his upper arm.

His eyes drew together in annoyance at first, and then he nearly stumbled as he got a closer look at her. "Yes," he said, regaining his balance, "how can I help you?"

"I'm Georgina Adams," she said simply, "and I was hoping to talk to you for a few moments. Are you in a hurry to get anywhere?"

"Well, I – yes, sort of," he said, running his fingers through the front of his hair. "I have some work to do, but I guess it can wait. I don't think we know each other."

She put her hand out and shook his. "We do now," she said.

They settled onto a couple of stools at a trendy bar a few doors down. He had noticed her limp and cast, and had, in a very gentlemanly way, taken her bag, held doors for her, and helped her to get comfortable in her seat. "Are you alright?" he finally asked.

"Yes, I'm fine," she said. "I was in a little bit of an accident, but I'm coming right along. It will be a while before I'm back in the gym."

"I know how that can be," he said, but Georgina doubted it. There was not much muscle mass beneath his clothing, and Georgina didn't think he had ever seen the inside of a gym. She told him that she was investigating Ingrid's murder for Konig, and that she had come across his manuscript. He immediately became cagey, while Georgina became intrigued.

"Yes, I was very sorry to hear about that," he said, taking a sip from his drink and pausing, "it seems to mean I won't be getting paid for the manuscript. But that's alright. What's that compared to the fact that she's dead, after all?" He made an attempt at a sympathetic expression.

Georgina pulled the manuscript out of her bag, and slapped it onto the bar. "You might not have been getting paid anyway," she said. "She wasn't completely happy with your first draft."

Todd flipped through the first few pages, and noted all of the red print. His eyebrows drew together in annoyance, and he picked up the whole manuscript and propped it in his lap, slowly turning pages as he breathed heavily. Finally, as he neared the end, his expression had eased from tension to something resembling amusement. "Well, I guess you're right," he said. "It doesn't make it any easier that she's gone, and so violently, but apparently this was going to take a lot more work."

"Well, you'll have more time to work on the book you're writing about the murder," Georgina said.

He looked at her with an open mouth, which slowly turned into a grin. "You got me," he said.

"Don't want to spend the rest of your career at Town & Country?" Georgina asked.

"Not really," he said. He took another, longer pull on his drink, and then turned to her. "Okay. It looks like you could use some information from me, or otherwise you wouldn't have approached me. Obviously, I could use some information from you." He turned his shoulders a little more squarely towards her in something he must have thought was a sexy move, and said, "I think we could help each other."

Georgina stifled a laugh by taking a sip of her own drink. She put her poker face back on, and said, "I think that's distinctly possible. Although I've already read everything you've got in that manuscript. What else could there be?"

Now he smiled for real. "What else could there be? How about everything that Ingrid *didn't* want in her book?"

"Oh, now that makes sense," she said. "I'm sure she wanted something that was a tribute to her life, but she wanted to edit out the things that didn't fit in."

"Well," he said, "the book was supposed to serve two purposes. It was supposed to be a 'tribute to her life' as you said, but it was also supposed to chronicle her art collecting. She'd already been given permission to sell it in the gift shop of the Metropolitan Museum."

"Was that the only publishing deal she had?" Georgina asked, laughing.

"Basically," he said. "It was a vanity publication. She was having it printed herself, and some guy from Sotheby's was doing the photography of her collection, and writing the portion on the acquisition of the collection."

"But you were writing the portion about her life," Georgina said. "That was by far the most interesting. The rest is just an academic exercise."

"Yes," he said. "That was absolutely true. And I did some good research. It wasn't easy. Her parents weren't born here." He motioned for the bartender to bring him another bourbon. "Can I get you a refresher?"

Georgina said, "Yes, please," but caught the bartender's eye when Todd wasn't looking and mouthed, "no alcohol," and pointed to herself. The bartender smiled, and served Todd his bourbon, and Georgina another gin and tonic, minus the gin. She said, "It must have been really difficult to track them down, then."

"It was damned difficult," Todd said, "I tracked them down, then found where they lived on Long Island, scared up the papers... found out that Ingrid's father was fucking around with his secretary, and she killed him. Believe me, *that* didn't make it into the first draft."

"Ingrid killed him?" Georgina asked, surprised.

"Nope, sorry," he said. "I have to be a little more careful with the order of my pronouns. The secretary killed him. Horrible story. He got her pregnant, and then was going to leave her. She stabbed him to death in the apartment he kept her in, and then lost the baby when she was in prison. Terrible story."

"Oh, Ingrid," Georgina thought, "that's tough to put behind you. I think I understand you a little bit better."

"But I'm doing all of the giving," Todd said, giving her a leer. "What do you have in return?"

"Well, I've got some practically nude photographs of Ingrid's Argentinian lover. He was killed with her," Georgina said. "They might be nice for the section of black-and-white pics in the middle of the book. Do you want them?"

"Damn right I do," he said. "Plus, she had some photo albums," he was thinking shrewdly now, "she had promised me that I could choose some of those photos for the book."

"I've got those now," Georgina said.

He looked at her squarely, not knowing how to proceed.

"What else do you have?" Georgina asked.

"Well," he admitted, "the murder was the best of it. I found a shitload of material on her husband's affairs before they got divorced, and after. I'm not sure that helps you." He was thinking.

"It will be nice for your book, though," she said. "Family life is always interesting, especially when there's a little twist. They had a bunch of great kids, though," she said. "That's wholesome."

"Ha, ha," he laughed loud enough for a couple of other bar patrons to look over, "Wholesome? That's not exactly true. She hated her kids. They were all losers. Not like jail time, or check fraud losers, but they were practically paralyzed. They couldn't do anything without her money. And one of them got killed when they were young. It was a weird story – hushed up. A drowning. I'm looking into that, too. These people are way too apt to die before their time to just be unlucky."

"Oh!" Georgina managed to look surprised.

"Oh, yeah," he said. "In fact, I'm looking at the kids as possible suspects in Ingrid's murder." He looked very pleased with himself. He looked back at her for affirmation.

If it Could Happen to Her

"Well," she smiled, "that's an interesting theory. What's the motive?"

"Money," he said, "what else?" gesturing with his drink, a little bit of which slopped over the side onto the bar. The bartender came over and wiped it up, with a wary look at Todd.

"Well, I'll give you a little hint," she said, then stopped, as though she were second-guessing herself, "well, you've been good to me. I'll tell you something you didn't hear from me. The kids weren't going to get anything from the will. And they knew it."

His face fell. "Shit," he said. "Well, it still makes for a good story."

"True," she said, finishing her drink. "Todd, do you have your notes anywhere around here handy?"

"They're at my apartment," he said, smiling into his drink, clearly thinking he was about to get lucky.

Georgina had Jason drive them to Todd's shitty fourth-floor walkup apartment. Her leg was screaming by the time she reached the top, and she wanted nothing more than to smash a vase over Todd's foolish head and take off with his files.

He poured her a glass of wine, which she left untouched next to his laptop computer, as he showed her his intricately-organized files. "It's great," he said, clearly a bit of a tech geek like herself. "I've scanned a lot of this stuff, and I was able to get the microfiches of the old newspaper files downloaded, too. All of this new technology stuff is making my job a heck of a lot easier."

"It's fascinating," Georgina said, looking on with apparent marvel as he moved among his files.

"I can show you some of this stuff," he said, "but a lot of it is confidential." He shifted back and forth on his computer stool.

"Oh, I understand," she said. "In fact, I'm not sure I'd be able to make heads or tails of it."

"It's not that tough. I could teach you." He smiled indulgently, and then said, "If you'll excuse me for a minute, I have to go visit the little boy's room."

"Oh, that's fine," Georgina said, smiling.

As soon as he stepped out of the room and she heard his footfalls on the hardwood hallway flooring, she whipped out several memory cards from her purse. One after the other, she dragged copies of Todd's files onto the cards. Her heart beat faster as she worked – his computer was fast, and the downloading was working quickly, but it only took so long to go to the bathroom. As she finished downloading the last of his files, she realized that he was probably brushing his teeth, too. She smiled, and put the last memory card into her purse.

When he came out, she was putting her coat on. His face fell. "I'm sorry," she said. "I'd really like to stay, but my leg is killing me, and I think I've had a little more to drink than I should have." She reached over and scrawled her throw-away phone number onto a notepad next to the computer. "Why don't you give me a call sometime in the next couple of days, and we can plan a nice dinner, maybe at my place?" She smiled over at him. "I'd like to pick your brain a little more."

He managed to regain some of his swagger as he accepted the telephone number. "I'll give you a ring, then," he said

Once Georgina had perused the material Todd had on his computer, which was fairly run-of-the-mill, but there were a few things she hadn't known before, she started wondering if Ingrid had office space, or storage space somewhere. Maybe she even had a techie like Jack of her own, to take care of her computer files, or other technological aspects of her recording system that she hadn't entrusted to her security company. She called Daniel Levine again. "Daniel," she said, "if Ingrid were going to have a storage facility, or even a little office for herself somewhere, do you think we could find it?"

"Phww," he exhaled. "That might be tough. She had an unbelievable amount of real estate, and it was owned through various corporations… it would be really difficult to know. You're not thinking bank safe deposit boxes or anything like that?"

"Not really. I'm thinking about something private. And if she wanted a little bit of secrecy, she wouldn't have her name all over it. But, she'd want to be able to get to it herself, so she probably opened it and loaded it herself."

"Hmm," he said, "We can do a fairly simple run through the credit cards, and see if she was paying for storage. If she was paying in cash, we wouldn't get anything," he said.

"Yeah, but most of those places make you present an ID, and a credit card, even if you pay in cash, right? In case you stop paying? So they can make their money until they pull your stuff out and auction it off? Since she's dead, there's got to be a bill coming due or slightly overdue," she asked.

"I think you're right about that," he said. "Let me have one of our guys look around in the financials, and see if he can find anything like that. What are you looking for?" he asked.

"I'm still not positive," she said, pulling her folder out of the garbage, looking at it again, stuffing it into her right-hand drawer, and slamming it shut.

"Okay," he said. "Well, I'll let you know. They're reading the will today. Did you know that?" he asked.

"Yes, I did," she said. "But I think the kids knew not to expect anything. At least, I think so. They're counting pretty hard on that $20 million, so I think the reading will just be a formality they have to sit through."

"Right. I don't imagine it will be a very festive atmosphere," he said. "How's the arm, by the way?"

"It's still attached, but it hurts like hell, and itches even worse," she said. "I can't wait to get this cast off."

"Well, I'll make sure Lloyd's throws in a little extra onto your fee for blood loss and bone breakage," he said.

"Oh, thanks," she said, hanging up.

She opened up her drawer, and looked at her folder again. "I'm taking a really big chance," she said out loud to herself. "If I'm wrong, this could go very badly." She chewed on her lower lip and twirled a piece of her hair around her working index finger, then rubbed her cast. She was getting ready to set a trap, but she still didn't have the bait she needed. However there might not be a better time to approach all of the children as a group. They'll be in a certain mood after the reading of the will, and it won't be a good mood.

"Well, I'm going to try it," she said, and picked up the telephone.

If it Could Happen to Her

Chapter Fourteen

Georgina placed a call to Frederick at the penthouse. His voice was still gruff from sleep. "Frederick, I hope I didn't wake you," she said with concern.

"No, no," he said, "Not at all. We're stirring around here. Magrit's little guy is up around 6:30. I think it's partially because they're jet-lagged, but I also think little guys just always get up that early. What can I do for you?"

"Well, I understand you're going to be reading your mother's will today," Georgina said.

"Yes," he said, simply.

"If you don't mind my asking," she said, "where are you going to read it? I would like to sit down with all of you, including Ingrid and Matthew, after you're done."

She could tell it was on the tip of his tongue to ask her, "what about?" but he stopped himself, knowing it had to do with the insurance payout, and was turning it over in his head. "Oh, well, certainly," he finally said, almost cheerfully.

"I hope he doesn't think I'll choose that moment to hand it all over," she thought to herself.

"We'll be at the lawyer's office. It's Cranmore & Wilson, not too far away from here, I think," he said distractedly. She could hear the shuffling of papers in the background.

"Don't worry about the address," she said, "I know where they are. Umm…" she said, scratching her chin. "Why don't we meet when you're finished at, say, the Colony?"

"Oh," he said, "well, that's convenient, and I suppose it's appropriate," he said. "Would you like to get a table, or should I?"

"I'll get a room," she said. "What time are you going over to Cranmore?"

"It's scheduled for 1:00, and I don't think it should take very long. There's a video our mother wanted us to watch, so we'll be viewing that, too."

The hair stood up on the back of Georgina's neck. "Really?" she said.

"Yes, Wes Cranmore tells me it's just her reading the will herself. Apparently it's done quite frequently these days, to stop anyone from saying the testator wasn't competent."

"Oh, of course," Georgina said. Cranmore certainly hadn't supplied Konig with a copy of any video will, and Geoffrey Sr. hadn't thought to pass a copy along, either. "Could be nothing," she thought. "If she's just reading the will out loud, they might not have thought it was relevant." But she found herself wishing she could be there in that room while they watched the videotape of their mother disinheriting them. It will certainly sting more than just hearing it in the lawyer's bland monotone as he reads it.

"I'll have the room ready starting at 1:00," Georgina said, "and I'll have some heavy hors d'oeuvres, pastry, tea and coffee available." To herself, she added, "and some liquor, if anybody needs any, which I'll bet you will."

"Do you think you can wrangle everybody, Frederick, or should I call around and speak to everyone individually?"

"No, I can tell them at the meeting. They'll know what it's about, and they'll come. Do you want Dad, too?"

"Not really," Georgina said. "This doesn't have anything to do with him. If he insists, then, of course, let him join us, because there wouldn't be any harm in it, I suppose, but you can tell him I just wanted to talk to the children. He might not put up a fuss."

"It's a 50-50 bet, Georgina. I'm surprised more often than not with Dad, so I'll just plan for the worst, and hope for the best."

"Shouldn't we all?" Georgina joked.

She managed to get a small chuckle out of the sleepy Frederick. She put down the phone, before quickly picking it up again and dialing. "Daniel," she said after being put through, "why don't we have a copy of the video will?"

"The what?" he asked.

"Frederick Musgrave has just told me he's going to be watching his mother disinherit him *on camera*, instead of in print – at least that's what he's been told. What do we know from Cranmore?"

"I certainly didn't know that," Daniel said. "Let me find out." He hung up, and Georgina sat twiddling her thumbs while she waited for his return phone call. She didn't wait long. "They've got it. They're claiming it was a mistake that they supplied the executed copy of the paper will, but not the DVD containing the video will. They said that, since it has no legal significance, really, they didn't think it was important. I've informed Geoffrey Musgrave's office of the omission. He's sure to raise the roof, but they're claiming it's nothing. It's just Ingrid sitting there in the lawyer's offices, reading the will out loud."

"I want it!" she yelled, just about to bite her thumbnail, but thinking of her manicure and stopping herself. "How soon can I get it?"

"They're going to make a copy immediately, and they're going to messenger one over to me," he said.

"Have them messenger it over to me, too. I want to see it before I see those kids. I have an appointment with them sometime between 1:00 and 3:00, and I have to be there waiting at 1:00."

"It'll be tight," he said.

"Please, Daniel," Georgina pleaded, desperately wanting to know what those kids were going to see before they saw her.

"I'll try," he said. "That's all I can say."

She put down the phone. "Fuck!" she said.

"That's fine language," Armeda said, bringing in a silver tray with a teapot and cup. She poured Georgina a bracing, strong cup of English breakfast tea, and left the room. Georgina added milk and sugar, paced and drank her tea while she observed her board. She poured another cup and took it with her to the bathroom. All during her shower, she listened for the sound of the doorbell, without hearing it. "Anything come for me?" she asked Armeda. She was still wet, and wrapped in a Frette towel, after she had painstakingly showered without getting her cast wet.

"No," Armeda said, "but Joseph's here to do your hair."

"Well," she said, frowning at Joseph, who was seated on one of the bergeres in the front hall with his big beauty box, "thank God for that." She spun back around to her bedroom, and Joseph followed her.

Joseph blowdried her hair as she stewed and waited. When he left, she dressed in black to befit the scene ahead of her, with a polished Dior suit, and phoned Daniel Levine one more time before leaving for the Colony. "It's not here yet," she whined.

"I know," he said. "We don't have it either. I called over there just a half hour ago, and they said it was 'in process.' What's so important about it, anyway?" he asked.

"I don't know," she said. "I just want my head to be in the same place their heads are when I talk to them. It's got to suck to hear it from your dead mother's own lips that she's disinheriting you, whether you're expecting it or not. And who knows whether she decided to include some asides, some words of wisdom, a curse... I won't know unless I see it."

"I understand that," Daniel said.

"I should have had this weeks ago," Georgina said, stamping her feet on the carpet.

"I understand that," he said, firmly. "But do the best you can."

"I will," she said, hanging up.

Georgina waited as long as she could at her apartment, and then rushed down into the elevator and into her car, arriving with Jason at the Colony Club at 1:10. She had left instructions with Armeda that if a package came for her while she was gone, to have it sent to the Colony after her. The attendants at the Colony didn't even bat an eye when Georgina requested the availability of a DVD player, in case she needed one. They were well-trained, and *never* asked questions. They assured her one would be at her disposal if and when she called for it. She telephoned Armeda and Daniel about every 15 minutes, until the Musgrave children arrived at around 2:30. Then she told Armeda and Daniel, "no calls. It's too late. I'll look at it after I'm done with them. Damn it."

The children looked as though they had been beaten with clubs. They had clearly shared transportation to the Club, because they arrived simultaneously, and it seems as though a conversation had ended as they arrived. Georgina welcomed them in the foyer of the club, and brought them back to the room she had provided. For the next 20 minutes, she ministered to them, as they were clearly shaken. She helped the staff to provide coffee, tee, pastries and hot hors d'oeuvres, and got them all seated and fairly comfortable. "I hope you'll permit me," Georgina said, "but it is past noon…" she watched as an attendant opened the doors to an armoire which contained an elaborate bar, stocked with Baccarat glasses, and high-end liquor. "I hope you won't be insulted…" she continued.

"On the contrary," said Matthew, getting up and immediately pouring himself a Glenfiddich on the rocks. "Ingrid, my dear, can I tempt you?" Frederick's wife wrinkled her nose, but no one else seemed to flinch at the relationship between the two siblings.

"Yes, please," she said, "but I'd love a gin and tonic. I ought to wait a few months, and enjoy the first one at the beginning of summer, but I'm throwing convention aside," she said, in an attempt at humor. Her eyelids were swollen, and her eyes were red from crying.

"I'll have one, too, Matthew," Luanne said quietly, "if it's not an imposition."

"Not at all," he said. Matthew fixed their drinks, and sat down between Luanne and Ingrid. Luanne took her glass, and reached out with the other hand and rubbed the top of Matthew's right hand. He opened it, and held hands with her for a moment, before taking it to his lips, and giving it a quick kiss.

Georgina couldn't help but notice that all of the children were on the verge of tears. They all were conducting themselves with a 'stiff upper lip,' but they had clearly all had a shock. Frederick got up and offered drinks to the other two ladies. Rika primly requested only tonic water, with a slice of lime, but Magrit wanted a Heineken, which he was able to locate in a refrigerator hidden in the lower cabinet. He helped himself to the same Glenfiddich his older brother had.

Once everyone was seated, sipping drinks, Georgina broke the silent ice by saying, "Is everything quite alright?"

The children quietly all looked around the table at one another. "Not completely unexpected, really," Matthew said, sipping his cocktail again, and leaning closer to Ingrid, "but a bit of a disappointment."

Georgina waited.

Frederick took the lead. "She left us nothing," he said. "I believe she said she had provided for us sufficiently during her lifetime –"

"Ha, ha," Magrit started laughing, but quickly put her hand over her mouth, and tilted her head down.

Frederick looked over at her with surprising sympathy, "—that she had provided for us sufficiently during her lifetime, and that she wished *herself*," he bit out the word, "to be memorialized in a wing at the Metropolitan Museum of Art, under her name, where her extraordinary collection of art could be enjoyed by anyone who wished to view it."

"And that's it," Matthew spoke up, getting up from the table and pouring himself another Scotch. "As I said," he repeated, with his back to the group as he took a large gulp, "not completely unexpected."

Everyone's eyes were on him with sympathy. Georgina realized perhaps it was the first time in years they had been united in anything like a group, but under terrible circumstances. "As Matthew said, Georgina," Frederick said, "it's a bit of a disappointment, but not completely unexpected." He cleared his throat. "We're fine, obviously. We've got trust funds, and annuities, that will take care of us. So, we're fine." He reached over and held his wife's hand. "We were, quite frankly, hoping, Georgina, you would have some good news for us. We know there were policies for each of us, in the amount of $10 million, and because Mother died in an accident, it would be $20 million. What have you discovered?"

"And what have you determined?" Matthew continued, turning around from the bar with his second glass already near empty.

"I have determined nothing so far," Georgina said, and stayed quiet for a moment to let that sink in. "However, what I have determined is that more investigation needs to be done." She saw shoulders sinking around the room. Frederick put his elbow on the table, and his head in his hand, and his wife put her hand on his back. "There have been two murders, that of your mother, and her friend, Bartolomeo. There has been another murder, just last week, of Ms. Larson, the woman who kept house for your mother."

Frederick lifted his head at that. "What? Miss Larson is dead?" he said.

"You didn't know?" Georgina asked.

"No, I didn't know," he said loudly. "I didn't fucking know. What the hell is going on?" Tears filled his eyes as his wife whispered comforting words into his ear.

"She was killed last week. She was discovered hanging from her shower rod," Georgina said.

"She killed herself?" Rika asked.

"No," Georgina said. It was made to look that way, but she did not kill herself. She was murdered."

"Oh, Jesus," Magrit said, putting both hands over mouth, then over her entire face, then doubling over and crying. Frederick reached over and wrapped an arm around her shoulders. "Steady. Steady," he said.

The rest of them just looked stunned. "Look," Georgina said softly. "I want to work with you. I, personally, think you've been screwed. Here's what I know so far," she said. She sat back in her chair, rubbed her cast, and said, "the man who broke my arm in my garage was named Johnny Stone. He's currently in a coma, and can't tell us anything." She looked around the table slowly at each face as she told her story. "He's the youngest member of a family Ms. Larson used to work for before she worked for your mother. His family owns the drycleaners in town." So far, she was getting blank looks all around. "Jerry Stone, Johnny's older brother, runs the drycleaner, and was close with Ms. Larson, had lunch with her every now and again, etc., and she lived in the apartment upstairs. His little brother was reportedly meeting with 'important people' in the days before your mother was killed. Ms. Larson was also killed last week, and as soon as it happened, Jerry Stone went missing with his family. They said they were going on vacation, but we can't get in touch with them. From that alone, we can't help but be suspicious that, in some way, they were involved in your mother's death, and, obviously, Bart's death."

If it Could Happen to Her

"Well, if it seems so damn clear," Matthew said, his words beginning to slur, "then why are we sitting here wondering when you're going to be kind enough to give us our money and let us get on with our lives?" His voice rose at the end. Luanne put her hand on his back, "Calm down, Matthew."

"The reason I can't give you your money and let you get on with your lives," Georgina said, "is because it's not clear the robbery was the only motive for your mother's murder. Your mother was home the night of the robbery. She usually wasn't. They came with guns, and killed her and Bart right away. The only reason they would have done that is if they intended to do it. They weren't surprised they were at home. Professional burglars would never take the risk of adding murder to burglary. They would have come in, taken what they wanted, and left, and exposed themselves to nothing more than 10 to 20 years, based on their records. But, adding murder to the mix, a whole different level of attention gets drawn on, lots more police are assigned, and the fine people of Cambridge, Connecticut will insist that someone fall, and fall hard. If they just wanted the pretty pictures and sculptures, that's what they would have done. Period."

Nobody said a word, but she had everyone's attention. "So, it quite simply doesn't make sense. Plus, you don't have a good relationship with your mother. None of you do. Or with your father, for that matter. I had access to the Will about two weeks before you did, so I knew you weren't getting anything." Frederick sat back in his chair, and glared at her. "Frederick," she said, answering the look, "you weren't happy your mother wouldn't buy you your townhouse. Everybody who was anybody in San Francisco already thought you owned it. It would have been embarrassing, and you've already admitted you had a fight about it." He started to open his mouth, but she said, "Magrit." Magrit looked up at her with tear-filled eyes. "You've had trouble for several years, and you've been trying to get it together, but your mother didn't even have one picture of your son in her house." Magrit softly started crying again. "Ingrid, and Matthew, do I even need to tell you why your mother had a problem with you?" Matthews's ears were fire red, and red blotches were starting to appear high on his cheekbones. "And Luanne, you were always around with your hand out for the cause of the moment." Luanne looked at her steadily, but her lower lip shook.

And now she had to play the card she hadn't yet turned over. "And your mom decided to make her will into a video, didn't she? It couldn't have been very fun to look at. She knew she was disinheriting you, but she decided to do it as close to 'in person' as she possibly could." They were shifting in their chairs now. Georgina knew that any moment they were either going to toss a drink at her or leave. "Your mom liked making videos," Georgina said. She let that sink in, and there was silence around the room. "I know more than you think," she said, reaching to pick up her tote bag. "As I said, I'm willing to work with you, but there are limits to how much I'm willing to overlook. Please feel free to keep the room, and have a talk. I suggest that you do. See if you can't come up with some way to convince me none of you had anything to do with it. Or," she said, "convince the person who did do it, to admit it, for the sake of the rest of you." She got up from her chair and walked out the door.

"You're a fucking cunt, Georgina Adams!" she head Matthew yell, and heard a Baccarat glass smash against the door she had just closed behind her.

"You're not the first person who's told me that," Georgina said, as she walked out. Her heart was pounding, and, despite knowing they were all degenerates of one sort or another, and that one of them surely arranged for their own mother's death, she couldn't help feeling sorry for them. They were a sad, sorry bunch. She met Jason in front of the Colony, and went back to her apartment. "Now, we see what happens," she said to herself, rubbing her cast.

She went back to her apartment, and poured herself a large glass of Pinot Noir. The damn video still hadn't show up yet, and Daniel Levine couldn't explain why. Her arm was killing her, so she didn't mind adding a Vicodin to the mix. She needed a complete mental disconnect for just a little while, she told herself. She went into her room, changed into a silk gown, and curled up in her bed with the remote control. She switched around, trying various channels, and watching several reality shows, and parts of several movies. By the time she finished the glass of wine, she could feel the Vicodin working as well. Her arm felt better, and she had a nice little buzz. As she started watching an episode of "Columbo," she thought about those kids. She looked around the table at the Club again, in her mind's eye, thinking how each one of them had been messed up in way of another. Let alone the oldest child, Geoffrey, Jr., who hadn't even made it into adulthood at all. She sat up in her bed very quickly, giving herself a dizzy spell. She sat quietly for a moment, letting her head steady itself, then she got out of bed and pulled on her robe.

She jogged down the hallway in her bathrobe, into her office. She opened up her computer, and started looking through newspaper archive files about the boy's death. He drowned, she remembered. But that's all she remembered. She didn't know any of them at the time. She patiently sorted through the files she found on LexisNexis, and found that Geoffrey Musgrave, Jr. had been killed in an accidental drowning while the family was vacationing at a campground in the Adirondacks. He had been 10 years old. She read all of the newspaper accounts from that time, but discovered nothing more. She found several more mentions of his death in general interest articles about either the family, or Geoffrey Musgrave Sr., but these just referred to his death in a very brief way. Georgina sank back into her chair. "I wonder," she said. She pulled out the file that held her theory, and wrote for about 20 minutes.

Armeda walked into the room, took a quick disapproving look at the glass of wine Georgina was drinking in the middle of the afternoon, but said nothing about it as she handed Georgina a package. "Finally," Georgina said, as she ripped open the envelope. She tipped out the plastic case carrying the DVD, and a letter from Cranmore and Wilson, apologizing for the omission, and reiterating that the video will had no legal significance whatsoever, was merely a reading of the written will, and that the written will was considered to be the Last Will and Testament of Ingrid Musgrave.

Georgina got up from her chair, and turned on the television in her office. She inserted the DVD into the side of it, took the remote and returned to her leather chair. She tipped the chair back and put her feet on the desk, crossing her ankles. There was no prelude. Immediately, she saw Ingrid Musgrave, seated in a crimson-upholstered bergere chair, with stacks of legal books behind her, dressed in a black and white Chanel suit Georgina remembered from last season. She sat tall, with her legs properly crossed at the ankles, and her knees tilted slightly to the side. She had on a pair of reading glasses, and she started reading. Her voice was strong and clear, and Georgina experienced a little bit of what her children must have felt when they watched it. It was creepy to see a dead person on tape. Ingrid read through all of the boilerplate sections of the will, dealing with executorship, trusteeship, etc. When she got down to the bequests, she read them one after another, small bequests and annuities for servants, the large bequest to the Metropolitan Museum of Art. When she got to the part about disinheriting her children, she looked up into the camera, over the tops of her reading glasses, several times as she read the offending portion of the will. "Wow, way to twist the knife, Ingrid," Georgina said, taking a sip of wine.

At the end of the reading, Ingrid put the will in her lap and took off her reading glasses. Georgina put her feet back down on the floor and leaned forward over her desk. "I will assume that you are all present. Geoffrey,

Luanne, Ingrid Jr., Matthew, Ingrid, Frederick and Magrit. Geoffrey, we had a very good marriage, and when that was over, you were a very good friend. I hope you will miss me." She said this with a straight face.

"Jesus, you were full of yourself, Ingrid," Georgina said, on the edge of her seat.

"As for you children – I did the best I could. I had hoped for better for all of you. You are all still young, and there is still time for you to make lives for yourselves that you can be proud of. In order to do that, there are things that all of you are going to have to put behind you. You know what they are. And I know what they are. You may not think I was a particularly attentive mother, but I took great interest in what all of you were doing. I was always aware of your activities. Don't think that I don't know what your weaknesses are. I do."

"No wonder those children looked like they'd been beaten up," Georgina said, sorry she had had to add to their discomfort with her own brutishly frankness. "Well, better to get it all over with at once," she thought.

"Nevertheless, I do love all of you. You're my children. I remember bringing all of you into this world, and I cherished you all. I hope the very, very best for all of you." At that, the recording ended.

Chapter Fifteen

Georgina sat back in her chair and thought about the words Ingrid had chosen to use. Was there a veiled threat in there? "I was always aware of your activities – you know what your weaknesses are. I know what they are," Georgina repeated to herself. "Those are fighting words," she thought. "First of all, what kind of a mother would do that to their children? Her one last chance to mend fences and leave her kids with a good memory, and she chose to pour lemon juice on their wounds."

Well, until she found out if her meeting with the children was any kind of a success, she was going to have to continue to follow up on the only other promising angle of the case. Where the heck were the Stones? The Rolling Stones, the Skipping Stones.

She called Detective Trigilio in Cambridge and found him still in, even though it was nearly 5:30 p.m. It was nice to know he wasn't a clock-puncher. "Have you gotten anything back on the toxicology?" she asked.

"Just the standard stuff, but they're testing for blood alcohol level, cocaine, stuff like that. And she didn't have any of that," he said. "I'm asking for something a little more detailed, because I want to know if somebody slipped her a mickey to make her a little easier to handle."

"A mickey," Georgina laughed. "They're looking for GHB, or benzodiazepines?" she asked.

"Yeah, roofies, stuff like that," he said. "I'll let you know if I find anything."

"Well, listen," she said, "I understand you've got some of your friends watching over at Johnny Stone's girlfriend's place."

"Yep," he said. "I understand you guys do, too."

"Yes, but I don't want you to be surprised when they tell you I was over there," she said.

"You're going to question her again?" he asked.

"I wouldn't call it questioning, exactly," Georgina said. "At the hospital, I told her I was just terribly concerned – that I didn't mean to hurt him so badly, even though he was trying to kill me. I'm going to turn up with, like, a tray of cookies, or something, and ask how she's doing."

"Yeah, right," he said. "I'd like to be there. Do you have a problem with that?"

"No," she said, "but how am I going to turn up with a plate of cookies and a cop?"

"Yeah," he said, "that makes sense." She waited while he thought it through. "How about this? You go in and talk with her, with a little something extra pinned to your blouse? And I can listen from outside. It's not perfect, but it's the best we've got."

"I'm pretty sure that's illegal," she said, not really minding.

"Well, it won't be for admission, obviously – unless, of course, you get something really good. Then we'll figure out a way to get it in."

"Okay," she said, "but I'm leaving here in about 15 minutes. I can't wait for you to catch up."

"I'll be there," he said

Georgina went into her large closet and switched on the inset lights that revealed her clothes collection, kept protectively in glass-faced, mahogany-trimmed cupboards, and stored at the optimum temperature and humidity. Beneath the shorter cabinets were drawers which held clothes perfectly folded and stored, and along the top of the cabinets were carefully aligned rows and rows of Georgina's collection of handbags. She had a fondness for whatever Marc Jacobs was doing for Louis Vuitton, and accumulated the trendy items, though she seldom used them. She generally stuck with her faithful Speedys, Neverfulls and Keepalls for use on a daily basis. She also had a fair collection of Chanel, and Hermés, all lined up lovingly, and kept in their dust bags, with tiny little tags bearing a small photograph of the handbag inside. Her shoes were kept the same way, lined up along the bottom of her evening gowns, with photographs on the shoe boxes as well. All tastefully done by a personal assistant who came in once each season and organized it for her.

She got down on her knees and, with her good arm, drew out a drawer filled with t-shirts and sweatshirts she generally used for horseback riding – things she didn't mind getting dirty, and that she enjoyed having a little roughed-up, even though still crisply laundered and evenly and perfectly folded. Finding a plain white t-shirt was easy, and a scruffy sweatshirt which said "Skibbereen." It was a very good riding school she had trained at briefly in Orchard Park, New York, one summer when she was younger, but she doubted Betsy would know that. All she would know, Georgina hoped, is that she looked like someone Betsy could relate to. She found a pair of well-worn jeans, and a small black Bottega Veneta purse, which had cost a fortune, but which had no visible logos, and didn't look posh. She found a simple black elastic in one of the drawers in her bathroom, and she drew her hair into a

If it Could Happen to Her

slightly messy ponytail. It was going to be slightly messy anyway, because she could only use one hand to do it, but the end result was perfect. Perfectly imperfect, rather.

She had on no visible jewelry, and she let her fading bruises show. She stepped back from the mirror and liked the impression. She could pass for low-end.

She walked into the kitchen and sniffed. "Mmmm… yummy," she said, as she watched Armeda pulling out a length of aluminum foil to cover up a plate of warm chocolate chip cookies. "Oh, Gees," Georgina said, noticing a Portmerion dish that was part of her everyday dinner china. "you can't put it on one of those plates. You have to put it on a paper plate."

"A paper plate?" Armeda asked, her hands on hips. "What the heck is a paper plate?"

Georgina moaned as she rummaged through her cupboards. Indeed, they had no paper plates. "Well, just put them onto the tinfoil, and stack them haphazardly, and put the tinfoil over them. I'll carry them flat."

"You carry them *nice*," Armeda said, annoyed as she moved the cookies from the lovely plate to the tinfoil. She picked up the spatula and gave Georgina's knuckles a gentle rap with it. "I don't bake for nothing," she said.

"Thanks, Armeda," Georgina said, walking out of the apartment. She met Jason downstairs, and he drove her as far as five blocks away from Betsy's apartment in Brooklyn. She got out of her car, and Jason watched carefully as she waited for, and flagged down, a taxi to take her the rest of the way. The driver gave her a really nasty look at first, but he didn't mind the $100 bill she pressed into his hand. She got out a block away from Betsy's door, and looked around for Detective Trigilio, without seeming like she was looking. Almost immediately, she sensed somebody coming up behind her, and she visibly flinched before she realized it was him.

"Sorry," he said, smiling, hands up in the air. "Don't kick my ass."

Georgina smiled, too. "Well even you might take me with one broken arm," she said. "Is she in there?"

"She's in there," he said.

"What do you want me to do?"

"I want you to wear this," he said, holding up what looked like one of Georgina's grandmother's brooches. It was about the size of a silver dollar, and encrusted with fake diamonds and pearls.

"Are you kidding me?" she laughed.

If it Could Happen to Her

"What's wrong with this?" he said.

"It would take too long to explain," she said, taking the brooch, looking it over, and reaching over her head to pin it to her ponytail elastic. She shook her head a couple of times, and reached up to feel that it hadn't moved. "That's okay," she said, "Can you hear me now? Can you hear me now?"

Trigilio looked over her shoulder, and nodded. "Yep. They can hear you. Go be sweet to Betsy. She's suffered a terrible loss." He reached for the foil, and tried to sneak a cookie out. "Those are for criminals only," Georgina said pulling them away.

She went to Betsy's door and sat on the stoop, with the cookies next to her, seemingly looking through her purse. She sat there, doing the same thing, for about 10 minutes, before a guy in a green mechanic-looking uniform walked up the stairs past her. "Hang on, please" she said, picking up her purse, and fumbling with the cookies with her good arm. She smiled at the guy, and tried not to drop them.

"Oh, here," he said, "let me." He smiled back at her. He held the cookies for her while he reached to open the outer door to the brownstone building with his keys. He held the door for her as she walked through, and opened the other door for her as well, after he picked up his mail. Out in his car, Detective Trigilio shook his head.

"Thanks," she said, giving him her best smile. She had noted, while he was checking his mail that Betsy Davis lived in Apartment 1C, so she gave him one last flirtatious glance as she walked down to Betsy's apartment. She knocked on the door, and waited a few minutes before hearing, "Hang on!" Betsy appeared at the door, dressed in a slightly different version of the same outfit she had seen on her at the hospital – t-shirt and sweats.

"Oh!" she said, reaching up to smooth her hair, which she also had in an untidy ponytail. "Hello. I wasn't expecting anybody," she said.

"Well, I didn't know what to say if I just called," Georgina said, "so I thought I'd just bake some cookies, and see if you had some time for some girl talk. I just wanted to hear how Johnny's doing, and you're doing, you know," Georgina said, half turning away, as though she expected not to be asked in. "Anyway, I guess I can just drop them off."

"No," Betsy said, opening the door further, "come on in. I'm not doing anything." She stepped back and allowed Georgina entrance into a house that smelled faintly of marijuana, and strongly of cigarettes and beer. "I can't really remember your name," she said, "I'm sorry."

If it Could Happen to Her

"I'm Georgina," she said, handing over the tinfoil-wrapped cookies.

"Thanks!" Betsy said. She walked into the small galley kitchen off the living room. The living room itself consisted of the gray stained shag carpeting she was expecting from Daniel Levine's report, together with mismatched end tables, a glass-topped coffee table with glass rings, small smudges of food, and an overflowing ashtray in front of a sort-of velour navy blue couch and reclining chair. Georgina took a deep breath and settled herself. It was not her favorite kind of environment, but she had to envision it as an experiment. She looked at the cigarette butts in the ashtray and saw the Newports she had expected. She was proud of herself as she drew out a fresh pack from her purse that she had stopped to get on her way. "Do you mind if I smoke?" she asked, pulling out a red Bic lighter she also purchased at the convenience store three blocks away.

"No," Betsy said, "I smoke, too. Oh, Newports… we're just like sisters," Betsy smiled, and put the cookies down on the coffee table. "Do you mind if I bum one? I was just about to run out to the store."

"No," Georgina said, "help yourself. I just got a pack." She lit Betsy's cigarette, and leaned back on the couch which held a faint odor that Georgina couldn't identify, but which smelled too close to cat pee for comfort. "Steady, girl," she told herself, as she took a haul on the Newport. She used to smoke Gauloises in boarding school and college, but gave up the habit soon afterward.

"How did you find out where I lived?" Betsy asked.

"I just looked in the phone book after one of the nurses told me your last name," Georgina said, smiling to herself, wondering what Betsy would think if she knew for a moment the scrutiny she had been under the past week.

Betsy went over to the refrigerator, "Beer?" she asked.

"Sure," Georgina said. Betsy came back with two Bud longnecks uncapped. She handed one to Georgina. "So," she said, looking at the television, which was broadcasting the 'Real Housewives of Atlanta,' "how are things going?"

"You know," Betsy said, puttering around a little bit, and making an effort to tidy up the apartment which Georgina felt that only a great deal of lighter fluid and a match could remedy, "pretty good. I miss Johnny. He used to kind of help out around here."

"How's he doing?" Georgina asked. "I've felt like going to the hospital, but I haven't, somehow, gotten over there."

"He's okay," Betsy said. "You know. The same." She sat down on the chair next to Georgina, took a big drag from her cigarette, and blew it up into the air. They both watched the television for a minute. "Can you believe the houses these bitches have?" Betsy said.

"They're nice," Georgina said.

"No shit," Betsy said. "I just need to find me a basketball player, and I guess I'd be all set."

Georgina laughed.

"Do you want to see some pictures?" Betsy asked.

"I'd love to," Georgina said.

Betsy brought over a photo album that had seen a lot of use. She flipped past the first half or so of the pictures, referring to her "loser" brother, and her "bitch" of a mother as she flew past her early life, and then, near the end, there were two or three pages of Johnny. Georgina got the privilege of seeing a couple of pics out at picnics with friends, or things like that, where Betsy had taken pictures with Johnny mugging at the camera. He was even uglier conscious than he was unconscious, Georgina thought. There was even one where someone else had taken the camera, so the two of them could be photographed together.

"That's really nice," Georgina said, closing the album. "Have you been in to see him today?"

"No," Betsy said, "not today," gesturing toward the pack for another cigarette.

Georgina pushed them towards her. "Help yourself," she said.

"I feel bad. I should be there every day, you know, in case he wakes up. But that asshole doctor, he doesn't tell me anything. But, what he does tell me is he doesn't know if he's ever going to wake up. So, sometimes I feel stupid sitting there." Betsy rubbed her fingers between her eyebrows.

"No," Georgina said. "Don't feel bad. How do you know what's going to happen? If he's going to be like that forever, you can't just sit by his side forever. You've got a life to live, too."

"Really," Betsy said, feeling better that Georgina agreed with her. "I mean, I'll go over again, you know, every once in awhile, but I can't go over there every day. I mean, if he's not coming back, and that thing he was working on isn't going to pan out, then I'm going to have to start looking for a job again," she said, taking a big haul from her cigarette, clearly not thrilled at the prospect.

"I wish I could find out what he was into for you," Georgina said. "I

If it Could Happen to Her

mean, you're practically his widow, and if he was into anything illegal, I mean, you know, but something where somebody else wound up with a lot of money, well... I got my arm broken, and you've got your fiancée in the hospital. That's not right," she said. "If somebody else made out."

"You know," Betsy said, sitting back in her chair, "I was thinking the same thing. But what can you do?"

"Well," Georgina asked, lighting up another Newport, and drinking from her longneck, "has Johnny ever been in trouble before?"

"He was inside for a while a couple of times," Betsy said, "but never for anything serious. When he was young, he robbed some houses of some of the rich people who lived in the same neighborhood as him. He came from money," she said with pride.

"Oh," Georgina said, with her eyebrows raised.

"Yeah," Betsy said, "but then his big brother stole the family business out from underneath him, and put him on an allowance," Johnny said. "He sat back in the office and made all the money, and he wanted Johnny to work at the counter, and run the machines. Johnny said, hell no."

"Did you ever meet his brother?" Georgina asked.

"No," she laughed. "I sat outside in the car once, while Johnny ran inside his brother's big frickin' house. He ran inside and picked up his check. His brother gave him a check once every couple of weeks, but it was nothing compared to what his brother was bringing down, obviously. And I wasn't good enough to be invited inside. Johnny didn't even go in himself. His brother handed it to him at the door and didn't even ask him in. Nice family, right?"

"Yeah," Georgina agreed.

"But Johnny thought he was going to do better," Betsy said. "He had ambition, you know?"

"Sure," Georgina said. "So what was he doing with those people you told me about?" Georgina asked. "Was it a business or something?"

"I thought so," Betsy said. "He said it was bigtime, and when he said bigtime, you know he meant it. I mean, that house of his brother's... Johnny told me it cost more than a million dollars," she whispered the amazing amount.

"Did he tell you anything about it?" Georgina asked, conscious that Detective Trigilio was listening, and hoping she could get something out of her.

"Not really," Betsy said, "just that he thought he was going to be doing

If it Could Happen to Her

really well."

"Has anybody called here looking for him since he's been in the hospital?"

"Nope," Betsy said, stubbing out her second Newport, and lighting a third. "I hoped they would, because, you know, if something happened, and he deserved a share, then I should be the one to take care of it for him," she said.

"Sure," Georgina agreed. Just then, the mobile phone inside her purse started ringing. She had planned to turn off the ringer, but she had forgotten. She picked it up and saw Daniel Levine's number appear. "My fucking ex," she said to Betsy, as she got up and walked across the room with one finger in her ear.

"Yeah?" Georgina said roughly.

"Where are you?" he barked.

"I'm wherever the hell I want to be," she said. "You don't own me." She looked over at Betsy and winked, who smiled in return.

"O-kay," he said slowly. "I guess I have no idea what you're up to. I can only hope you're working. But I thought it might interest you to know that Ingrid and Matthew Musgrave are dead. They've been murdered, in their home, and we're fired. Geoffrey Musgrave just fired us."

Georgina went white. "You can't possibly be kidding me," she said.

"No, I'm not kidding you. What the hell did you do, Georgina? You said you wanted to play a game? What did you do?" he asked, his voice getting gradually louder.

"What happened?" Georgina said, "I have to get over there."

"No, you can't," Daniel said. "We're fired. F-I-R-E-D, fired. What the fuck did you do?"

"I blew some dust off the shelves, Daniel!" she shouted. She immediately realized she had Betsy as a rapt audience. "I'll call you back in a minute," she said.

"Don't –" he managed to say before she hung up.

Georgina turned off her phone with the flick of a button. "Fucking dick," she said.

"Aren't they all?" Betsy said.

"Listen, Betsy," Georgina said, "I have to run. I have to see what this is about." She rolled her eyes.

"I know what that's like," Betsy said.

"Listen," Georgina said, "hand onto that pack of cigs. I just got a carton."

"Thanks," Betsy said, "that's nice of you," she got up and saw her to door. "And thanks for the cookies."

"You're welcome," Georgina said. "I just wish I could have stayed longer. Next time I will." She gave her best smile as the door closed behind her. As soon as it did, she broke into a jog, and turned on her phone again, calling Daniel immediately. "I was just visiting with Betsy, what the fuck happened?"

"They're both dead. Matthew's throat's cut, and it looks like Ingrid's got her head bashed in, but the only reason I know that is because I have a few friends at NYPD. We're off it." He was pissed. Losing millions of dollars made him very pissed.

"Let me call Geoffrey," she said, hanging up on him. She stood in the alcove where the residents of Betsy's building received their mail. She dialed Geoffrey in Bedford, and, not finding him there, dialed the penthouse. He wasn't there, either, but Frederick was, and he was beside himself. Georgina managed to get him to give her Geoffrey's mobile phone number. She dialed it, and heard a shouted, "Hello?"

"Geoffrey, it's Georgina," she said, "what's going on?"

"'What's going on?' she says," he said, mocking her, "aren't I paying you people a fucking fortune to be telling *me* what's going on? My family is fucking dropping like flies, and you guys aren't doing shit. You're asking *me* what's going on?"

"Mr. Musgrave..." she said.

"I'm on my way into the city to see what's going on for myself. You guys are supposed to be fucking handling this," he choked up for a moment. "I didn't necessarily think the world of those kids, but I didn't want to see them dead, either."

"Mr. Musgrave..." she tried again.

"Just shut the fuck up. You're fucking up royally and you're fucking fired. With you assholes working for me, I'll probably end up dead myself. Fucking professionals," he said, hanging up.

Georgina ran outside, waved at Trigilio's car and went around the corner. She waited for him to catch up, filled him in, quickly, and then dialed the phone again, calling Daniel. "Daniel. I'm still working on it. Do I have authorization to go over there to the scene? I'm here with Detective Trigilio. I'm sure he'd like to go, too." She looked up at Trigilio, and waited for Daniel's response.

"No," he said. "We're fired." He hung up on her.

"Fuck," she said. She took the phone and thumped it against her head two or three times, put her good hand on her hip and walked in circles. Trigilio didn't say anything, just watched her. She punched in Geoffrey Musgrave's number again.

"What!" he yelled.

"Don't you yell at me, you moron," she yelled back. "I just broke out of an interview with the closest contact we've got to one of the guys who killed your ex-wife, to call you and find out why we're fired. *We're* fired? You fuck up your family five ways to Sunday, we start sorting it out, and push somebody into action – somebody who now *kills* Little Ingrid and Matthew and *we're* fucking fired? You're an idiot. Tomorrow morning, you'll probably find a bomb under your Bentley, you stupid shit. We're the closest you've come to any kind of information, and you're firing *us*? *You're* fucking fired, you son of a bitch. I'm going to Armani right now to buy a new black suit for your funeral. Asshole." She hung up the phone.

"Nice phone manners," Trigilio said.

"Shut up," she said, practically holding her breath and she walked around in circles, staring at her phone. In precisely two minutes, it rang back. "I'm sorry," Geoffrey Musgrave barked, "find out what happened."

"Will do," Georgina said, cheerfully. She dialed Daniel back. "We're back on. Musgrave just hired us back. I'm on my way over to the scene. I'm bringing Detective Trigilio over there with me. He's either OK'd as Cambridge, working on a related case, or he's with us, okay?"

Daniel Levine breathed a huge sigh of relief. "Okay."

Georgina hung up. "Come with me," she said, dashing the three blocks to where she left Jason and her car.

Chapter Sixteen

Georgina jumped into Trigilio's car and rode along with him, with Jason following along behind. They got there in a hurry, too, because Trigilio snapped his light to the top of his car, and all of the other traffic moved out of their way. With Georgina's Lincoln Town Car racing along behind, Georgina thought they must have looked like a terribly important motorcade.

She gave Trigilio directions to Ingrid and Matthew's townhouse, while she chewed on her bottom lip and looked out the passenger side window. She wondered if she should tell Trigilio what she had said to the children after the reading of the Will, but she decided against it. She felt badly enough already. It's not like she actually killed them herself, but she certainly didn't help matters. She had stirred the pot, and, because of it, two more people were dead. She couldn't wait to talk to Dr. Gregson about it, but, for now, she had to put it out of her head so that she could work.

"So," Trigilio said, breaking into the silence, "tell me about these two," he said. "They're the ones that were living together, right?"

She took a deep breath. "Right. And quite a few people were under the impression that they were living together as husband and wife, too," she said, looking over at him.

"Oh, Gees," he said, curling his upper lip. "Rich people," he finally said, as though that explained it all. "Were they old, young, what?"

"They weren't old, and they weren't really young, either. Early to late forties, I believe," Georgina said. "They were both pretty out of shape, too. If they were shot, it doesn't really matter, but if it was something else, they wouldn't have been able to put up any kind of fight. If anything, I think they'd try to run."

They arrived at the scene and observed three or four marked police cars pulled up in front, and the Medical Examiner's van, already at the scene. "Oh, I hope they haven't moved anybody yet," Georgina moaned. She jumped out of Trigilio's car as fast as she could. He left it parked out amongst the rest of the marked vehicles, with the light still on top, to ensure it wouldn't be towed away while he was inside.

As they approached the house, a uniformed police officer stepped forward and put out his arm. "Sir – Ma'am," he said, "I'm afraid you're going to have to step back."

Trigilio pulled out his badge and showed it to the officer.

The officer looked at it. "You're from Cambridge, Connecticut?" the officer said with a bit of a smile.

Trigilio didn't seem to like that smile, for some reason. "Well, that's good. You can read. It says Cambridge, Connecticut. Why don't you tell me who the lead detective is on this, Officer? And then go get him for me."

The officer took another step forward, and said, "I understand that you're a fellow officer, but I'm afraid I'm going to have to ask you to step back. I'll go inside and check and see if the lead detective has any time for you. I'm going to have to tell you that I doubt it."

"Alright, son," Trigilio said, smiling. "I understand."

The officer turned and started walking toward the townhouse door.

"No, son," Trigilio said, "wait here," he said, pointing down at the officer's feet. He pulled out his telephone and started dialing. "What's your name?" he asked the officer.

"Sergeant Blalock," he said, turning back toward the door again.

"Sergeant Blalock, if you turn your back on me again, I'm going to make you pay for it," Trigilio said.

Blalock turned around, eyes narrowed, and was about to say something when Trigilio said, "Jackson, it's Trigilio from out in Connecticut. Yeah. Ha, ha. You, too. No, actually I'm up here right now. A couple of murders I'm working on down there are connected to a couple of murders that happened up here just now. No, like, right now, at 13 Garden Place. I've got a Sergeant Blalock here who tells me that the lead detective probably won't have time for me, and that I should be stepping back out of the way. Are you still Commissioner around here, or what?"

When Sergeant Blalock realized that Detective Trigilio was talking directly to Police Commissioner Jackson Murphy, he hung his head.

Trigilio said, "Do you want to talk to him? Okay." He handed the telephone to Sergeant Blalock.

"Yes, Sir," Sergeant Blalock said. "Yes, Sir. Yes, Sir. Yes, Sir. Absolutely, Sir. Thank you, Sir." He handed Detective Trigilio back his phone, "I apologize, Detective Trigilio. Please come this way. Is the young lady with you?"

"Yes, she is. She's with Konig, and she's with me."

"Yes, Sir," Sergeant Blalock said, turning to lead them up to the townhouse.

"You have the mobile phone number of Jackson Murphy?" Georgina

If it Could Happen to Her

said, smiling.

"It would appear that way," Trigilio said, pleased with himself as they walked toward the front door.

"Can I have it?" she asked.

"No way," he smiled.

"You keep getting more and more useful all the time," she said.

The officer walked up to the front door, and asked them, politely, to wait there briefly while he went to find the lead detective, who he guaranteed would not keep them waiting.

"I'm not exactly dressed to impress," Georgina said, looking at her cast, her faded jeans and sweatshirt, knowing her hair was in a messy ponytail.

"It was appropriate to talk to Betsy," Trigilio said, looking her over again. "I can do the talking here, and make sure that you hear everything you need to hear."

"Thanks," she said.

A surprisingly young-looking, sharp-dressed detective met them at the door of the townhouse. He was about 6 feet tall, with nearly black hair, possibly part Hispanic, Georgina guessed from his complexion, and with a nice suit, crisp white shirt, and a nice pair of shoes. "Pretty boy," she thought. "I'll bet we're looking at the Chief of Police about 15 years down the road."

"Detective Trigilio," he said, holding out his hand, "I'm Detective Summers, Mark Summers," he said. "I guess you've got some connection in Cambridge, Connecticut we need to check out? What's going on down there?"

"Well," Trigilio said. "The mother of these two kids was worth slightly less than $200 million dollars, and she was shot dead in her home in Cambridge, Connecticut about two weeks ago, along with a companion. We've since had another murder that we're convinced is connected. This," he said, gesturing at Georgina, "is Georgina Adams. She's from Konig. Excuse her appearance, but she was working with us on something undercover when we got the call. She's been working on these kids, and the other kids, because of the insurance."

"Good insurance?" Detective Summers asked, looking at Georgina.

"The best," she said. "Lloyd's policies for each of the kids, and there are three others left. $10 million each, or $20 million each, depending on what I find out."

"So what's going on here?" Detective Trigilio asked.

"It's messy," Detective Summers warned. "We're not letting many

If it Could Happen to Her

people in, because there's blood just freakin' everywhere."

Georgina swallowed down the lump that rose in her throat. "Can we get in?" she asked. "I was here to interview them just a few days ago. I know exactly where everything was."

Detective Summers looked at her again, and then back inside, "well, that would be helpful," he said. "You, of course, Detective Trigilio – you know what you're doing. I'm going to give you some booties and gloves, okay? No problems with latex?"

"No," they both said, getting properly attired.

Trigilio stepped aside, and let Georgina walk in first. Bloodbath wouldn't even describe it. The front hallway, which had struck Georgina as the charming entrance to a middle-aged couple's pleasant home, with its staircase up the side covered in floral carpet, and its cheerful paintings, was now covered in blood spatter – the walls, the hardwood floor, the carpet – everything.

"I've got to ask you to be real careful," Detective Summers said. "The only other guys in here right now are the ID guys who are doing the photos, the sample collection, and the fingerprinting, and the medical examiner, who's looking them over before we take them away. There's hardly anyplace to walk. The first one's here," he said, taking them to the left into a comfortable sitting room Georgina had only seen briefly when she visited.

"Anything seem different to you?" Detective Summers asked.

Georgina looked over at him quickly, to see if he was kidding. She saw that he wasn't. "Other than the obvious," she said, "no. Everything seems to be where it was." She looked around. "Those Staffordshire figurines are expensive, and I can see his Rolex on his wrist," she said quietly.

Matthew Musgrave lay on the floor, wearing a pair of khaki trousers, navy blue Stubbs & Wooton needlepoint slippers, a blue button-down oxford shirt and a navy cardigan. He was lying on his side, both hands up around his neck, in a clearly vain attempt to stop the flow of arterial blood from the gaping wound there. Georgina carefully moved closer, and saw that his throat had been cut nearly from ear to ear. "I wonder what kind of strength that must have taken?" she said.

"It depends on the weapon," Detective Summers said. "We're looking for it, but it's not obvious that it's here. It's not lying around, and I'd be surprised if we find it cleaned off and placed politely back in a drawer."

"Me, too," Georgina said, looking around the rest of the room. A few tables had been overturned, curios lay broken on the floor, blood was smeared over the surfaces of the couch and chair, and the wall showed the arcing pattern of arterial blood spatter.

"Again, anything out of the ordinary?" Detective Summers asked Georgina, "aside from the obvious?"

"No," she said. "I didn't spend much time in this room. I saw it briefly, but we talked in the kitchen."

"Well," Detective Summers said, "that's where we're headed next."

Georgina took a closer look at Matthew. "He couldn't have put up much of a fight after that attack," she said.

"No, but she did," Summers said, turning and tip-toeing his way out of the sitting room. Georgina and Trigilio followed him past the staircase, observing paintings knocked off the wall, the clear smear of a bloody hand on the wall, and the area rugs which had been pushed askew. "She's here," he said, stepping into the kitchen and revealing Ingrid Musgrave, Jr.'s body on the floor, over in front of the oven. She was clad in a housecoat which may once have been a blue gingham, but which was now covered in red blood. Her head and face had been abused so badly it was difficult to look at, and Georgina thought she might even have had trouble identifying her if she didn't remember her physical shape, and the jewelry she wore. "We've got our murder weapon, here," Summers said, pointing to a cast iron frying pan on the tiled floor in front of the sink. "She was stabbed as well as bludgeoned. We're being real careful with fibers in here, because there was a fight."

Georgina could see that for herself. All of the canisters lay on their sides, or on the floor. The patterned dishtowels Georgina had seen on her first visit lay soaking up the pools of blood – broken dishes and glasses were everywhere. "I've got to ask you guys to be careful, too," Summers said. "Not to insult you, but just because there's literally blood and glass everywhere, and we don't want anybody to get hurt."

"Plus you don't want our blood mixed up with theirs," Trigilio said quietly, looking about the room grimly.

"No," Summers said. "This is where our killer left some proof – if he left it. There was a fight. Clothes and hair have to be around here somewhere. And I would be very surprised if our perp weren't injured himself."

"Yeah," Trigilio said, stepping back and looking back down the hallway. He spoke low to Georgina. "Adams, what do you think? I think the doer hit the big guy quickly, to get him out of the way. That was a surprise. But the other one, she saw it coming. She got caught, maybe even started to put up a fight and either got stabbed in there, or got a ton of her brother's blood on her, because there's bloody handprints and spray on the floor and the wall – either hers or the doer's, on the wall on the way out of that room, and all down the hallway. Then there's some dripping blood there," he pointed to the hallway floor, "and there, and there, and there. Those are pretty big drops, too. I think our victim was already injured when she started down this hallway." He turned back around and looked at the kitchen, "But she put up a fight here, and the knife got taken away somehow," he said, "because she was finished off with a weapon of opportunity, that frying pan there. It looks like, at that point, the victim and the doer were both fighting for their lives."

"Little Ingrid lost," Georgina said quietly. She looked around. "Maybe she headed in here for a knife of her own," Georgina said.

Over Georgina's shoulder, Trigilio said to Summers, "Be real, real careful with the DNA. It's possible that we've got brothers and sisters killing each other."

"Oh, shit," Summers said, looking up from where he was examining some finger smears with his ID officers.

"Yeah," Trigilio said. "Makes it harder for your guys."

"Well, at least we know that," Summers said, looking at his ID officer, and getting a nod in response. "We can be very, very careful here, and make sure that they're very careful at the lab, too." He stood up. "Nice family," he said.

"They're the best," Georgina said. "Trigilio," she said, quietly, making sure she had his attention, "I have to tell you something."

He looked over at her, and then back at Summers. "So, Summers. You can count on me, and I can count on you?"

"That's what Jackson Murphy says, and that's good enough for me. Do me a favor, and give me a ring when you get back to Cambridge, and we'll give you everything we've got." Summers gave Trigilio a quick salute.

Trigilio returned it, and walked back toward the front of the house with Georgina. "Is this a public talk or a private talk?" Trigilio asked.

"That depends on whether or not you want to kill me afterwards," she said.

"Private it is," he said, holding out his right arm and leading her back to his car, leaving their booties and gloves with the officer at the front door.

They got in, and Georgina told him what she had done after the reading of the Will. She told him everything she said and did, and left nothing out.

Trigilio was silent for a moment, and then said, "Wow. You are a supreme head fucker-upper."

"There are days when I would take that as a compliment," she said quietly.

"Well," he said, gripping his steering wheel with both hands, "don't get me wrong. These are not good people, and at least one of them is a murderer. So, you do what you have to do. We're allowed to lie to suspects all the time, if we think that it's going to get us somewhere. But, man," he said, looking over at her, "that was just sheer psychological warfare. Some of those kids weren't murderers. I don't know." He shook his head.

"It obviously had the biggest effect on the killer, and we've certainly narrowed the list," she said.

"I know," he said.

"And let's not forget," she said, her voice raising, "that the reason that these two are dead is most likely because they were a part of it. There would be no reason to kill them otherwise."

"That's true," Trigilio said. "That hadn't occurred to me quite yet. But you're probably right. People make their beds."

Georgina started to chew on her right thumbnail.

"Now, now," Trigilio said, gently taking the hand away from her mouth. "Let's not ruin a perfect manicure. We've got a lot of work to do."

"Well, I'll tell you what I need to do," Georgina said. "I need to lay eyes on each one of those kids and see who's been in a fight. It might be just that simple."

Unfortunately, it wasn't. The Musgraves became immediately unavailable to everyone. Georgina couldn't even find out from their father where they were.

"Don't raise your voice to me, Adams! I can't find them, either. They're not at my place in the City anymore," he said. "Frederick and his wife and Magrit and her kid all cleared out. My maid tells me that they packed. Not everything, but they packed. And I can't get Luanne at her place."

"Give me their cell phone numbers," Georgina said. "Maybe Daniel can use a little GPS magic and find them."

"I don't know their goddamn cell phone numbers," he said, his voice cracking. "They always called me," he said. "They always called me. Always wanting something. Now I don't even know how many are left."

"I'm sure they're fine, Mr. Musgrave," she said, trying to calm him down, and keep him focused. "I'm sure they're a little bit scared, and they don't know who to trust. They haven't gone far," she said. "And they'll be back."

And they were. Less than 24 hours later, Geoffrey Musgrave called to tell Georgina that he had located his children. "They went to the frickin' Ritz," he said, still managing to be disgusted with them. "On my tab. The Ritz called me, and said they had booked a three-bedroom suite. They're all there. At least they were a few hours ago. I think they're headed back to my place. There's going to be a service the day after tomorrow, and you'll be able to talk to them after that, I'm sure." He sounded old and tired, not much like the man Georgina had met just a few days ago.

"Mr. Musgrave," she said, pleadingly, "I really shouldn't wait that long to see them. I should see them all right away. I need to question them about what happened to Ingrid and Matthew," she said, thinking to herself that she also wanted to get a good look at them. She knew that every day that went by, swelling went down, and redness faded. The battle scars that the killer had received would be starting to disappear.

"I don't know what to tell you, Adams," he said wearily. "Try to call them at my place." He hung up.

Georgina did try, repeatedly, to reach the children by phone. She obtained their cell phone numbers from Konig's offices (which had resources she didn't), and they weren't picking up. She phoned the penthouse on Fifth Avenue, and Luanne's place, but wasn't able to get any further than voicemail. She then had Jason drive her to both places, where she was told, on Fifth Avenue, that no one was at home, and at Luanne's place, where her ringing of the doorbell met with silence, and the lights were seemingly off. If they wanted to not be at home when they actually were, they were certainly rich enough to pull it off.

"Damn it!" Georgina said to herself as she got back into her car. "Where are those fuckers?"

Jason knew a rhetorical question when he heard one, and didn't respond.

Georgina sat up straight, wrenching her arm as she did so. "Ouch," she said, moving her cast into a more comfortable position. "Jason, can you take me down to that place in Cambridge, Connecticut I told you about?"

"Yes, Ma'am," Jason said.

Georgina reached into her Louis Vuitton Neverful totebag, and pulled out her bottle of painkillers. She popped one, and swallowed it dry.

If it Could Happen to Her

Chapter Seventeen

On the way down to Cambridge, Georgina warned Jason of the intricacies of Ingrid Musgrave's security system. When he reached the driveway, he said to Georgina, "Okay?"

"Okay," she said, looking at her watch. Jason spun down the driveway, and they both jumped out at the end. It was dark by the time they got there, and impossible to tell if anyone was there, because the automatic lights Georgina had noted earlier had popped on all over the house, making it look occupied. Georgina used her key, dashed in and punched in the security code. She moved quickly around the house, with Jason on her heels, seeing if she could determine any sign someone had been occupying the house. Unfortunately, she found nothing. Wherever the children had gone after the Ritz, they hadn't come to Mummy's house in Connecticut.

"Shit," Georgina said. She set the alarm again, and Jason rushed her to the end of the driveway. After spending so much time driving down here, only to face disappointment, Georgina made a quick decision to stop by at Jerry Stone's house, to see if anybody was around. She knew Detective Trigilio would kill her, but she didn't want to wait, either. She gave Jason directions.

As they pulled down the street the Stones lived on, she asked Jason to turn off the headlights, and had him park across the street a few doors down. There were lights on at the Stone's house, but after watching the automatic lights at Ingrid's house, Georgina knew that meant nothing. Then she saw a shadow cross a window with the shades drawn. "Oh, yeah," she said, smiling. She reached for her phone and called Detective Trigilio.

"I happened to be in the neighborhood," Georgina said, "and I happened to notice there are signs of life at the Stone's house," she said cheerfully.

"Don't you dare!" Trigilio said.

"Get over here as quickly as you want to," Georgina said. "I'm going in to say hi."

"Wait for me, damn it!" he said. "Adams, I waited for you. I won't forget it if you fuck me over."

"I'm sitting here, for Christ's sake," she said. "I'll give you ten minutes, but I'm not screwing this up, just because you need to do your hair before you get in the car."

"Don't move without me," he growled again, and hung up.

Exactly 11 minutes later, Georgina saw Trigilio's car pull in behind hers.

She was glad she had waited. Jason got out, went around, and opened her door. Detective Trigilio came up shrugging his jacket onto his shoulders, and looking like he wanted to strangle Georgina. Jason gave him a glare, and some body language, stepping in front of Georgina, to discourage it.

Trigilio glared back at Jason as Georgina smiled. "He'd go to jail for me, Trigilio. Don't make me prove it."

"It's not worth it, anyway," he said, buttoning his jacket, straightening his tie, and giving Jason one last look. "Let's see who's home."

"I'll ring the bell in front," she said, "like I'm a neighbor or something. They don't know me. You make sure nobody tries to sneak out the back."

Trigilio looked up at the house. "Thank you for the tips on police procedure. How do you know these aren't automatic lights?"

"They might be, but, as far as I know, they don't make automatic shadows that move around."

"They should," he said, heading back around the rear of the house.

Georgina went up to the front door while Jason hung back behind the car. Not in view, but not inside, either, just in case he needed to jump in and help. She smoothed her hair, which she already knew was perfect, and pinched her cheeks to add a little color. She had a dark gray fur jacket on, and with her Louis Vuitton tote bag hooked into the crook of her arm, she looked right in place in this neighborhood. But, she also knew the Stones might not be expecting, or wanting, company. She reached forward and rang the bell.

She breathed deeply, as she wondered whether anyone would answer, or whether they would end up facing the bad end of Detective Trigilio's gun out the back door. But, the door opened in front of her. She was met with the nervously-smiling face of a well-tended, late-40-something slim blond woman. "Hi," she said, holding the door open only about a foot, with one hand holding it tight. "Can I help you?"

"I'm Georgina Adams," Georgina said. "Is your husband at home?"

"What's this about?" Brenda Stone said, closing the door opening down to about half a foot.

"I just want to talk to him, Mrs. Stone. Please. There's nowhere for him to go. My bodyguard is out front, and there's a police detective at your back door.

She watched the color drain from Brenda Stone's face. "Brenda," a male voice said behind her, "I've got it," Jeffrey Stone said, pulling the door open. Georgina felt, rather than saw, Jason appear behind her right shoulder. "Who's that?" Jerry Stone said, about to close the door.

"That's my driver," Georgina said. "As soon as he's sure I'm okay, he'll go back to the car and wait for me – Detective!" she shouted. Trigilio came coolly around the corner, quite obviously re-holstering his pistol.

Georgina turned and saw Jason headed back toward the car. "Can we talk to you for a minute, Jerry?" asked Trigilio.

Jerry Stone stood looking from one of them to the other, a look of resignation on his face, and then opened the door.

They sat in his living room. Trigilio and Georgina sat next to one another, Georgina leaning back comfortably, and Trigilio, leaning forward with his elbows on his knees, his hands together, fingers intertwined, staring at Jerry with less than friendliness in his eyes. Jerry's wife Brenda brought in a tray of tea and cookies, and put it on the coffee table between them, then sat down next to her husband.

"So," Trigilio said, "we saw the luggage in the hallway. Very nice luggage." He smiled at Brenda Stone, who blushed as she sipped her tea. "Coming or going?" this question was clearly directed at Jerry Stone.

Jerry Stone sat sunken into his couch shoulders slouched together. "Both," he said, looking at his hands and not at either of them.

"What's that supposed to mean?" Trigilio said, taking a magazine, neatly stacked on the coffee table, rolling it and tapping Jerry on the knee with it.

"It means, Detective," Jerry said, looking up with tired, red eyes which were now brimming with tears, "that I had just come back from running away for a few days, and I was getting ready to run away for a few more days."

"Why?" Trigilio asked.

"Because I didn't know what the fuck else to do!" Jerry exploded, his voice cracking.

His wife reached over and put her hand on his knee, rubbing it twice, then reaching to take his hand.

"Detective," Brenda Stone said, "my husband and I have shamefully avoided our responsibilities for the past few days." Georgina noticed she had black circles under her eyes, too. Jerry Stone hung his head. "We should have come right out and told you everything we knew, or thought we knew..." she stuttered for a moment, "but we weren't even sure if we knew anything, so we didn't know..." her lower lip began to tremble, and she took a deep breath as a tear ran down her cheek from her left eye.

Jerry squeezed her hand tighter. "We don't know what the fuck we

If it Could Happen to Her

know," he said. "Sorry, hon'," he said to his wife. "I know my shithead brother did this to you, right?" He pointed at Georgina's arm. "You kicked his ass and put him in the hospital, and he's probably a vegetable, right?"

"Don't raise your voice," Detective Trigilio said, raising his own, "you knew Ms. Larson got killed upstairs, right?"

"I didn't know for sure she got killed. I knew she was dead, but I didn't know for sure what happened. I knew my brother was running with a shitty crowd, but he always did… nothing like this had ever happened before. It was only ever – embarrassing."

"It's more than fucking embarrassing, now, isn't it?" Trigilio said, "Sorry, hon'," he directed at Mrs. Stone.

"Easy," Georgina said, her hand touching Detective Trigilio's elbow lightly. "She doesn't like coarse language. There's nothing wrong with that."

"It's a little late for pleasantries," Trigilio said, taking a deep breath, and sitting up, adjusting his gun.

"I'm sorry, Detective," Brenda said, "Don't worry about me. I don't have the luxury right now of pleasantries, and, frankly, I don't think I deserve them. We should have called you right away, and offered ourselves to you for interview, with anything we knew or possibly could have known – anything that would help. But my husband loved Ms. Larson. He loved her. She raised him, and helped him take care of his brothers and sisters, and he would never, never have hurt her."

"Where are your shitty brothers and sisters, by the way?" Trigilio asked.

"I spoke to Jackie," Brenda said calmly. Jerry turned and looked at her quickly. "Brenda…" he said.

"Jackie," Trigilio said, interrupting Jerry, "which one of the crappy bunch is that?"

"She's the second one. Younger than Jerry," Brenda continued, as though Jerry hadn't said anything. "She's got a couple of kids, and they're a little bit here, there and everywhere."

"What did she have to say?" Trigilio asked.

"Not much," Brenda said. "She was staying in a motel with her kids, and had left her apartment. She was calling for money, so that she could stay there a while longer."

"What was she hiding from?" Trigilio asked.

"I don't think she even knew," Brenda said. "She said that Johnny had gotten in some trouble, and her boyfriend had suggested that she hide for awhile."

"Who's her boyfriend?" Georgina asked.

"Robert Lanier," Brenda said. "He's a friend of Johnny's, and he's the father of Jackie's youngest."

Georgina showed no reaction at the mention of that name, but inside she was celebrating. She knew Trigilio was, too, but she marveled at his ability to hide it, as well.

"Where's this motel?" Trigilio asked.

"It's the Shangri-La, out on Route 42," Brenda said. "They're in Room 5."

Trigilio took out his phone and called the station. He had another detective called in to go over to the Shangri-La, and bring in Jackie Stone for a talk.

"She's got children," Brenda said, interrupting him. "Let them know they can bring them here."

Trigilio nodded and did so, knowing that the children might well end up in foster care if he didn't.

As Trigilio hung up the phone, Jerry leaned over and put his right hand over his eyes. He started to cry. His wife reached up and rubbed his shoulder, putting her head down, and waiting for him to speak. "I don't know who did this. And I know what you're talking about. You're not just talking about Ms. Larson. You're talking about Mrs. Musgrave, too, right? You think Johnny did it."

"Johnny's coma has made him only slightly stupider than he already was," Detective Trigilio said coldly. "There's no way he did it alone. Who do you know?"

"I didn't hang out with him. I gave him money, and he had an account I set up for him. I put money into it every month so he'd keep away. Sometimes he'd still stop by for checks, though. I wanted my wife and kids to have a good life, and all of my brothers and sisters – all of them – are worthless. I didn't want to have much to do with them."

"Who do you know?" Detective Trigilio said, again.

Jerry Stone breathed deeply. "He hung out with that loser Robert Lanier, and another guy named Matthew Ellston. They were joined at the hip whenever one of them wasn't in the joint. They all worked at the drycleaner at one time or another, but I've had to fire them each about five times. Come in late... lift from the till..."

If it Could Happen to Her

"Those names sound familiar. But we're talking about way more than lifting from the till, Jerry," Trigilio said, leaning forward. "We're talking about the murder for hire of Mrs. Musgrave. We're talking about the attempted murder of Miss Adams, here, and we're talking about the murder of your precious Ms. Larson and her cute little dog. We're also talking about two more corpses we found in Brooklyn this morning."

"What's that," Jerry said, lifting his head, tears running down his face, "Who? Who's dead now?"

"Well, we know your brother didn't do it, Jerry," Trigilio said, "but we don't know where you were."

"So I killed people?" He said, standing up and leaning forward. "I don't even know who's dead," he said, putting his fingers up to his chest, "I don't even know what you're talking about."

"Sit down, Jerry," Trigilio said.

"What are you talking about, Detective?" Brenda said, calmly, as Jerry sat.

Georgina had been watching how Brenda deftly handled the situation. Letting Jerry talk until she thought he should be quiet, and then letting him shout when they could use a break in the tension. "Where were you, Brenda?" Georgina asked, quietly. "And where were you going when we got here?"

Brenda looked over at Georgina coolly, "Who are you, again?"

"I apologize," Georgina said, moving forward, and offering her good hand for a handshake. "Your husband seems to know who I am. I'm Georgina Adams. Your brother-in-law broke my arm." Brenda limply shook Georgina's fingertips. "I'm an investigator with Konig, and I'm investigating the murder of Ingrid Musgrave. It's worth a lot to my clients to find out what happened to her." Georgina said this calmly, her eye locked on Brenda, knowing this was the stronger, and smarter, of the two partners in the marriage. If Jerry hadn't had sense enough to hang onto her, he may well have ended up a lot more like his siblings.

"Konig," Jerry said slowly, "private detectives?"

"Yep," Georgina said, shrugging her shoulders and smiling.

"Very expensive private detectives," Brenda said. "Insurance money?"

"Lots of it," Georgina said.

"We were in Puerto Rico," Brenda said. "We have a condominium down there. We came back earlier today, to see if we could find out what had happened while we were gone, and we were going to go back there tomorrow morning. It's lovely this time of year."

"It's never been my cup of tea," Georgina said, lifting her cup to her lips.

Brenda looked at her coldly. "We've got plane tickets, and we've got neighbors who we saw down there. I don't know who got killed, but we didn't do it."

"Tell me about the day Ms. Larson got killed," Trigilio said.

Jerry sat slumped sideways on his couch, his forehead held up by his left hand. "I wasn't there that day. It was my day off. I was here at home, watching TV, taking sedatives because I'm so fucking worried about what my idiot brother was up to before he wound up in the hospital. Then Pat Monroe from my office calls me and tells me the guy from the deli who delivers her lunch can't get inside her apartment. He gets the key and lets himself inside, and finds her... her and the dog. He freaks, calls me, calls the cops. I puked, and told Brenda, and then we just packed some bags. I couldn't deal."

"Tell me what you know about Ingrid Musgrave," Trigilio said evenly.

"Nothing, but I can guess," Jerry said, sitting with his elbows on his knees, kneading his hands together. "Johnny came here bragging a few weeks ago, saying he was going to have a house bigger than this someday, and then maybe I'd stop by to pick up a check from him every now and again. 'Sure,' I said. I just laughed. He said stuff like that all the time. Could never get anything together, but he was greedy, greedy, greedy. The last time he came by, he had those losers in the car with him. I said, 'Why are you hanging out with those crooks again? You could go back in the joint just for being in the car with them.' And I didn't like him bringing them to my house." He looked over at Detective Trigilio, "He was still on parole from his last stupid burglary – two blocks away from here," Jerry laughed, shaking his head. "My fucking neighbors. And do you know how he got caught? He dropped his wallet. He was that stupid. They called me, and I told them to feel free to call the police. But, anyway, he said to me that these guys were really smart, and that they were planners, and they had some really good ideas. Big money." Jerry rolled his eyes. "I just told him to be careful. There was nothing else I could do." He threw his hands up in the air.

"How long ago did you see these two guys?" Georgina asked. "A few weeks ago? Can you be more specific?"

"Not really," Jerry said. "I wish I could."

"Well, we'll see what we can do to find them," she said, looking over at Trigilio.

If it Could Happen to Her

Trigilio stood up. "And I'd unpack those bags if I were you. You said you came back to find out what's going on. You just did. You no longer have permission to go down to Puerto Rico because it's lovely down there this time of year. I expect to be able to find you, either here or at the drycleaner, for the foreseeable future. I want some cell phone numbers, too, and I want the ones that you answer."

After Trigilio got the information he wanted, he left some paler, but noticeably calmer, Stones. "They're not criminals," Georgina said, once they got to the side of her car.

"You figured that out all by yourself?" Trigilio said.

"Well, I could see her pushed to it – mess with her kids or something like that, she's got a mean streak – but they ran because they were scared. They're back. I don't think they're going anywhere. Especially if they just signed on to take care of three little kids. They're going to have their hands full"

"Well, I'm going back to the damn station to talk to Jackie when she gets there. I've got a lot more reason to be looking for these losers Robert Lanier and Matthew Ellston. They're in default with their parole officers for about two months, and their last known addresses are under new tenancy. They split without paying the rent," he said.

"Well, they're somewhere – I hate to state the obvious," Georgina said. "I'm going to Konig in the morning to chat with Daniel Levine. I think he almost burst an aneurysm when Mr. Musgrave fired us, and then hired us back. I'm going to make nice-nice, and I'm also going to try to get more information about these guys. Sometimes we can find out a little faster than the cops." She said this with a smile.

"Want to make it a race?" Trigilio said, smiling as her opened his car door.

"Want to make it interesting?" Georgina asked.

"Hmm…" he said. "How about if you find them first, I buy you a year's worth of that fancy coffee you like?"

"Not that it matters, but if you find them first?" Georgina asked.

"I get to post that picture I took of you in the crooked ponytail and the sweatshirt on the Cambridge Police Department website," he said, getting into his car.

"You took a picture of me? What? With your phone?" she said, going over to his car as he started it up. "That's illegal, you know."

"No, it's not," he said, as he pulled away.

If it Could Happen to Her

"My attorney will explain it to you!" she yelled as he drove away.

Georgina sat in the chair across from Daniel Levine the following morning, watching him as he and one of his computer techs worked on a couple of different computers, running down leads on the losers named Robert Lanier and Matthew Ellston. "Finding fine upstanding citizens is a lot easier than finding losers," Daniel said.

"You've got birth dates and Social Security numbers – how hard could it be?" Georgina said, examining her cuticles.

"Again," Daniel said, furrowing his eyebrows at her, "you're talking about fine upstanding citizens. Scumbags sleep on other scumbag friends' couches. That's much more difficult to track down. And knowing Little Johnny is in the hospital would surely make them want to hide, unless they want to share his room, or worse."

"Well, they've got all that stuff. It won't fit in a duffle bag. Haven't they tried to sell any of it?" she asked.

"Apparently not," said George, the tech who was tapping away on a laptop on Daniel's other desk. "We haven't gotten a hit on one single thing. Usually bozos like this give something to their girlfriend, or their mother, or something, and it gets hocked pretty quickly."

"Jerry Stone's sister didn't have anything?" Georgina asked. They had already received the statement that Jackie Stone had given, and the results of the search of her apartment.

"Nope," he said. "We've got nothing so far. And the art, and the sculpture, et cetera, that's high-end stuff. They would have already planned where it was going to go."

"Or the person who hired them just took delivery," Georgina said.

"Hmm?" Both Daniel and George looked up at her.

"Maybe the person who hired them gave them a list, with the locations of everything he or she wanted them to get, and just had them deliver it, for an extra fee. It probably wasn't even anywhere near what it was worth. Those idiots wouldn't know the difference between a Picasso and a velvet painting of Elvis," Georgina said.

"Right," Daniel said, sitting back from his computer. "Shit. That means it's probably all sitting in a storage facility somewhere, and it's not coming out until they damn well want it to come out."

"Somebody smart is involved, but it's not Lanier, Ellston or Little

178

Johnny. But, find them, and it won't be hard to find out who paid them," she said.

"Yeah," Daniel said. "And it would be nice to find those freakin' Musgrave kids, too. If there's one thing that's harder to find than a scumbag, it's an extremely rich person who doesn't want to be found."

"I'll bet they're all in the apartment on Fifth Avenue," Georgina said. "But you don't have enough for a warrant to get in there and see. You'll have to take their maid's word for the fact that they're not." She got up and swung her tote bag onto her shoulder. "I have a feeling I'm just going to have to wait until the memorial service for Little Ingrid and Matthew. It's tomorrow, and I'm invited."

"Oh, yeah?" Daniel said. "Well, that's appropriate, considering your little speech at the Colony."

Georgina glared at him. "I only told them the truth," she said.

"Look," Daniel said, "I'm not so upset that a couple of people who were probably involved in a murder for hire got what was coming to them, but you almost got us fired. That, I do care about." He paused. "Anyway. What are you going to do?"

"Well, I'm going to the service," she said. "I'm going to the brunch afterwards, too. Nothing as fancy as the one for their mother, but I've really got to get a look at those people. One of them was fighting for their life a mere few days ago, and there have got to be some injuries. They can cover up bruises on their body, but if they got scratched or hit in the face, I'll still be able to see that."

"You're sure it's one of them?" Daniel said.

"I'm pretty sure," she said.

"But why would the other kids stick by the one who did Little Ingrid and Matthew? You might be able to hide those bruises and scratches now, but as soon as it happened, there's no way. They had to know. Why would they stay together?"

"That I don't know," she said, standing at his door with her arms crossed, gazing out his window. "Maybe there's some bizarre sense of loyalty. Maybe they're just fucking scared, and they're afraid they're next if they don't stick together. I don't know."

"And why did they invite you to the memorial service?" Daniel asked.

"They didn't. Their father did. After I asked to be invited. But he still claims he doesn't know where they are. I asked him to check out the Fifth

Avenue apartment, because there's no way the maid is going to get in his way, but he said he wouldn't do it. He sounds out of it. He's down in Bedford, and I'm guessing he's heavily medicated, either with alcohol or sedatives. He was slurring his words, and I couldn't get him to focus. He's really doesn't give a shit right now."

"That's probably why he's still paying us," Daniel said.

"Well, you'd better hope his prescription doesn't run out until I find out who did it," Georgina said, flinging his door open on her way out.

If it Could Happen to Her

<u>Chapter Eighteen</u>

Georgina chose another black suit to wear to the service for Little Ingrid and Matthew. This time there wasn't going to be a funeral, per se – just a brief memorial service. And this time it would be at their father's club, the Union. Georgina wasn't sure if these different circumstances were because of the unusual nature of the children's relationship to one another, the fact that they had far fewer "friends" than Ingrid Sr. had, or just because the family was all "funeraled-out." Three murdered members of one nuclear family in two weeks were more than most people could handle. She was just glad she had been able to convince Mr. Musgrave to invite her. She wasn't confident of it when she had called him and requested to be there, but his substance-induced stupor had helped a great deal.

Georgina walked into the Union Club, and was discretely directed to a room off to the rear and the left of the main dining room. There was no sign marking the door, indicating the occasion. Mr. Musgrave was there, along with his wife, and the officiant, a tall slender cleric with a distinguished head of gray-white hair, whom Georgina did not know. She could guess he was Episcopalian, but she didn't recognize him from Trinity. None of the children were there yet, and Georgina cursed to herself, hoping they weren't planning on skipping it. They had been ducking her for the past few days, but she needed them to be here today.

She walked up to Mr. Musgrave, and put a hand gently on his shoulder. Even with his expensive plastic surgery, he looked as though he had aged another 15 years in the past few days. He looked up at her with puffy, glazed eyes, and dilated pupils. He did not smell of alcohol, so she imagined that he was probably fairly loaded up with prescription medication. He took her hand, and shook it, but he didn't rise. "I'm tired of this," he said, looking glumly at the podium up front – there were no caskets there, the bodies were still with the Medical Examiner – "I'm just really freakin' tired of this, Adams. Figure it out. Take care of it. I'll take care of you if you take care of this."

"Mr. Musgrave, I…" she began.

"I know you don't need the money, Adams," he said, with a little bit of his normal fire, "but name the charity – how about that?"

"That sounds good," she said gently.

"Just take care of it," he said.

"I will," she said, turning to see the other children walking into the room in a group.

Magrit entered first, holding her little boy in her arms, his arms around her neck, and his legs around her waist. When she saw Georgina, she froze, and her eyes first registered surprise, and then something close to hatred. "I'm definitely persona non grata for some people around here," Georgina thought. Behind Magrit came Rika and Frederick, and he wasn't nearly as subtle as his sister in his feelings. "What the fuck are you doing here?" he said, moving toward her quickly. Georgina thought he might actually strike her. That would not ordinarily have presented a problem for her, but with her broken arm, it wouldn't have been a fair fight. Luckily, Rika grabbed him from behind, slowing him down a bit, and his father rose in front of him, placing himself between Frederick and Georgina.

"She's here because I asked her to be here," he said.

"Ladies and gentlemen," the officiant said, coming forward, his voice raised, but with calm authority. His white collar immediately entitled him to some respect, and his presence slowed things down for a moment, "let us please remember why we are here today. We are here to celebrate the lives of two people who have gone on to a better place. Petty matters of this world can wait – don't you agree?"

"Yes, Sir," Frederick said apologetically, turning toward his wife, who stared daggers at Georgina while she led him to a chair.

"You're absolutely right," Luanne said from behind him. She pointedly avoided any kind of eye contact whatsoever.

Georgina had quickly scanned all of them, and had seen nothing to indicate any of them had recently been in a struggle. The chilly March weather was working against her, as the only visible parts of their body were their faces. All of them were wearing overcoats and gloves. She observed their hands as they removed their gloves, and found their seats, but was unable to see any wounds. "This isn't going to be easy," she thought.

Georgina sat through the officiant's presentation concerning the lives of Little Ingrid and Matthew. He spoke of their shop, their friends, their hobbies, and their particular charities. It was a downright cheerful portrait of a happy, normal brother and sister. He mentioned nothing about their unusual relationship, or the fact that they were murdered, obviously. He had clearly been provided with the information by someone, since no one from the family spoke. A framed photograph of each sibling faced the small gathering on his either side, along with a simple bouquet of white lilies. "This is lame,"

If it Could Happen to Her

Georgina thought. "I hope I have better than this when my time comes."

The officiant wrapped things up very quickly. The family members had all sat through the service without crying, but there had clearly been tears over the course of the past few days. They all had puffy eyes, and a glazed look that resembled their father's. When the officiant finished his speech, everyone sat still for a moment, as though not knowing what to do.

Luanne was the first one to stand. She said, "I would like everyone to join me at my apartment for a small brunch. Georgina," she said, looking vaguely in Georgina's direction, but not meeting her eye, "I understand my father has invited you, so please feel free to come. I would appreciate it if you wouldn't cause a scene." She turned and grabbed her coat, pulling it over her shoulders as she left.

The others did the same thing. Georgina followed them downstairs, and waited and watched as they all got into the same limousine. Mr. Musgrave got into his own car with his wife. Georgina walked up to Jason where he waited, and hopped in, following behind. She had been to Luanne's apartment before, and wondered how it would comfortably fit the eight people she had invited to join her. Georgina couldn't even remember that much seating. Luanne had been so proud of the simplicity of her home life. Today, it was inconvenient. Why wouldn't they have something right there at the Union, or back at the Fifth Avenue apartment? Or a restaurant? It was more than inconvenient – it was odd.

Georgina sat back and wondered how in the world she would be able to examine them physically. None of them looked like they'd been in a fight. She'd examined all of their exposed skin very carefully for visible bruises or scratches, and had seen none. Could she be wrong? Perhaps she could get Mr. Musgrave to at least ask them to roll up their sleeves.

She arrived nearly simultaneously with the rest of them, but waited to be the last to get out of her car. They all made their way silently up to Luanne's apartment. Magrit's little boy eased the tension a little bit by needing to be changed, and then needing to be laid down for his nap. Luanne and Magrit surrounded him with pillows on her bed, and he drifted back off to sleep almost immediately, having already fallen asleep in the car.

They all found places in the petite living room, where Luanne had catered a small brunch, with scrambled eggs, bacon, sausage, English muffins, bagels and pastry. Mr. Musgrave made a brave attempt to prepare a plate, but it sat in his lap untouched. No one ate much, and Georgina merely sipped on a cup of

If it Could Happen to Her

English breakfast tea while she waited for the two women to reappear from putting Tommy down.

"He's out again," Magrit said, smiling wearily and sitting down. "It's been a busy few days for him, and he's not used to being in so many different places. I honestly can't wait to get back to London, for his sake, so he can be back in his own room, and his own preschool, and get some continuity going for him again."

Georgina was very happy to hear that from Magrit. She had learned a lot, and the child had clearly changed her life for the better. Children had a way of doing that, Georgina knew.

"You should stay in New York," Luanne said, pouring herself a cup of coffee, "and have him go to the school I'm making. It would be wonderful for him."

"I'm sure it would be wonderful," Magrit said, showing surprising grit, "but London is home for us now. I don't care what happens here. I'm going back to London the day after tomorrow. I don't care if we get the insurance money or not. I'm going."

The room was silent for a moment, after Magrit had the nerve to speak about the unspeakable. "Don't be hasty," Frederick said, glancing over at Georgina, who he knew held those cards, "you don't know what will happen."

"I don't," she said. "And I don't care, either."

"Magrit," Mr. Musgrave said, his voice husky, and his words slurred "I would be happy if you would stay here, in New York, or at least in the United States." He paused for a moment. "I'd like to be a better father to you, and have a chance to be a good grandfather to your little boy."

Magrit looked stunned. Everyone was silent for a moment, not quite knowing what to do with this sort of expression of affection from their father – but Luanne spoke up, "Father, did you know that a child's personality is nearly fully formed by the time that they're six years old?"

"What?" Mr. Musgrave said, looking over at Luanne with confusion.

"A child's personality is nearly fully formed by the time that they're six years old," she repeated.

"What the fuck does that have to do with anything?" he asked.

"I just wasn't sure that you knew that," Luanne said.

Mr. Musgrave looked perplexedly at his wife, who was every bit as confused as he was. Frederick was the one to speak up, with a distinct edge in his voice, "Luanne, I think Father is trying to make a point. I'm not sure what you're trying to do."

"I'm trying to make a point, too, Frederick. It doesn't matter what he does now. It's too late to be a good father to any of us. And it's nearly half too late for him to be a good grandfather to Tommy," Luanne said, calmly taking a seat, and crossing her ankles.

"Father," Magrit said, "I do appreciate what you're trying to say." She spoke to her father, but stared at Luanne. "And I would like it very much if you would take a more active role in my son's life. I think it would be wonderful if he spent more time with his grandfather, and I would like to spend more time with you as well." She looked back over at him, made a small smile, and took a sip from her cup, tears welling in her eyes. Her father got up and went over. He got onto his knees and wrapped his arms around her. She gave in, and leaned against his shoulder, crying softly. Mr. Musgrave looked around at the others, and said, "and that goes for all of you. I've been a shit. We've all been shits in our way. But it's my responsibility. I'm the father. Things are going to be different from now on."

Georgina watched as Frederick smiled at his father, swallowing to keep the tears from welling in his own eyes, and then she looked over and saw Luanne continue to sip on her tea, as thought nothing momentous was occurring. She thought Luanne's behavior was unusual, to say the least, but perhaps she wasn't quite as ready to bury the hatchet as her siblings were.

At that moment, however, Georgina's mobile phone had the temerity to ring. She reached into her bag quickly and silenced it, very embarrassed to be interrupting such an important moment, especially as a non-family member.

"That's rude," Luanne said. "These technological conveniences of modern life were made to connect us, but they have made our humanity so much more..." she searched for the word, "... disconnected."

"I apologize," Georgina said, but when she saw it was Trigilio, she took her telephone out into the hallway, closing the door behind her and walking a few steps down the hallway. She answered it, saying, "I'm at the funeral brunch, for Christ's sake. You know that. What could possibly be so important?"

"Well, if you're not interested, I'll let you get back to your doughnuts," he said.

"No, I'm sorry. Tell me." She knew he wouldn't have interrupted if he didn't have something big.

"I found Robert Lanier and Matthew Ellston," he said.

If it Could Happen to Her

"You're kidding me?" she said, trying to keep her voice down, because she didn't want to be overheard, but wanting to scream out loud.

"I'm not kidding you. But they're going to tell us even less than Little Johnny," he said.

"Why is that?" she asked, her heart sinking.

"Because they're dead. Both of them."

"Fuck," she said, reaching to throw her phone against the wall, but then thinking better of it. "What happened?"

"Queens Police got a call. Shots fired. Showed up to find these two guys dead in the shitty apartment they'd apparently been staying in since the robbery."

"Did anybody see anything?" Georgina asked.

Trigilio laughed. "In Queens?"

Georgina didn't have time for the humor, and she was worried. "What the hell are we going to do now?" she said.

"Well, you're there with the kids, you stay on that," he said. "I'm heading out to Queens right now, and I'm going to help tear things apart over there. I'll find something that ties them to this, I promise you."

"Is the stuff there?" she asked.

"Apparently not – none of it," he said. "I asked the guys who were there, and they said the place was covered with beer bottles and pizza boxes and Chinese food containers. And... a few guns and a bag of cash. A big duffle bag filled with a lot of cash. The person that shot them up clearly spent a few minutes looking for it, but it was hid pretty good, and they wouldn't have had much time after the shots were fired, so... now that they know there's a tie-in, and it's pretty damn clear, they're waiting for me. I'm driving right now."

"So they couldn't have done it alone, Trigilio. You don't believe that, do you? That cash means somebody paid them."

He paused for a moment. "No, I don't believe that, but it is a pretty good close to my case. And this was a shooting again, Georgina, it wasn't a knife like the two Musgrave kids. It might not be perfect, and I hate to see rich people get off, but I don't know what I can do. They might not have done it alone, but it sure looks like they damn well did it. The ballistics on the guns will put the bow on the package, and then, that might be it." He paused for a moment, feeling sorry for her, and maybe wrestling with his own conscience, "All I can say to you is, keep working it, and see what happens. I'll do what I can."

If it Could Happen to Her

Georgina hung up and felt like crying. What kind of proof was she going to find now? It seemed obvious that those three men had committed the robbery and killed Ingrid and Bartolomeo, but there was no way they planned everything themselves. The artwork, jewelry and sculpture stolen from Ingrid Musgrave's house was in storage somewhere, and those guys had cash only. They were sitting tight with a bunch of cash. She could only hope the police there could find a clue to where the merchandise was held, or some way to tie the cash to the person who paid them.

But there was nothing she could do about that. She hoped Trigilio wouldn't be quick to close it up. She thought of Matthew and Little Ingrid's blood-covered bodies, and thought that, no matter how they lived their lives, they deserved better. The only thing left for Georgina to do was to go back into Luanne's apartment, and see what was happening with the Bizarro Brady Bunch.

She walked in, and found Frederick now hugging his father. There were only two people in the room who didn't look thrilled. Heather sat nervously sipping on her cup of tea, perhaps calculating in her head how this new-found family closeness would cut into her and the twins' share of Mr. Musgrave's inheritance. Luanne still sat in her chair, but she had put her cup down. Her hands were folded in front of her. Georgina quietly closed the door behind her. Magrit was crying, and hugging Rika. "Well," Georgina thought to herself, "if nothing else comes out of this, perhaps this might be a halfway-decent family." Unfortunately, she was still convinced one of them was a murderer. That didn't help.

Even Heather managed a timid smile at the hugs being exchanged, and the happy tears. Everybody, in fact, seemed to be at least half-heartedly taking part in the happy little get-together except Luanne. In fact, she seemed to be concentrating on her hands, folded in her lap, which Georgina noticed were clasped so tightly, the knuckles were white.

Luanne said, "Father, this is all very nice. But are you going to just try to be a better father, or are you going to give us some money?" she said, examining her fingernails.

Everyone looked over at Luanne. "I already give you money, Luanne," Mr. Musgrave said quietly.

"Not nearly enough to start my school, and not nearly enough to make up for all of the heartache you've caused," she said, refusing to look up at him. "If we don't get the insurance money from Mother, then I'll need at least two million dollars from you to start my school. It's important."

"I think we can talk about that some other time, Luanne," Mr. Musgrave said, his jaw set tightly.

"Don't bother. That's what I thought you'd say," she said.

Frederick said, his voice low and grave, "Luanne, are you okay?"

"Yes," she said, "of course." She brushed imaginary lint off her skirt, smoothed it around her knees and got up, walking into her bedroom.

Magrit and Frederick exchanged looks. Everyone seemed to be at a loss for words for a moment, until Mr. Musgrave said. "What's going on with her?"

Frederick said, "I think maybe she's just overcome." But he didn't sound convinced.

"Frederick..." Magrit said very quietly.

He shook his head, and Georgina felt immediately that she knew what was going on. "Magrit," Georgina said quietly, "do you want to tell me something?"

Magrit looked over at Frederick again, "No, I don't think so."

Georgina said, "Magrit, she's in there with your son."

Magrit's eyes popped open, as she considered that. "Georgina..." she looked over at Frederick again, and seemed to receive an unspoken permission of some sort. "There is something..."

Mr. Musgrave stood up and stared at her. All of the glaze in his eyes seemed to suddenly be gone. He was clearly undergoing what, in college, Georgina used to call an 'un-high-ing experience.'

"What's up, Magrit?" Luanne said, coming out of the room, casually twirling a black nine millimeter pistol around her index finger. "What do you want to tell our dear Georgina?"

Magrit stood up and turned to face Luanne, seeming torn between wanting to run, and wanting to dash past Luanne to protect her child. "You shouldn't have that, Luanne," Magrit said. "It's not safe."

Luanne laughed a strange, high-pitched laugh. "It's not safe?" she said, holding the gun out, as if giving Magrit a better look at it. "No. It's not supposed to be safe. That's its purpose. Its purpose is to not be safe."

"Luanne," Georgina said. "Magrit's right. It's not safe for you, either. It's an unsafe thing for you to have. It's important for you to be safe. You're an important person." She used her most soothing voice, reaching back into some of her clinical classes on dealing with crisis.

"I feel important, Georgina," Luanne said. "That's not the problem. I've worked through all of that." Luanne stopped twirling the gun, and pointed it at her father's stomach. "It's too late, Daddy," she said, and fired.

Mr. Musgrave immediately clutched his belly and dropped to his knees. His wife knelt beside him, and put her hand over his, holding him up with her other arm. "Oh, my God, Geoffrey!" she wailed.

"I also learned that stomach wounds are the most painful form of gunshot wound," Luanne said. "I can't remember where I read that."

Frederick moved Rika behind him as Magrit took the opportunity to dash back into the bedroom to get Tommy. Georgina heard the door slam and lock, but Luanne didn't seem to notice. "Luanne, what the hell are you doing?" He put his hands out, gesturing in a downward, calming motion. He looked over at his father, and then back at Luanne, "We had this handled, Luanne. We agreed that we had this handled. We could handle it. We still can."

"No, no, Frederick," Luanne said, pointing the gun at him. "Magrit was just about to tell Georgina what happened to poor Little Ingrid and Matthew, those perverts. Those disgusting perverts who turned into who they are because they didn't have the proper amount of maternal and paternal affection," she said, leaning down towards her father, her face only a few feet away from his – where he now lay on the floor in a fetal position – and yelling directly at him. "A child needs to know that their parents love them, and that the world is a safe place."

Georgina knew if her arm weren't broken, she would easily be able to take Luanne and get the weapon away, but she didn't trust herself in her present condition. She watched, however, to see if an opportunity presented itself. Luanne was clearly unhinged at the moment, and wasn't even really paying attention to the gun in her hand.

"You're right, Luanne," Georgina said. "You are 100% right, in theory," she said, speaking in what she hoped was a normal, teaching, sort of tone of voice. "However, there are instances where repairs can certainly be made in the human psyche. You will have to agree with me. Look at how far you've come, after what you've been through."

Frederick looked over at Georgina like she was crazy, but Georgina knew who she was talking to. "You've been through several depressive episodes, and several failed relationships, but you've managed to put a really quality idea together – your school. And you've put your priorities in order," she said, looking at Luanne with encouragement in her eyes when Luanne finally looked over at her. Georgina thought she saw a flicker there of a woman seeking to be

If it Could Happen to Her

understood. "You live in a very nice, very tidy apartment that suits your needs very well. You're not acquisitive, like so many other people in your position might be, for your own sake. You want to make a difference."

"That's absolutely right," Luanne said, standing straighter now, and reaching up to smooth her hair. "I'm sorry, Father," she said. "Obviously that was an overreaction on my part."

"I've got her," Georgina thought, moving a few steps closer to Luanne, trying to figure out how to ask for the gun, and for one moment thinking that it might be over.

"You are a fucking Looney Tune, Luanne," her father said, spitting out the words with a little bit of blood, and Georgina's heart sank. She saw Luanne's face harden again, and as she brought up the gun a second time, Georgina felt she could risk taking action. She grabbed the gun with her good right arm, spun, and pinned Luanne's arm under her armpit, pointing the gun at the floor.

"Luanne, please let it go," Georgina said, holding the gun firmly, and wedging her finger underneath the trigger as best she could. Unfortunately, Luanne had her own left arm free, and she grabbed Georgina's hair and pulled, hard. "Ow, damn," Georgina said. "Could somebody lend a hand here?" She was trying to hold the gun pointed down at the floor, while her head was being pulled back. And the tip of her finger was being smashed by Luanne's attempts to squeeze the trigger. Frederick made the mistake of grabbing Luanne around the neck and spinning her around. He was larger, and surprisingly strong, and by spinning her around, Georgina lost her grip on the gun, and her finger slipped out from behind the trigger.

Luanne fired the gun almost immediately, and Georgina felt something like a punch, and a burning sensation on the back of her thigh. "I'm hit," she said, pushing backwards, and hoping to get Luanne off balance. Frederick pulled backward, and they all tumbled to the floor. Georgina ended up underneath Frederick, and he lost his grip on Luanne. She rolled up to her feet and pointed the gun wildly around room, but Magrit was already hiding in the bedroom, and her father and his wife were clearly no threat, as they attempted to tend to his wound. She pointed the gun at Georgina and Frederick as they lay on the floor. Georgina reached back and rubbed her lower thigh, her hand coming up sticky with blood.

"I'm sorry about that, Georgina, but, really, you have to learn how to mind your own business," Luanne said. She reached up and mechanically

If it Could Happen to Her

smoothed her hair again, and pulled her skirt straight, while holding the gun on Georgina and Frederick. She reached for her purse, which was on the floor to the side of the buffet table, and placed it carefully on her shoulder. "Now, feel free to make yourselves at home, but I would appreciate it if you would all allow me some private time to get my thoughts together."

Georgina saw, out of the corner of her eye, Mr. Musgrave's young wife clamping her hand over her husband's mouth, so he couldn't say anything. Luanne backed out of the apartment and shut the door.

"Shit," Georgina said, reaching with her one good arm, and pulling up her skirt. She saw an entrance and an exit wound, but they were shallow enough to be almost a graze. She tugged the Hermes scarf from around her neck, and rolled it up, using it to stop the bleeding. She was lucky.

She looked around at the rest of them, and saw Frederick and Rika going over to look at their father, whose color was growing increasingly pale. "Hang in there, Father," Frederick said, as he reached for his Blackberry and called 9-1-1. "Georgina, are you alright?" He put his hand over his father's and Heather's, attempting to stop the flow of blood.

"I will be," she said.

If it Could Happen to Her

Chapter Nineteen

They spent the next several hours together in New York-Presbyterian, being stitched up, tended to, and talking to police. Magrit, Frederick, Rika and Heather were able to give fairly accurate accounts of what had happened to the local police, while leaving out the more complicated nature of how it fit into the big picture. The uniformed officers were so busy filling in their blanks, and gathering information to try to locate Luanne and her car, that they didn't notice their minor evasions. Georgina had suggested that, if possible – and short of obstruction of justice – they wait to tell their entire story to Detective Trigilio. She wanted him to hear the first version, so that there was no mistake, and so he would have no excuses to either kill her, or drop this angle of the case.

While Georgina's wounds were being sewn up, she remained on the telephone nearly constantly with Trigilio, while he drove from one crime scene to another, trying to figure out where Luanne might have gone, waiting for him to show up at the hospital, and hearing what he had found in the crappy apartment that Little Johnny's buddies had been staying in. "They were clearly laying low," Trigilio said. "They'd turned over the material, and they'd been paid, but they were either smart enough to lay low, and not start spending, or somebody gave them that advice. Or maybe even paid them only half, and told them another half was coming if they laid low. Unfortunately, all that was coming to them was a couple of bullets. Do you really see this Luanne chick pulling off all of this? I mean, all of it? Planning this elaborate scheme for the robbery and murder, then killing her own brother and sister in a bloody, nasty and very personal way, and shooting these two dumb idiots? Little Johnny's starting to look like the lucky one of the bunch."

"Yes, I can believe it, Trigilio. I'm having a hole in my leg from one of Luanne's bullets sewn up as we speak." Georgina looked down and observed the work of the plastic surgeon who was gingerly sewing up the flesh wound near the middle of her outer thigh.

"I'm not saying she's not crazy, but, man..." he said, "this takes crazy, plus smart, plus determined, plus cold-blooded, plus a hell of a lot of other things. Is she all of those things?"

"I think so, Trigilio. I really think so. And I think it goes way, way back," Georgina said. Then she looked over and saw Frederick approaching, through the glass walls of her small room within the larger emergency room.

If it Could Happen to Her

She asked Trigilio to hang on for a minute, and she asked Frederick, "what are they saying about your dad?" The nurse who had just finished dressing Georgina's wound left.

"He's in surgery, but he'll live," Frederick said, sitting down in a chair next to her bed in the emergency room. "Please, feel free to finish your call. I don't want to interrupt."

"I can't," Georgina said, "we were talking about you."

Frederick's face flushed.

"It's the cop from down in New Jersey who's coming up here to put all of the pieces together," she said, "and you'd better not bother with any bullshit, because I don't have any patience for it, and he'll probably just slap some handcuffs on the whole bunch of you."

"We deserve it," he said, looking away.

Georgina went back to Trigilio, "Frederick is here with me, and we're all going to be waiting for you." She turned back to Frederick, "Where is everybody else?"

"Magrit and Tommy are downstairs in the daycare center, so he can play a little, and Rika's keeping Heather company."

"Where are you now?" Georgina asked Trigilio.

"I'm pulling in," he said. "I'm going to be parking and with you in minutes."

"Well," Georgina said, looking over at Frederick, "I'll be asking Frederick to get everybody together here in my room. The locals have done some surface questioning, filling in the blanks, and they're looking for Luanne, but they've got a lot more to tell you, I expect." Frederick nodded without speaking, and left the room.

When he came back, he had everyone except Heather with him. Tommy, the boy, was being cared for temporarily down in the daycare center, so that Magrit could join them, and Rika stood by his side, holding onto his arm. Trigilio had arrived by then, and had already admired the hole in Georgina's leg, by lifting up the corner of her hospital gown as the nurse practitioner prepared to put a bandage on it. "Not bad," he said. "It will make for some nice storytelling the next time you have to wear a bikini."

She slapped his hand, and readjusted her gown. "I have a great plastic surgeon. In six months, you'll never be able to tell it was there."

"Well, that's nice," Trigilio said. "I hope Konig gives you extra money for bloodshed, because you're certainly taking a beating on their behalf. I've been a cop for more than 28 years, and I've still never been shot."

"Yet," Georgina said, grumpily rubbing her leg with her good hand, once the bandage was on.

The children stood nervously shifting about while Trigilio and Georgina spoke, but now Frederick interrupted, "Did you want to ask us anything, Detective? It's been a terrible day. We've got our father upstairs in surgery to keep an eye on, and Magrit here has a little boy in the day care center. We'd like to get him home as soon as possible."

"I don't suggest you take him anywhere except the apartment on Fifth," Georgina said, "and if I were you, I'd get an armed security guard to stay downstairs in the lobby until they've got your sister."

Frederick's eyes opened wide. He clearly hadn't thought of that.

"Well, I certainly wouldn't want to inconvenience you folks, or add to your terrible day. Why don't I just get NYPD back here and tell them what you did? You can wear handcuffs back to their station, and relax there. Get some 'me' time," he flipped open his telephone and began to dial.

"I'm sorry, Detective," Frederick quickly said. "I'm – we're in no position to be complaining. Ask us whatever you want. I apologize."

Trigilio closed his phone. "I guess my first question to you folks is, who knew what, and when?" Trigilio began.

Nobody answered right away, so Georgina jumped in. "I'll help you get started. Did any of you help Luanne to plan your mother's murder?"

"Oh, Jesus, no," Frederick said, turning even paler, if that was possible.

"No, no," Magrit said. "We only knew something was wrong – that something was wrong with Luanne when Matthew and Ingrid died. She came to the apartment..." she looked at Frederick and Rika, who nodded.

"She came to the apartment, and she was a mess." She turned and sat down on the plastic chair Frederick had brought in from the hallway. He brought another chair for Rika while Magrit told her story. "She was wearing a big trench coat to cover everything, and to get through the lobby without anybody noticing, but once she got into the apartment, she took the coat off, and she was covered in blood," Magrit started crying.

"We didn't know what to say, or what to do," Frederick said, "except try to take care of her. She was almost catatonic. I honestly don't think that she was responsible, mentally, for what happened. Magrit had to help to hold her up in the shower, to get her clean. Then, we bandaged her up, just tucked her into bed, and, in the morning, it was like nothing had happened."

"Before this lovely, invigorating shower, which destroyed God-knows how much physical evidence, I assume she explained to you what she had done?" Trigilio asked, trying to be patient with these people who had harbored, at the very least, a double-murderer for several days.

"She said, 'I've killed Ingrid and Matthew,'" Magrit said. "Just like that. She stood there, while we took her clothes off of her and stuffed them into garbage bags..." Trilgilio's ears got red as he thought about the sheer destruction of evidence that they were so casually admitting to. "She said it, like you would say 'I'd like the tomato soup instead of the minestrone.' It was that simple. It made it even more frightening."

"Rika had some sedatives, so we gave her two of them, and put her to bed in one of the guest rooms. One of us stayed with her all night, but she never moved," Frederick said, looking out through the windowed wall, "just slept there all night, with her hands together under the side of her head like a little girl."

"Some little girl," Trigilio said. "I wish I had the crime scene photos from your brother and sisters' house to show you what your 'little girl' can do when she's upset. Even though we were wearing booties, we had to practically play "Twister" to get around the place without stepping in blood or tissue, or brain matter," he said, "Remember, Adams?" Frederick flinched, and Magrit covered her face with both hands.

"I will never forget," she said. "Frederick, Luanne cut Matthew's throat from ear to ear before he had a chance to fight back, and then she repeatedly stabbed and slashed at Ingrid..." she spoke louder, to drown out the sound of Magrit's crying, "chasing her through at least three rooms before finishing her off by bashing in her skull with a frying pan in the kitchen. I couldn't even identify her except for the jewelry she was wearing." Georgina let it all hang in the air for a moment, as Magrit sobbed. "This is who you've been protecting the past few days," she said, "and if you don't think that she'd do the same to you if you got in her way, you'd be very much mistaken."

"Well, I assume you're looking for her," Frederick said. "I don't know where she keeps her car, except that she probably keeps it near her apartment. I've never spent enough time there to know whether there's underground parking, or if she parks on the street. She drives a Subaru Forester from a couple of years ago, white, but I couldn't begin to tell you the license plate number, or even what state it's registered in."

"We've got the car covered," Trigilio said. "It's gone, but we've got an all-points out on it. If she's running around in it, or planning to take the Thruway anywhere, we'll have her."

"So, I guess you're assuming she had Mother killed as well," Frederick said quietly.

"Did she admit that to you, while she was unburdening her soul?" Georgina asked sarcastically, angry herself by what the family had already concealed.

"No, she didn't," he said.

"Did you ask?"

"No," he said, quietly, "I didn't." He paused. "I didn't want to hear the answer, but there's really nothing else to think, is there?" he asked out loud, to no one in particular. "She's a killer," he said.

"And Matthew and Little Ingrid were probably in on it with her," Georgina said.

Magrit looked up, surprised, "Why do you say that?" Having just come from their memorial service, and heard how they were brutally murdered, she wasn't yet ready to hear that they also probably helped to have her mother killed.

"Why else kill them?" Georgina said. "Would they have been smart enough to figure it out themselves, and confront her with it? They didn't seem too terribly concerned about it when I met with them. They were probably the most estranged of all of you from your mother, and her death wasn't any terrible blow to them. I doubt they would have investigated, and agitated Luanne to the point where she would have attacked them. So, like I said, why else kill them? I think they all planned it together, and then something happened, and it went very, very wrong."

Trigilio listened quietly with his arms folded while Georgina spun her tale.

"She didn't shoot them, after all. I mean, today she came out, twirling her gun on her finger, and she was ready for a confrontation. But that day, she used what she could find. She probably killed Matthew with one of his own knives, and she stabbed Ingrid with the same knife and finished her off with her own cookware. Something went very, very wrong in their evil little partnership that day." Georgina cleared her throat. "Either way," she said, reaching for her Blackberry, "They paid for it. Luanne will, too, if I have anything to do with it."

"What are you going to tell Lloyd's?" Rika asked.

"Shut up, Rika," Frederick and Magrit said, nearly in unison.

"I'll have to give that some thought," Georgina said, getting ready to dial Daniel Levine's number. "You're complicit, at least in the murders of your brother and sister. But the policies are on Mummy, so, as I said, I'll have to give it some thought. Now, if you'll excuse me," she said, "I have to consult with a colleague. You're going to Fifth Avenue? All of you?" she asked.

"Yes," Frederick said, "We'll all go there, and we'll get an extra security guard, and we'll wait there to hear from you. If we hear from Luanne…" he said, reading Georgina's quick glance, "we will attempt to convince her to come to us, and we will immediately contact both you, and the police."

"In that order," Georgina said.

"I don't fucking think so," Trigilio said.

Frederick nodded to both of them, but didn't agree or disagree. Georgina was sure that she would be the first to hear if Luanne turned up on Fifth Avenue.

"So where is she going to go, Doc?" Trigilio said, pulling up a chair.

Georgina smiled at the reference. "Well, she's not going back to her apartment. She not going to Matthew and Little Ingrid's place, and she's definitely not going to Fifth Avenue."

"We've got a police car sitting in the driveway of the place in Cambridge," Trigilio said, "but didn't her mother have a place up here on the Upper East Side?"

"She did," Georgina said. "And she had a place down in Hobe Sound, but I don't know if Luanne had access, and I'm pretty sure she knows somebody's staying there. Let me make sure that Dan Levine is having those places covered."

"He'll do that?" Trigilio asked.

"Are you kidding?" Georgina smiled. "I just saved Lloyd's $20 million for sure – Luanne's share. And I've got damn near enough evidence to prove that she had her mother killed, which changes accidental to deliberate, and changes $20 million each to the two leftover kids to $10 million. I've changed over $100 million in potential exposure to $20 million already. He'll be happy to stake out those places. They'll do whatever the hell I tell them to do," she said, smiling and dialing Levine's number.

Levine gratefully acquiesced to everything that Georgina demanded. He set up security at both Ingrid's home in Hobe Sound, and the apartment on the Upper East Side. Trigilio quietly waited until she got off the phone. "If you'll step outside for a moment, Detective, I'll get my clothes on."

"Are you discharged?" he asked.

"I'm not under arrest," she said, gingerly testing her weight on her leg, "and I go where I want to." The painkillers they had given her had a comforting familiarity, and were working rather well to dull the pain, but walking was going to be difficult without a crutch, or at least a cane. "Trigilio," she said, as she got dressed around her wounded leg, and her wounded arm, "I'm going to need to hang onto your arm on the way out of here."

"I'm pretty sturdy," he said, from our in the hallway. "But, tell me this, Adams. Why did she do it?"

"Which one?" Georgina asked.

"The first one," he said. "All of the rest were done to cover up the first, even if they didn't bother her very much. But why did she arrange to have her own mother killed?"

Georgina tried to figure out how to tell him her theory, and her vague suspicions about a video that could be the answer to the whole thing – how they had all reacted to Ingrid's video will, and the hint that there might be more to be seen – how when she'd searched Ingrid's house for videos and video equipment, it had already been searched, and the equipment she had found suggested that Ingrid had the capability of recording everything that happened under her roof. But, to tell Trigilio that, she'd have to confess to robbing Ingrid's house, and she wasn't quite ready to do that. "Money isn't good enough for you?" she asked, avoiding the question.

"I guess," she heard him say, "but why now? Why so elaborate? And why so fucked up? She doesn't strike me as a psychopath."

"No," Georgina said, "she's not smart enough, and she's certainly not organized enough."

"Psychopath's are smart?" Trigilio asked.

"The one's I've known have been very smart."

"How many is that?" he asked, laughing.

"Too many," she said, not laughing.

"So," he said, "tell me about Luanne."

"Well," she said, wrapping her scarf around her shoulders, and limping into the hallway, "I think she's damaged."

Trigilio put his arm out, and Georgina tossed her jacket over it before she took a hold of it to steady herself. They walked out together, with him holding

If it Could Happen to Her

her up. "Tell me something I don't know."

"Well, she's not just normally damaged, although there really isn't any such thing. I think that she was born with some difficulties, and some pathology that might have been recognized, and treated. She was dyslexic, and that was also never treated. But, I think that she's got an overstimulated response to perceived threats."

"She sees enemies that aren't there?" he asked.

"Maybe," Georgina said. "I know that she hears insults where there aren't any. And I think she honestly feels that she's just protecting herself. She doesn't think that she's done anything wrong. Plus, she's got a bizarre form of fixation complex." They reached Trigilio's car, and he carefully helped her to find a comfortable way to sit in the passenger seat. She was half-sideways and grimacing in pain, so Trigilio pretended not to notice that she wasn't wearing her seatbelt. "I know that every year or two, she's got a new cause that she becomes enamored of. She gets really into it, and it becomes everything she's about, and she devotes all of her time to it, until the next thing comes along and touches what might loosely be called her heart. Right now it's that damn school that she can't stop talking about. She's trying to make her mark, and be important, but she can't go the distance with anything. She's been married and divorced several times. She attempted suicide several times, and never very seriously."

"What's very seriously?" Trigilio laughed, as her turned the key and started the car.

"Death," Georgina said. "People who really want to die will kill themselves. They'll do it. People who 'try' to kill themselves, and get saved, or whatever, are just trying to get a reaction."

"So, if she were on your couch, Doc?" Trigilio asked.

"I'm not a clinician," Georgina said, "but I would call her a psychopath. I think that there was a time, probably before adolescence or soon thereafter, when she might have been helped with therapy and medication, but she's gone now."

"I would say so," Trigilio said. They drove in silence for a while, while Trigilio headed back to Georgina's apartment. She had checked on Geoffrey Musgrave's condition, and found that he was out of surgery, in recovery, and stable. The children had used the security company Georgina recommended to arrange for security at the hospital, and at the Fifth Avenue apartment where they were all now headed.

If it Could Happen to Her

Trigilio turned Georgina over to the doorman of her building, who helped her up to apartment, into the scolding arms of Armeda. "My goodness, shot!" she screamed.

"I'm not dead, so please stop screaming," Georgina said. "Please do me a favor and get me one of my father's walking sticks from the umbrella stand."

Armeda did that, and then helped Georgina back to her bedroom, where she helped her change from the black suit that she was still wearing, and which Georgina was pleased to see didn't have any holes or blood on it. It was damned expensive. She changed into a tank top and a pair of pajama bottoms, and a cashmere sweater. The entire process was incredibly painful, and as soon as Armeda left her alone, assured that she was going straight to bed, Georgina took another painkiller. She spent a few moments, removing her makeup and washing her face, waiting for Armeda to go back to her room. Then, she quietly limped along to her office, using her father's mahogany walking stick with the brass head of a falcon. She turned on the lights, and moved her chair over in front of her murder board. She sat and looked at it, mulling it over as it was, thinking about the changes that needed to be made, and wondering what changes were yet to come. She moved Ingrid and Matthew over near the rest of the dead, and made a note to herself to get some of the scene photographs. They wouldn't be a cheerful addition to her home's décor, but they would remind what she was dealing with.

To a great extent, she might well be out of it. She may never see Luanne Musgrave Balin again. They would catch her. There was no way they wouldn't catch her. She wasn't smart enough, and she needed much, much longer to plan, in order to pull off anything intricate. Luanne would do something stupid like try to check into a Holiday Inn with cash, and they'd have her. Georgina could imagine that planning her mother's murder may have taken years. But when it came time to kill Matthew and Little Ingrid, she had the will, and the fortitude, to do it, but not the intelligence to do it in such a way that she could get away with it.

And her performance today was geared for maximum attention. She wasn't trying to get away with anything today. She shot her father in front of everybody, and there was no running away, very far, from that.

Georgina opened up her computer and printed various things that she needed to organize her thoughts, and continued to reorganize her murder board until she felt it reflected what she knew. At some point in the near future, she was going to have to turn it into a written report, and receive a handsome cut of

If it Could Happen to Her

the payment that Konig would get from Lloyd's. She would donate the money. She always did. But she liked to see the check first, and deposit it, before she wrote a separate one to the charity of her choice. And now, once Mr. Musgrave had his check-writing capabilities back, she was going to remind him of that big donation he promised to her. The New York Public Library would have a much more comfortable operating budget next year. And he wouldn't be feeling very warm, fuzzy thoughts about Luanne right now. No matter how much he claimed he wanted to be a better father to his first family, there was no way he meant Luanne anymore. Stomach wounds were incredibly painful – Luanne was right about that.

Now, Georgina added some things to the murder board that she had been keeping in the tiny manila folder she had created to house her case solution. Needless to say, it was damn near flawless, except it needed to be updated with two more murders, a further attempted murder on Geoffrey Musgrave, and what she must charitably admit was an accidental shooting, of herself. The file had contained the information on Luanne's brother, Geoffrey, Jr., and his drowning accident in 1990.

Georgina read through it again, and printed out a picture of Geoffrey, Jr. from a yearbook photo from Groton. She was looking at a younger version of Geoffrey Musgrave, but much more handsome. He had a long list of activities to go along with his picture, including Class President, Football, Baseball Basketball, and honor roll. This was truly a golden boy. "I can see why losing your first child, and a child like this, would take the winds out of any family's sails," Georgina said out loud to herself, looking at the photo. She was pretty sure she knew what had happened, but there was no way she could confirm it. Maybe someday, she'd let Geoffrey, Sr. know what she thought… or maybe not.

Georgina finally limped off to the kitchen to pour herself a glass of milk, with some Bailey's to give it flavor, then she struggled off to her bed, the stiffness already setting in. Taking another painkiller, she sipped her milk and picked up her remote control, finding Poirot on PBS, and settling herself into her soft warm sheets and comforter, with a pillow propped under her injured leg, to keep some of the pressure off of it. She was positive this would put her off her feet for another couple of days – which she wasn't happy about, with Luanne still out there, and the case file un-concluded. But there was nothing she could do to track Luanne down herself, so she let Konig and the police do their job, hoping the phone would ring to tell her they had her – "just not until after 10:00 a.m. tomorrow morning," she told herself before allowing her eyes to drift shut.

Chapter Twenty

Georgina spent the next day in even more pain than the day before. She kept herself fairly well cushioned with pain-killers, and enjoyed the ministrations of another private nurse, and the fussing of Armeda, constantly fluffing pillows and readjusting her cashmere blanket to keep her comfortable. She was again stationed on the giant chaise lounge in her living room, in front of the television. She had tried to read, but had found her eyes going over the same sentences again and again, without comprehension. She was simply too distracted to focus. She gave herself up to a "Dateline" marathon of real-life murder mysteries, the phone within an arm's reach. Walter stopped by at lunchtime with high-end takeout, and then went back to work.

She periodically checked in with Detective Trigilio, and when she absolutely had to get up, she used her father's walking stick, held in her good hand. She thought she really would enjoy the "bonus" she was going to get from Lloyd's for her physical injuries. Even though she wouldn't keep it, she would enjoy the idea of it. She had certainly earned it. "How's the leg?" Trigilio asked each time she called.

"I can get around," Georgina said, "but I'm unbelievably sore." Unfortunately, she got the same update from him each time she rang. "Nothing. Nobody's seen her. We're looking. Sometimes it takes time..." a litany of police platitudes she'd heard a million times before, and which she quickly tired of.

Trigilio tired of her, too, by mid-afternoon. "Damn it, Doc," he yelled, "you'll be the first one I call when we've got anything, I swear! Give me at least another two hours before you call me again." He hung up. Georgina pouted and complained, and dozed for the remainder of the afternoon. She called him once again around 6:00 p.m., when her nurse was packing up to leave. "Nothing yet. I'm on call. If they call me, I'll call you," he said.

Armeda finally went to bed at 10:00, not happy that Georgina had decided to spend the night on the chaise. "I'm not moving," Georgina said, while flipping through channels with the remote control.

"You'd be much more comfortable," Armeda said, her hands on her hips, trying to look stern in her absurdly colorful, flowered, terry cloth bathrobe. "Human beings were meant to sleep in a bed," she said, as Georgina ignored her.

"Goodnight!" Georgina yelled, as Armeda stomped off to her room.

If it Could Happen to Her

Georgina drifted off again as she watched a movie. She woke about an hour later, as her mobile phone rang next to her. She snatched it up, hoping it was Trigilio. She sat straight up as she heard the modulated tones of Luanne Balin's cultured voice. "Hello, Georgina," she said.

"Hello, Luanne," Georgina said, being very careful to keep her voice calm as well.

"How are you?" Luanne asked, "your leg, I mean? I called the hospital to get father's condition, and yours – he's stable, by the way."

"That's good to hear," Georgina said.

"Yes, I'm very glad about that. And they said that you weren't there. I hoped – assumed, really – that meant you weren't hurt too badly."

"Well, I'm sore, but I'll be alright," Georgina said. "Where are you, Luanne?"

"Actually, I'm just down the block from your place," Luanne said. "I was hoping to stop by and talk to you. I apologize for the hour, but considering the circumstances, I wanted to say that I'm sorry, in person – taking personal responsibility for my actions."

"Thank you, Luanne," Georgina said. "I'm still up, and I would love the company. Could you do me a favor, though?" Georgina asked. She couldn't risk Armeda getting hurt. "Just have the doorman ring my mobile, and I'll let you in myself. I don't want to wake my housekeeper."

"Of course," Luanne chirped, "very thoughtful of you."

The moment she rang off, Georgina quickly called the doorman to give him her mobile number, instruct him to allow Luanne up, and then also allow the police up when they arrived, but *not* to mention the police to Luanne.

"Are you sure, Ms. Adams?" he asked.

"Absolutely," she said, hanging up and calling Trigilio, as she limped into her office. She spun dials on the safe concealed behind a painting, as the phone rang. "Jesus, Adams," he said grouchily, "I'll let you know…" he began.

"Be quiet," Georgina said. "She's here. She's on her way up. Call NYPD, and have them come up quiet. My doorman is expecting them."

"She hasn't shot you enough in the past 48 hours?" Trigilio yelled, as she hung up, and turned off her ringer. She opened the safe, and took out a 9mm Sig Sauer which was already loaded. She tucked it into the Hermes scarf she had fashioned into a sling. Then, she went around to her desk to grab an extremely sensitive digital audio recorder from her middle drawer. She tucked

If it Could Happen to Her

that into her sling as well, making sure that they were secure.

Then she went to the front door of her apartment and waited for Luanne, who didn't keep her waiting long. The elevator opened, and Georgina greeted her with a smile, leaning heavily on the cane, to seem like less of a threat. She could only assume that Luanne was still armed.

Luanne looked remarkably well put-together for someone who had been on the run for nearly two days. "Smart to stay in the city," Georgina thought, "instead of trying to leave." She'd have been caught in her car, at the bus station, the airport – anywhere she would have gone to start running.

"So, you need a hand?" Luanne asked with a concern, reaching for Georgina's elbow. Georgina saw that Luanne had her purse on her shoulder, and assumed the gun was in it.

"Thanks," Georgina said, smiling. "This actually gives me an excuse to use my father's old walking stick." She held it up to show Luanne.

"How lovely," she said, "and how charmingly sentimental."

"Please come in," Georgina said, moving aside and closing the door behind her, leaving it unlocked.

She led Luanne into the living room, where they sat opposite each other in large white bergere chairs flanking her fireplace. Luanne put her purse on the floor next to the leg of her chair, Georgina was relieved to see.

Luanne crossed her ankles and folded her hands. "Georgina, I hardly know where to begin. Clearly, I've over-reacted, and I'm going to have to take responsibility for what I've done. I've spoken with my attorney, and I'm going to make arrangements to turn myself in."

Georgina opened her mouth, about to speak, but Luanne continued.

"Obviously, there are extenuating circumstances, and my lawyer feels confident that it will be taken into consideration."

"That's wonderful, Luanne," Georgina said, seething inside that this bitch thought that 'extenuating circumstances' justified the murder of seven people, and the shooting of two others. "I mean, you weren't personally responsible for some of it, technically. No matter how much you'd like to take responsibility."

"No," Luanne said, sitting back more comfortably in her chair. "I didn't kill Mother or Bart, after all, Robert and Matthew and John took care of that. It's indefensible, but I simply didn't have it in me."

"And I'm willing to bet you didn't kill Ms. Larsen, either," Georgina said, leaning back and mirroring Luanne's body language.

If it Could Happen to Her

"No, Robert and Matthew took care of that, as well," Luanne said wearily.

"So, when they died," Georgina said, looking down at her fingernails, "they were just murderers."

"Exactly," Luanne said. "I felt badly deceiving them, but they wouldn't have anything to offer the world. I actually felt worse lying to them, than shooting them, though that may sound strange."

"No," Georgina said. "You're not a liar, Luanne."

"No. Exactly," she said.

Georgina already had everything she needed. "And as for Matthew and Little Ingrid…" she didn't finish the sentence.

Luanne looked sharply at Georgina, "There was something terribly wrong with them, and I'm convinced that if I hadn't killed them, they would have killed me."

"That sounds like self-defense to me. So what was going on with your mother?" Georgina asked quietly, not half believing it was this easy to put the last nail in Luanne's coffin.

"That's a little more complicated," Luanne said, "I loved my mother, but there was a very dark side of her, a selfish, dark side, and she always frightened me, and my brothers and sisters. All of us. But I decided to stand up to her. And I warned her, too. I think, for once, I scared her."

"Thus, the codicil," Georgina thought. Out loud, she said, "so that's what made you do it? I though, perhaps, there was something symbolic in the fact that you had them take her art."

Luanne threw her head back and laughed. Georgina smiled, but couldn't think of anything more jarring that could have happened at that moment. Luanne leaned forward and tapped Georgina on the knee, "You always just 'get' me, Georgina. That was true. You're so right. Mother loved that stuff more than she loved us – so I took it. I was happy to take it. If it weren't for how much those pieces of junk meant to the children who would attend my school, I probably would have set fire to the whole lot."

"You did save it?" Georgina asked.

"Yes," Luanne said. "It's in a storage unit in Greenwich, a few miles from Mother's house. I met the guys, and just took the truck from them. They didn't know what they had. They just had a list. It was damned difficult moving all of those things, too."

"I can imagine," Georgina said, thinking that she now had absolutely

If it Could Happen to Her

everything that she needed. Luanne wasn't going to get a deal. "What did your mother have on you, Luanne?" Georgina asked.

"What do you mean?" Luanne said icily.

"Why did you and Matthew and Ingrid have her killed?" Georgina asked. "That's really what started everything. Did she have something on you, and them?"

Color began to rise in Luanne's cheeks. "Certainly not." Luanne said.

"I said you weren't a liar, but that's not true, is it? You lied to me just now when you said that you didn't have it in you to murder. But you knew you did," Georgina said.

"I don't know what you mean," Luanne said, her hands trembling, even though she held them tightly together.

"You killed your brother, didn't you, when you were little?"

Luanne inhaled deeply and stood up.

"Why did you do that? Was he a little too perfect? A little too popular? Good in school? A natural leader? Everything you always wanted to be, but couldn't?"

Luanne took a step toward Georgina, "I found the tape," she said, stopping Luanne in her tracks. "I've got it. Is that why you had them steal the safe? Is that where you thought it was?"

"I don't know what you mean," Luanne said, turning pale.

"You're a pervert, Luanne," Georgina said, smiling.

Luanne turned around and grabbed her purse. Georgina pulled out her gun and shot her in the foot. Luanne went down, screaming.

"It's also extremely painful to be shot in the foot, Luanne. So many bones," Georgina said, leaning over her, and tossing her purse away. A glance proved the gun was, indeed, inside.

Luanne rolled on her back, holding her shin and wailing. Georgina went around behind her, and with her good arm, slowly pulled the white chair away, so Luanne wouldn't get blood on it.

At that moment, four uniformed NYPD officers burst in, with Georgina's doorman on their heels. Armeda was right behind, observing the situation, screaming and running back into the kitchen. Georgina put her one arm up, and said, "my gun is here in my sling, and her gun is in that purse." She let the policeman take her gun, and she informed him that the other gun was used in another shooting earlier today.

She smiled as she saw Armeda run back in, with towels and a garbage bag, sitting down to wrap up Luanne bleeding foot. As the police called for paramedics and Luanne screamed, Armeda turned to Georgina and said, "it's all on the hardwood, not on the carpet, thank goodness."

"The carpet!" Luanne screamed, as the police cuffed her.

"You're not worth the price of this carpet, Luanne. It's incredibly expensive, and irreplaceable," Georgina said, leaning down. "You killed your brother, then your mother, then your other brother and sister, and you're responsible for so much death and destruction, it's nearly impossible to keep track. And there are no extenuating circumstances. Those children you wanted to teach need to be protected from people like *you*. Anyone who would have a three-way with her own brother and sister…" Georgina said very quietly as Luanne grew wild-eyed. "Luanne, I'm going to take that recording, and post it on the Internet, where it will exist forever. Just search the key words sex, incest, perversion, murder…" She smiled at Luanne, and moved back as Luanne bucked and screamed and spit. All four officers had to subdue her.

Finally, and it seemed like forever, the paramedics came and sedated Luanne, temporarily dressing her wound and taking her to a waiting ambulance.

Trigilio walked in just as they were taking her out on a stretcher. He looked at Georgina, standing in the foyer, and said, "I'm glad it's not the other way around," he said.

"Me, too," Georgina said, smiling.

Armeda walked in and said, "one of those haz-mat cleaners is coming to get that darn blood off the wood. I'm not going to touch it."

Trigilio smiled at her. "Well, I don't think Luanne's going to tell me much, but I might as well ride along." He turned to the front door.

"She doesn't need to tell you anything," Georgina said, taking the recorder out of her scarf. "She told me." She tossed it to Trigilio, who caught it with one hand.

He looked at it and smiled. "Nice."

"I want the recorder back," Georgina said.

"It's evidence," Trigilio said, closing the door behind him.

Georgina smiled, and looked around her. She took a deep breath, and yelled, "Armeda, I'm going to bed for the next three days!"

"You go right ahead," Armeda yelled back, from the kitchen.

Georgina went into her bathroom, took two of her painkillers, and crawled into her poofy, comfortable bed, and soon fell asleep.

Chapter Twenty-One

"Little Johnny eventually died, too. That's another one on my tab," Georgina said, her head on the soft leather arm of Dr. Gregson's couch.

"You don't really think you're responsible for any of these deaths, do you?" he asked. "You can't legitimately take responsibility for other people's actions. You know that. You haven't killed anyone."

"No, I guess I don't really think that, but Little Johnny died at my hand. Even if it was a few weeks later."

"That was self-defense," Dr. Gregson said sternly, "and you know it. You're not indulging in some self-pity right now, are you?"

"No," she said. "Well, maybe, yes," she admitted. "I'm enjoying a little self-pity right now."

"Well, you put a very bad person away," he said. "How do you feel about that?"

"Good," she said, definitively. A smile even toyed with the edges of her lips.

"Do you want to talk any more about that night?" he asked.

"Maybe," she said.

"You never had a tape?"

"No. I guessed."

"A pretty good guess," he said. "Are you saying that you deliberately brought on a psychotic break?"

"She was on the verge of one, I could tell. So I pushed a few buttons."

"But you knew where they were. Do you think that's ethical?"

"I'm not a clinician," she said

"True, but don't you think you have a greater responsibility than the average citizen?"

"No."

She paused, "and besides, psychiatric facilities tend to be much more comfortable than women's prisons."

He paused for a moment as well, "Yes, definitely. That's true." He once again took in her loose-fitting yoga pants, tank top, oversize cashmere sweater and ponytail. He had observed her clothing when she came in, but he felt she was ready for the question. "So, you've taken to your bed?"

She stiffened, but she was ready for the question, too. She knew it was coming. "Yes."

"What are you taking for medication?" he asked gently.

"Whatever I think will work," she said, plucking at one of the double-C Chanel-logoed buttons on her sweater.

"I see. Are you alright?"

"No," she said. "I'm not alright. I will be. But it's a fucked-up world out there, doctor. I want to avoid it sometimes. And I can afford it."

"Certainly, but…"

Georgina jumped up off the couch abruptly. "I think we're done here today."

"Same time next week?," he asked gently.

She didn't answer, just slowly made her way out the door with her cane. She went down in the elevator, holding her sweater closely around her. Jason awaited her at the curb, and flung her door open. He gently helped her get settled into the back, with her leg up. She pulled the cashmere blanket she had back there up around her neck, and curled into the corner of the back seat for the quick ride back to her apartment.